IN THE *Grey*

A. M. KUSI

This book is a work of fiction. Names, places, characters, organizations, events, and incidents are either products of the authors' imaginations or are used fictitiously. Any resemblance to actual persons, living or dead, or to businesses, companies, events, institutions, or locales is completely coincidental. Any trademarks, product names, service marks, and named features are assumed to be the property of their respective owners and are only used for references.

Published by A. M. Kusi 2021

amkusinovels@gmail.com

Visit our website at www.amkusi.com

Editor: Anna Bishop of CREATING ink

Sensitivity Edit: Renita McKinney of A Book A Day

Proofreader: Judy's Proofreading

Cover Design: Regina Wamba of ReginaWamba.com

ISBN: 978-1949781205

OTHER BOOKS BY A. M. KUSI

<u>A Fallen Star (eBook FREE on all retailers)</u>

(Book 1 in The Shattered Cove Series)

<u>Glass Secrets</u>

(Book 2 in The Shattered Cove Series)

<u>Defying Gravity</u>

(Book 3 in The Shattered Cove Series)

<u>The Lighthouse Inn</u>

(Book 4 in The Shattered Cove series)

<u>His True North</u>

(Book 5 in The Shattered Cove series)

<u>Brave Love</u>

(Book 7 in The Shattered Cove series)

<u>The Orchard Inn (eBook FREE on all retailers)</u>

(Book 1 in The Orchard Inn Romance Series)

<u>Conflict of Interest</u>

(Book 2 in The Orchard Inn Romance Series)

<u>Her Perfect Storm</u>

(Book 3 in The Orchard Inn Romance Series)

"There is a child within you longing to be seen, to be held, to be validated, and to be loved. Protect your inner child. Be the parent they've always wanted."
– Luna and Sol

"Unfortunately, there are wounds that time does not heal. Fortunately, healing is intentional and grief can be moved through."
— Empowered Through Grief

GET A FREE SHORT NOVEL

Join our newsletter to get a FREE short novel that's not available on any retailer. Plus updates about new releases, giveaways, pre-orders, sneak peeks, and more.

Visit the website below to join now.

WWW.AMKUSI.COM/NEWSLETTER

TABLE OF CONTENTS

TRIGGER WARNING

This book covers sensitive topics about self-harm and suicide that may be triggering for some readers.

1
———

EMMA

Emma wiped the sweat from her brow. Her hair stuck to her neck under the hot spotlights. Her chest heaved as adrenaline coursed through her veins. The cheers from the crowd were deafening. Closing her eyes, she relished the high—every atom buzzing and alive. Moments of happiness were fleeting in her life. But the stage was one place Emma didn't doubt she belonged. Here she was, Emma Sterling, rock goddess and lead singer of The Sirens.

She lifted the microphone to her lips as the last notes of the electric guitar ended. "Thank you, Nashville, and goodnight!"

Screams erupted and chants for a second encore echoed as she exited the stage, her bandmates at her heels. *Yes! What a goddamn high.*

"Here." Callie, their band manager, handed her a bottle of water as she sunk onto the couch in the green room.

"Thanks." Emma twisted the top before guzzling half the bottle.

"Taking care of you is my job." Callie winked. "And I'd be

more than happy to meet *all* your needs. Just say the word."

Emma let her eyes wander over the gorgeous woman's body. It wasn't the first time Callie had offered. But Emma didn't mix business and pleasure anymore. That was the deal they'd made as a group after Asher had stirred up trouble with the last manager by sleeping with him.

"Fuck, that was rough without Geo," Asher said, sliding in next to her, beer in hand. His dark eyes clouded over as an invisible weight descended upon the room.

She reached out and took his palm in hers. His long fingers wrapped around hers and squeezed.

"Geo will be back. He'll get through this. We have a lawyer working on an appeal." She offered him what she hoped was a comforting smile.

"He turned the suit down," Nicky said, blowing out a cloud of smoke before passing the blunt to Leo.

"Why would he do that?" Emma gasped.

"Because he thinks he deserves prison," Ravi grumbled.

"It was an accident. He didn't mean to——"

Leo held his hands up. "We know that. Tell it to Geo."

Emma shook her head and swallowed the lump in her throat. Just when they'd hit it big, achieved the dreams they'd fought so hard for as a team, Geo had been ripped out of their lives—all for a drunken mistake.

They'd lost their second guitarist, their best friend, and brother. *This can't get any worse.*

Missing Geo only added to the ache in her soul. She took another sip of water, trying to quell the nerves. The hollow pain increased as the high from performing wore off. No one cared about her dark family history on stage. Or her long string of ex-boyfriends and girlfriends, who never came close to filling the hole in the center of her heart. Reality slammed into her. Numbness sunk inside her bones like gravity. Wanting reared its ugly head once again. She was homesick for a place she'd never known, yearning for someone she'd never had.

Why wasn't she happier? Even before Geo had been taken away, a grey had settled over her life. Shadows had followed her ever since she could remember. She'd thought for sure making her dreams come true would chase them away for good and thrust her into the light. But this was like climbing Mount Kilimanjaro and the view being just *okay*.

Maybe there is something wrong with me. Why couldn't she feel anything unless it came with an adrenaline rush or endorphins?

Giggles filtered into the room as Callie let in the few VIPs and groupies.

"Oh my God! It's her!" someone screamed.

Emma braced herself for the onslaught of questions and pictures.

"Em? Your phone's been blowing up." Callie handed it to her.

Emma glanced at the screen and her heart stuttered.

Link.

Why would he be calling her? Her belly flipped and tumbled with nerves. He never called her, much less spoke to her when they were in the same room—as rare as that was. He put up with her for her stepdad's sake.

Her phone rang again.

Something isn't right.

She swiped the screen and answered, "Hello?"

"Emma—" His voice caught, fear bleeding into the space between them.

"What's wrong? Is Dad okay?"

Silence was her only answer.

No, no, no, no, no, no.

Emma stepped away from the noise.

A fan thrust a pad of paper and Sharpie in front of her face. "Can I get your autograph?"

Emma shook her head and pushed past her, finding a storage closet as dark as the cloud looming over her. "Link?" She choked back her rising panic.

His voice was gruff, haggard, like he was barely holding it together. She'd never heard him like this. "His heart . . . You need to come home."

"I'm coming." Emma pulled the phone away, ending the call with a shaky hand as her body trembled. Her lungs squeezed tight as she opened the door and walked back into the lounge. Laughs and squeals faded into the hum of background noise as the world around Emma darkened. The blackness of despair lapped at her feet.

"Em? Are you okay?" Callie sounded like she was in a wind tunnel.

Emma shook her head. "I have to get home. My dad—"

She swallowed. A new surge of adrenaline rocked through her body, sharpening her senses.

"I need a flight to Shattered Cove five minutes ago."

Callie nodded, seemingly understanding the importance. "Let's get you to the airport, then."

Dad is going to be okay. He had to be. He was the only one who'd ever really loved and cared for Emma, even though they weren't blood related. He was the only one who'd ever chosen her.

"There's a flight to Boston leaving in forty-five minutes," Callie offered.

"Book it." Emma ducked into the SUV, not bothering with her seat belt.

The driver broke the speed limits to get them to the airport. But something told her that—even with the fastest jet plane—it would be too late.

2

———

EMMA

Emma rushed through the hospital doors and past the front desk, her throat too clogged with emotion to speak. Her stomach twisted with anxiety as she made her way to the ICU. As she ran through the hall, each step was heavy with the weight of dread bearing down on her. Part of her wanted to rush forward and see her papa—the other was terrified of what she'd find. The double doors opened, and the tall figure of her stepbrother exited. She sucked in a sharp breath.

His solemn watery gaze flicked to hers. Grief shone back. "You're too late."

She shook her head. "No." Her chest squeezed tight. Pain lanced her rib cage as her heart was torn to shreds. Her eyes prickled. Blinking, she kept the tears at bay. *Shove it down.*

"He's gone—" Link's voice broke, his shoulders slumping. A devastated expression crumpled his beautiful, strong features.

She moved, wrapping her arms around him. His chest deflated before his hand splayed out against her lower back.

5

Even through the grief, his touch brought her comfort. She hoped hers did the same.

"Can I see him?" she asked.

Link pulled away and nodded, his bloodshot eyes looking anywhere but at her.

Maybe it was the shock that wracked her body, giving her the courage. She reached out, her hand running over his short beard, turning his face towards her. "Link?"

The pain that flashed in his eyes made her knees buckle. She wanted more than anything to take some of it from him, even if it meant adding to her own.

He blinked. "I gotta . . . get out of here." He slipped out of her grasp before disappearing down the corridor.

Emma buzzed the front desk to let her in. A nurse led her to a room in the farthest corner. The bitter scent of antiseptic burned her nose as she entered. The nurse said something, but it sounded like she was underwater. Emma's eyes were glued to the dark brown complexion of her papa. She stepped closer, one shaky foot in front of the other. His eyes were closed, like he was merely sleeping and would wake up any minute to tell her this was all a morbid joke. She reached her trembling hand out to cover his. Bile rose in her throat at the coolness of his skin.

"Papa, why? Why did you leave me too?"

Empty silence was her only answer. Anger roiled in her gut. Had he been sick and not told them? Had the doctors missed something? Had he had symptoms when she talked to him two days ago? She inhaled the tiniest breath of cleaner-tainted air. Her chest was so tight. This was the last time she would ever lay eyes on him. How could she say goodbye?

"I love you, with all my heart . . . Thank you, for everything you've done for me. For saving me . . . I'll never know why you chose me, but I'll forever be grateful." Emma leaned over him and kissed his cool cheek. She pulled back, slamming her eyes closed to imprison the tears, swallowing the onslaught of emotions as she always did. Numbness settled back into her bones.

Her nose stung. She had to get away before the tears erupted, before she broke apart. Emma ran out of the room in a haze. She needed to find Link. All they had was each other.

After searching the waiting room, she ended up in the cafeteria.

Where is he? Did he leave?

She sat in a chair, a wave of emotion crashing through her.

What if he leaves me now too?

It's not like they were close—not since she was a teenager.

Or maybe this is the end.

She shook her head. *No.* Despite his apparent dislike for her, Emma loved Link—more than she should. That had always been the problem.

"Emma?"

She looked up. Charli's concerned eyes studied her.

"Dad had a heart attack. And Link—I've never seen him this . . . distraught. I need to find him." Emma stood. Why had she sat? She must find him right away. It was so important. She—*Why can't I seem to focus?*

"Oh my God!" Charli wrapped her arms around her a moment before another set of arms pulled her close.

Remy. Her best friend was here.

"I'm here. Emma, sweetheart. I'm so sorry." Remy's voice cut through the fog.

What is she doing here?

Charli backed away.

"He's gone." Emma's voice sounded so far away.

The timid woman who worked at the High Tide Diner, Brynn, walked over and handed Remy a tissue.

Charli's phone rang loudly. She answered before darting out of the cafeteria. Emma hoped her friend was getting good news. The woman deserved some after the hell she'd been through this last year.

"I have to go." *Have to find Link.*

"Let me give you a ride," Remy offered.

Emma shook her head. "No, I had my bike in long-term parking at the airport. I'll be fine."

"It's okay if you're not."

Remy's words halted Emma's steps. She drew in a deep breath and turned as the mask she wore around her friends slipped into place. "I'll be okay. I just need some time." She hoped her expression was convincing.

Remy slowly nodded. "Let me know if you need anything. Come stay with Mikel and me if you want a place."

"Thanks." Emma spun around and numbly made her way down the hall towards the glowing red exit sign. The automatic doors swished open, and she hesitated, pausing as someone brushed past her. Was she ready to go out into a world where her father didn't exist anymore? Emma's hands trembled.

Link. Link needed her.

She placed one foot in front of the other making her way to the parking lot. The cold cut through her unzipped leather jacket. She welcomed the icy spikes of the New England January wind. Pain helped her focus, drew her out of her head. She slipped her helmet on and started the engine. After kicking her motorcycle into gear, she focused on the road ahead of her, never behind—nothing good ever came from her past.

Twenty minutes later, she pulled into Link's driveway. His

black Chevelle with white pinstripes and his tow truck took up most of the space. Memories flooded over her as she admired the shiny frame of the car he and their dad had spent hours rebuilding. Emma had helped when she was home too, but mostly she'd just watched and listened.

"No daughter of mine is gonna rely on someone else to change her oil," her dad had joked. He'd always pushed her to do things for herself. She had him to thank for being such an independent woman.

And now he's gone.

She climbed off her bike and headed to Link's door. She knocked, bouncing from one foot to the next nervously. She hadn't been here in years.

A grunt came from the other side, but he never came.

She knocked again and tried the handle. It was open, so she let herself in. "Link?"

"Go away," Link growled from the couch before tipping the tumbler of amber liquid to his lips. He drained the glass and then poured another. The dim light from a lone lamp illuminated half of him while leaving the other in shadow. He hunched over, elbows on his knees as his head hung low.

A small smile tipped the corner of Emma's mouth before she shut the door behind her. He'd told her to go away when they were kids, but he'd never meant it. Slipping off her Doc Martens, she responded as she always had, "Make me."

She slid next to him on the couch.

Link had already drained the second glass. His glazed eyes darted to her. "You going to drink or just run your mouth?"

She grabbed the bottle from his hand and took a long pull. It burned going down. She coughed and handed it back to him. "That tastes like shit. Do you have any tequila?"

He nodded towards the kitchen.

Emma got up and opened cupboards until she found what

she was looking for. She grabbed a couple of shot glasses, salt and, after scouring the fridge for any citrus, she settled on a bottle of lime juice. Beggars couldn't be choosers.

She set up her supplies on the coffee table as Link downed more bourbon.

"Auntie Yaa will fly in from Ghana in a week." He wiped his mouth with the back of his hand.

"I can't believe he's gone," she admitted.

Link stared at the empty cup, tears dripping over his face. "He's all I had left."

"Hey." Emma wrapped her arms around him, bringing him into her embrace. "We still have each other. I'm here for you . . . I know we haven't been close in a while, but we can fix that."

He nodded, pulling away enough to pour another glass of alcohol.

"Better slow down or you're gonna black out and have one hell of a headache tomorrow." Emma poured the tequila into the shot glasses.

"Maybe that's what I want," Link grumbled.

She looked at him, taking the time to study the strong cut of his jaw. His eyes were so dark, they were the color of a midnight sky—just like their dad's. The short dreadlocks on the top half of his head were pulled into a ponytail, the bottom half shaved in a fade. Her gaze wandered down his neck, over the prominent Adam's apple she wanted to taste, trailing his collarbone, to the wide expanse of his muscular naked chest and the defined eight-pack of abs. *Fuck.* Heat flooded her body, and it had nothing to do with the bourbon.

Of all the people in the world, why did Link have to affect her so?

"Jussss tonight," he said, obviously mistaking her silent ogling for concern at his overindulgence.

She lifted her shot glass. "Just tonight."

The corner of his mouth turned up as he clinked his glass to hers and downed the shot without the salt or the lime juice. He didn't even wince.

Anything to help ease the pain of his loss.

* * *

Countless drinks later, Emma had lost all sense of time. Her body buzzed with warm tingles. Her vision was fuzzy and her sense of balance all but gone. She belted out the lyrics to "Zipper" by Jason Derulo, which was blasting through Link's sound system, laughing as they danced around his living room. He sang, his deep voice soaring over the higher notes.

God, was there anything sexier than a man who could sing? Bolts of lust shot directly to her core. She reveled in anything to distract her from the pain of losing her papa, seeking out the fire that would surely burn her rather than the emotional pain of grief.

He stumbled, bringing his body closer to hers. Her breath caught. His glazed, bloodshot eyes glued to hers as his voice dropped an octave. She swallowed, and he licked his lips. Her urge to kiss him rose as his hands lowered to her waist.

She moved to the beat as the song changed. "Crazy in Love" by Sofia Karlberg poured through the speakers. She sang the lyrics, telling him everything she'd held in for years. His eyes darkened even more with intent and focused on her mouth. Was that desire sparking in them? Or was that tequila and wishful thinking? Did he feel the same as she did? Was that why he'd pushed her away for so long?

"Link?"

He didn't answer her, his eyes half-closed, staring at her mouth like it was the most interesting thing in the world.

He feels this too. She shouldn't—couldn't. He was her step-brother. But it was too hard to resist when she was desperate to *feel.* She leaned on tiptoes and ran her lips over his gently. The connection was like a bolt of lightning shocking her system. How many years had she fantasized about doing this? All her wildest imaginings fell short of just how powerful the energy pulsing between them was.

Link sucked in a gasp, as if too stunned to kiss her back.

Did I just fuck up?

He growled, grabbing the back of her neck as she stumbled towards the couch. He spun her around and pushed her onto the cushion before settling his weight over her. His tongue parted her lips. He tasted like bourbon and every fantasy she'd had come to life. Tightening his grip on her hip, he thrust against her. His hard arousal poked her belly.

She moaned. *Is this really happening? Am I dreaming?* The room spun.

Emma raked her teeth along his bottom lip. Link threaded his fingers through her hair, tugging the back of it, sending daggers of delicious pain through her.

"Fuck." Link pulled away, his lips glistening.

"Yes. Fuck me." The words spilled out in her haze.

He seemed to be at war with himself, hesitating.

Would he pull away and say this was all a mistake? Or would he give in to this magnetic attraction between them? It was time to put it all out there.

Looking him in the eyes, she did something she never had and made herself vulnerable. "Please?"

3

EMMA

Link's mouth crashed onto Emma's. Desire flooded her every cell. Pent-up need encompassed her in a hurricane of lust. She leaned against him, sending them tumbling over the edge of the couch to the ground. He grunted but never broke the kiss, as she climbed on top of him. After whipping her shirt off, she paused, taking the moment in. She savored the way his eyes burned with want for her. She slipped the black lace bra down her arms and tossed it.

"Fuck, your tits are perfect." Link reached and pinched her pink nipple before sitting up to take it in his mouth.

"Mmmmm." Emma held his head against her as he sucked and nipped, tugged and kneaded the soft flesh. She ground into him as his mouth continued its assault on her senses. Needing more, she cursed the layers of clothes between them.

After stumbling off him, she unbuttoned her jeans and tried to pull them from her. Why did skinny jeans have to be so hard to take off?

Crash!

The music abruptly stopped.

"Shit!" She laughed, taking in the fallen lamp on the floor and the unplugged stereo system. The only light left came from a small lamp in the other corner of the room.

Cool air rushed across her naked skin as he tore the pants the rest of the way off her. A flood of heat spiraled from her core to every extremity at the show of force. Wetness seeped from her pussy as his nose skimmed her inner thigh, breathing her in.

Why was that so sexy? Rough, calloused hands spread her wide. Chills raced across her skin, blooming into a wildfire of need. Anticipation wound around her like a thick fog as her core clenched.

One lick, right up the center, parted her slick, lower lips. She shivered and hissed, her eyes rolling back. His wet, warm soft tongue licked, and flicked, and swirled everywhere but her clit, teasing—tempting her with sweet torture. Everywhere he touched burned white hot as if he was searing her with his own desire.

Whimpering, she arched her back, trying to move his tongue to where she needed it most. He growled, pressing her belly down roughly as he sucked her clit into his mouth. The pain melded with the pleasure, sending her swirling into bliss.

"Yes! Link!" She grabbed his head, pulling his hair.

Raking his teeth over her clit, he added a finger inside her as he sat. Her juices glistened over his mouth and chin. He licked his lips, causing her whole body to shudder in response. The way his dark gaze locked on her brought a wave of sensual power rushing over her, drowning her in a flood of desire.

"Fuck me. *Please?*" There was that word again. She couldn't stop begging this man for everything he was willing to give. Emma was wanton and reckless. Nothing mattered but the hollow ache that only he could fill.

He stopped to play with her breasts. Fuck that. *Fuck me.*

Emma unbuttoned his pants and tore the zipper down before yanking his pants to his knees. She'd waited too long for this. They could do slow next time. Emma wanted him, and each second without him filling her felt like an eternity.

Shoving him backwards so he leaned against the couch, she crawled over him. His hazy surprise quickly morphed into a smirk. She settled onto his lap; his thick cock pressed against her slick folds as she kissed him. Her essence on his lips only added to the forbidden rush. This kiss was more intoxicating than the tequila, sending hot pulses of lust vibrating through her.

His hands explored her body, squeezing her ass as she lifted her hips enough to take his thick, hard cock into her hand.

"Fuuuuck," he gritted out before jerking her hips over him. In one swift motion, he was buried deep inside her.

"Oh, God!" A bolt of lightning striking her body couldn't have been more shocking to her system. No man had ever fit her like this. "You're fucking perfect," she moaned as she thrust her hips up and down, riding him. The abrasive rug cut into her knees; the alcohol numbed the pain. Every cell in her body buzzed, drunk on tequila and pleasure.

He sucked the white flesh of her breast into his mouth, marking her, as she clenched around him.

"So good. Better than I'd imagined," he mumbled into her neck.

He'd imagined this before?

Her thighs clenched over his as she held on to him, digging her nails into his shoulders. Pleasure wracked her body.

His fingers tangled in her pink-and-blue-tipped blond hair, tugging it back so she had no choice but to look at him. It was like he knew exactly what she liked—what she wanted.

"That's right, little bird. Come for me," he growled, lifting his hips to meet her thrust for thrust.

Sharp pricks of teeth bruised the tender flesh of her neck, sending her shooting past the stars and into a whole new plane of ecstasy as he tensed under her. His muscles bunched and grew taut under her touch, pulling her into a bourbon-and-sex-soaked kiss.

She panted. Her hard nipples pressed against his chest. Sweat glistened off his body, his eyes barely open. Her own were growing heavy. Spent and in a cloud of bliss, she rested her head against him.

Holy shit. I just had sex with Link.

After all the years she'd lusted after him, craved him, she finally had him. Emma may have lost one man today, but she'd gained another. They would have each other to get through this.

She closed her eyes, the steady rhythm of Link's heartbeat lulling her to sleep.

4

LINK

Who the fuck was playing the drums in his house? And why did his mouth feel like it was stuffed with cotton balls? Link cracked his eyes open. Big mistake. He winced at the light. Damnit. The percussion was coming from a splitting headache. He groaned and forced his gaze to survey his surroundings.

Why am I naked in my living room?

The soft body against his nudged closer.

Fuck, what did I do last night? Or maybe who *would be more accurate.*

He studied the naked backside of the blonde on his arm. She had a really nice ass. He moved his arm out from under her and sat carefully. Every muscle ached from spending the night on the hard floor. His head was pounding. The empty bottles of bourbon and tequila on the coffee table were explanation enough.

What was the last thing he remembered? He lowered his head in his hands.

Dad. The hospital. Emma. Home. Emma—shit. He jerked his head to the sleeping woman, panic filling his veins with ice.

There's no way.

He grabbed his sweatpants off the floor and slipped them on as he looked anywhere but at her. His lamp was in pieces in the corner. What the hell had they done?

She groaned and rubbed her face, turning around.

His heart stopped, stuck in his throat. "Fuck."

"Shhhh. Don't yell." She winced.

He'd fucked his sister. *Jesus Christ.* Bile rose. He stumbled to the bathroom just in time to empty his guts.

He flushed and brushed his teeth, needing to get rid of the rancid aftertaste. Wiping his hand across his mouth, he froze. Shame and guilt crashed over him. He smelled like her.

What would Dad think of me now? How could I have been so fucking stupid? I'm disgusting.

"You okay?" Emma appeared in the doorway, her hands stretched out with a glass of water and two pain pills.

He accepted them and guzzled down the water. She'd slipped on one of his T-shirts, but her legs were bare. His cock twitched in his pants.

There is something wrong with me.

She offered him a smile and then grabbed his mouthwash, swishing some in her mouth before spitting it back out.

Emma reached her arms around him. He tensed.

Emma turned her confused gaze to him, running her hand over his cheek. "Want to go back to bed?"

With her? Was she crazy?

"What . . . I mean . . . what happened last night?"

Her nose scrunched, and it was fucking adorable, which only made things worse. "Which part?"

"Why were we . . ." He moved his hand back and forth between them. "Naked. Did we . . .?"

"You don't remember any of it?" She looked almost sad.

"I remember you stopping by and bringing out the tequila."

She pulled away, wrapping her arms around herself. The motion tugged at his heart, but he stayed where he was, every muscle rigid with tension.

She smoothed the hair out of her face. "Last night is fuzzy, but I remember we had sex."

"Fuck!"

She flinched at his outburst before her eyes grew glassy. "I thought . . ."

"Look, I'm sorry. I can't believe I let this happen." Link pushed past her to the kitchen. *Coffee.* He needed caffeine and some toast before he dealt with this.

"You don't have anything to be sorry about." Emma followed him. This was her grief talking. It made sense she'd seek comfort from him. It's not like she'd actually want him otherwise.

He shook his head, anger rising at himself. "I fucked my sister. I'd say that's pretty messed up."

She stepped back as if he'd physically hit her. "We're not blood-related, Link. There isn't anything wrong with what we did."

He snapped. "Nothing wrong? Papa died yesterday, and what do I do? I fuck his daughter!"

"It's not as big of a deal as you're making it out to be. He never legally adopted me."

"Did we even use protection?" He searched the floor for any used condoms, but there was nothing. Maybe he'd put it in the trash? Surely, he'd disposed of the condom once they'd used it.

His gaze flicked to Emma, pleading with her to tell him they hadn't been totally reckless.

She bit her lip and winced, fear flashing for the first time in her blue eyes.

His gaze snagged on the red and purple bite marks on her neck. His stomach rolled. Had he hurt her?

"No, we didn't. Fuck. And I'm not on birth control because I've only been with women in the past few years."

"Aren't you a lesbian? How could you . . . I mean, we . . ."

She rolled her eyes, and damn it if it didn't make him want to bend her over his knee and turn that pretty, round ass pink. He shook his head, disgusted at himself for thinking it.

"I'm bisexual. Pansexual if you really want to know. I'm attracted to the person for who they are not their gender."

"Well, that's just the fucking cherry on top. I fucked my sister without a condom, and she's not on birth control." Panic squeezed his chest tight.

He couldn't be a dad. He wasn't ready for that type of commitment, but even more so, *he couldn't father a child with his stepsister.* This was also the last thing Emma needed after the shit show going on in the media with her band member going to prison.

She shook her head, anger and pain reflecting in her gaze. "I'll go to the pharmacy. Don't worry. I wouldn't want to impose on your life any more than I already have." She grabbed her pants and slipped them on before gathering the leather jacket off the chair and zipping it up as she rushed to the door.

"Em, that isn't—I didn't mean it like that. Just give me a damn minute to process this."

She turned to look at him, her gaze hopeful. "Do you regret last night?"

Yes. Without a doubt. "Don't you?"

The light in her eyes dimmed as her shoulders slumped.

"I'll be staying at Jasmine's inn. Let me know what you need from me for the funeral arrangements."

"Em—" He grabbed her wrist to halt her. Energy hummed along his arm. That hadn't been there before. It was like finally acting on the forbidden fantasy he'd fought for years had unleashed a tidal wave of emotions.

She turned, casting him a cautious glance.

He sighed. "Let's keep this between us. We never speak of this again. It's best for both of us. If word got out . . . Look, I don't want people to hear about it and start talking."

She didn't need the bad press. Papa had told him about the record label warning Emma's band they could be dropped after Geo's altercation.

Emma leaned in, so she was only a breath away. A mask of indifference covered her face, making her unreadable. Her gaze turned to ice. "Don't worry."

His shoulders relaxed as he sighed in relief. The last thing they needed was this small town knowing how badly he'd fucked up. His father would be so disappointed in him.

"I'm well versed in being fucked over and passed on," Emma finished before exiting his town house and slamming the door.

Her words socked him in the chest. "Fuck!" He punched the wall, pain lancing up his arm. It was nothing close to the heartache he'd caused Emma.

Protect her, son. She needs you more than you know. His father's words rang in his head.

What have I done?

5

EMMA

Emma ripped open the box and freed the one tiny pill before tossing the container into the garbage outside the pharmacy. She swallowed the tablet dry, hoping it would work and she wouldn't end up pregnant. *I'm not ready to be a mom.* Her career had just blown up, her father just died, and the would-be baby daddy made it clear he wanted nothing to do with her. Surely it would work—it was ninety-nine percent effective, after all. In a couple of weeks' time, she'd be whining about getting her period again.

Emotion clogged her throat—or was that the pill? Emma slipped on the helmet and started her motorcycle. The nice thing about the seacoast was that the winters were milder. There wasn't even a dusting of snow. But it was a nippy thirty-five degrees.

After pulling her leather gloves out of her pocket, she put them on before shifting into gear. Wind whipped through the rips in her jeans as she sped down the road.

After a few miles, the left side opened up revealing the crashing waves against a rocky shore. This was Shattered

Cove. No matter how much of the world she traveled and toured, this was the only place that would ever be *home*. Jasmine and her boyfriend Atlas's restaurant, Atlantis, whizzed by as she made her way to The Lighthouse Inn.

Another couple minutes and the white, Victorian-style building came into view. She parked her bike on the side of a gravel parking lot and grabbed the small backpack tied on the rear before she took her helmet off. Salty wind rushed against her, sending her pink-and-blue-highlighted blond hair tumbling into her face. Pressing it behind her ear, she took a deep breath, preparing herself to walk in and pretend everything was okay—just like always.

She just needed to say hello and then get settled in her room, where she could finally lie down and wallow.

The front door banged open as a little girl came rushing out. "Auntie Emma!" Zoey screeched before hugging her waist tight.

Emma wrapped her arm around her niece. "Hey, kiddo."

Zoey pulled back, her cheeks rosy, her dark hair twisted into two Dutch braids. "Mommy said you were coming. Can I take a ride on your mower-circle while you're here?"

Emma smiled at her niece and walked towards the inn. "Maybe. If your mom says it's okay."

Movement drew her gaze to the front door. Jasmine, her close friend since her teen years, leaned against the entry with her arms crossed. "Where is your coat, little miss?" Jasmine asked Zoey.

The girl ran ahead to her mom. "I forgot. Me wanted to see Auntie Emma!"

Jasmine patted her head and sent her inside before rolling her eyes.

"She gets more adorable every time I see her." Emma walked through the doorway and into the reception. High ceilings stretched above her, and a giant painting of a ship at sea adorned the wall to her left. Dark grey wood floors contrasted with the white walls perfectly, leading to the main desk of the inn.

"She keeps me busy, that's for sure." Jasmine shut the door behind them. "I'm so sorry about Solomon."

Emma nodded, her nose stinging at the reminder. *Just hold it together for a few more minutes.*

"Daddy! She's here!" Zoey's voice came from the kitchen.

Emma cut a questioning glance towards her friend.

Jasmine gave a cautious smile. "She asked Atlas if she could call him that a couple months ago."

Emma reached out and drew Jasmine into a hug. "I'm so happy for you. You deserve this."

"Are you hungry?" Atlas's deep voice interrupted their moment. Emma released Jasmine and turned to him. She'd only met the man a couple times over the holidays, but seeing the light in Jasmine's eyes for the first time spoke louder than any words of adoration for him could.

A pang of longing flit through her chest. *I wish I knew what it was like to be loved like that.*

"Em? Want a snack?" Jasmine's voice brought her back to the conversation. Sympathy glistened in her eyes.

"No. Sorry. I'm just really tired."

"Of course you are." Jasmine walked over to the desk at the other end of the room before grabbing something off of it and returning. "Here." She placed a set of keys in Emma's hand. "You've got the best suite all to yourself. Do you need anything special?"

Emma shook her head.

"Come by Atlantis anytime. Dinner's on me," Atlas said, picking up Zoey.

She forced a smile. "I appreciate it."

"Do you want help getting settled in your room?" Jasmine asked, reaching for Emma's backpack.

Emma shook her head and tugged her bag higher on her shoulder. "No, thanks. I just need some sleep." *And to be alone.*

Jasmine offered her one more tight hug and released her. "If you need *anything,* I'm here."

Emma walked past the desk and turned right into the common room with the L-shaped couch, turquoise pillows, and beach decor. She made her way up the grey wooden staircase to the Lighthouse suite. She put the key in and turned the knob.

The brightness hit her first. The walls and curtains were a crisp white. She set her helmet on top of the weathered dresser to her right. The wrought-iron king bed with a navy comforter was the only dark color in the whole room. After setting the keys on one of the bedside tables next to a honeycomb ceramic lamp, she dropped her backpack on the floor. With it, the last of her energy drained from her. The events of the last twenty-four hours caught up to her. She walked over to the giant window overlooking the ocean, taking time to admire the crashing waves. One after another, they rose, washed up the beach, then receded, only to do it all over again. If that wasn't the very definition of her life right now, she didn't know what was. Going through the motions, getting the same results. Predictable. Stuck in a never-ending cycle.

Why even bother trying?

Emma sighed and shut the curtain before making her way over to the small mini fridge. She grabbed a water and downed it as she entered the large bathroom with the lighthouse-painted door. She should enjoy the large tub with the jets, but she was too tired. She'd probably fall asleep in it.

Shucking off her clothing, she let it fall into a pile. Next to come off were her bracelets. Her muscles ached from the long ride from Boston airport to Shattered Cove on her bike, and the events of last night. Link hadn't been gentle—which was how she liked it. The fingerprint bruises on her hips were a painful reminder of both the best and most heartbreaking night of her life.

Swiveling to the mirror, she took herself in. Her hair was a wild mess from Link's fingers, and the helmet hadn't helped. Black eyeliner was smudged under her eyes, making her blue irises stand out. She ran a finger over her red chapped lips, both from being sucked and bitten by the man and the dehydration of drinking far too much. She never let go like that, not usually.

Just tonight. Link's words echoed in her mind. Just one night of insanity.

Her hand smoothed over the bite marks on her neck, a torturous reminder of what couldn't be. *I thought he finally saw me.*

She shook her head, the back of her eyes prickling. After turning the shower spray on, she waited until it was hot enough to climb under. Emma washed the lingering traces of his scent down the drain with the last of her hope.

Emma collapsed to her knees, letting the hot water pour over her face—unlike the tears she kept imprisoned inside. Here, Emma could let herself fall apart. She could cry for her father, for the mother who'd abandoned her, and for the man she loved and could never have. But they wouldn't come— stuffed too far down, unable to break free. She slapped her hand hard against her thigh. The sting burned her nerve endings.

I need to let this out. Need the pain to stop.

Her hands traced the hidden scars on her upper thighs and then her wrist. She squinted her eyes closed. The urge to take some of the control back flooded over her.

Eyeing the shaver warily, she stumbled upright and shut off the water before grabbing her towel. She needed to get away from the temptation.

After quickly drying her hair and body, she slipped beneath the grey sheets and closed her eyes. Exhaustion, in every sense of the word, swallowed her up as she drifted off to sleep.

* * *

The phone ringing woke her. Emma jolted upright, the sheets falling to her waist. Confusion spun around her.

Where am I?

Right, Jasmine's inn.

Ring!

Emma picked her phone out of the backpack on the floor before swiping it to answer.

"Hello?"

"Hello, Miss Sterling?" an older gentleman asked.

"Yeah?"

"This is Mike Driscoll. I'm the estate lawyer of Solomon Owusu."

Emma furrowed her brow. "I didn't realize he had a lawyer."

"Oh, yes. Mr. Owusu was a very thorough man. I'm sorry to hear of his passing."

"Thanks."

"Well, I'm calling to let you know I have the paperwork with his wishes upon his death to go over with you and his son, Lincoln. I'd like to schedule an appointment at your earliest convenience."

"He . . . um, in his culture, they do not speak about the

arrangements for a full week after the . . . passing. We'll have to wait until then."

"Of course. I'll get you on the schedule and send you over a date and time to see if that works for you?" he asked.

Emma nodded, even though he couldn't see. "Okay."

"Take care."

She tapped the screen to end the call. Sitting in silence, it all crashed over her at once.

Dad is gone. He's never coming back.

What was the last thing I said to him?

Did he know how much I loved him? How much I appreciated the life he'd given me and the one he'd saved me from? Did he know how grateful I am for his support and belief in me?

A quiet knock on the door interrupted her thoughts. She got up and grabbed the damp towel to cover her naked body as she opened it.

Jasmine held out a bottle of wine. "Thought you could use this."

Emma let her in and shut the door behind her. "Honestly, I think I drank enough last night to last me a while."

"Oh, sorry. You did look pretty rough when you got here."

Flashes of the previous evening assaulted Emma as she grabbed another bottle of water from the small fridge. She offered Jasmine one, but her friend shook her head.

"Do you need me to do some laundry?" Jasmine motioned to the towel.

"Actually, yeah. I've only got one clean outfit. I have some stuff at Dad's . . ." Emma's words stuck in her throat. She couldn't go there yet, knowing it would be empty.

"No problem. You can borrow some of mine." Jasmine crawled onto the bed, sitting against the headboard with a pillow tucked behind her. Emma opened her backpack, pulled out the spare pair of clothes she had, and dipped into the bathroom to change.

Once she was dressed, she climbed on next to Jasmine.

"So, where did you sleep last night?" her friend asked suspiciously.

Emma closed her eyes. The vivid image of Link's naked body beneath hers flashed through her mind.

Let's keep this between us. Link's words cut short the bittersweet memories. *What's one more secret? One more game of pretend?*

Emma shrugged. "A friend's."

Jasmine pushed against her shoulder playfully. "The kind of friend who leaves bite marks, huh?"

Panic stole Emma's breath. She'd forgotten about the marks. *Good thing I didn't tell her where I'd stayed.*

One of the many masks she wore slid into place. Emma smiled and waggled her eyebrows. "Those are the best types."

Jasmine laughed, but concern flashed in her green eyes.

"What?" Emma asked.

"Just don't make the same mistake I did. Sex offers only a temporary relief. Eventually, you have to face what you're running from before it destroys you." Jasmine spoke from her own experience.

Emma placed her hand over her friend's. "I know. Promise it was a one-time thing."

"I get it. Just know I'm here for you." Jasmine squeezed her hand.

"I can't believe he's gone," Emma confessed.

"Solomon was a good man. Can't tell you how many times he and Link fixed my old beater car for basically free," Jasmine mused.

"He was the very best." Solomon had been the only one to choose her in her life.

"What he did—taking you in after your mother left . . ."

Jasmine rested her palm on Emma's leg. "He was a kind man."

She was right. Not many people would take on another couple's daughter, but with her mother addicted to heroin and her father having died in a car accident, Solomon had been there. He was her mother's boyfriend before she'd relapsed. After the last fight between them, the first and only time she'd ever heard Solomon raise his voice, she'd woken to find her mother gone.

"Where is Mom?"

Papa Solomon took a deep breath before looking her in the eyes. "Your mother is gone."

"When is she coming back?" Would Emma have to leave too? Papa Solomon was the nicest out of all of her mom's boyfriends. He didn't try to get into her bedroom when she was changing or hit her like the others.

"She's not. At least, not until she can get healthy." His sad eyes told the truth. Her mother wouldn't be back—ever.

"Where do I go now?" Emma asked, hoping Solomon wouldn't send her to child services. Anything was better than that.

Solomon shifted closer, his kind eyes directed at her. "You're my daughter now. You'll stay here with me and my son as long as you want to."

That was the first time Emma had felt like someone truly loved her. In the moment, she hadn't known that was what it was, being starved of it her whole life.

That was the pivotal experience that changed her life. And maybe it was time to accept that the only person who would love her enough to choose her like that had just died.

And I wasn't even here to say goodbye.

Her lungs squeezed tight around the shards of glass of regret.

I failed him.

6

LINK

Link ran his fingers over the wooden armrest on the chair he was sitting in. His eyes swept to the antique desk with files piled on each corner of the otherwise organized area. The walls were lined with books, the scent of fresh coffee tinting the otherwise stale air. A few certificates of education hung on the wall, all awarded to Michael Driscoll, his father's estate lawyer.

The door behind him opened and shut. Soft feet padded towards the chair next to him. He didn't need to look over to know the sweet, strawberry smell was from Emma.

The old chair creaked as she sat. He cut a quick glance in her direction. It had been a week since she'd walked out his front door. Dark circles underlined her dull blue eyes. She tucked a stray strand of her blond hair that escaped her messy bun behind her ear. Her cloudy blue gaze met his as a lightning bolt of energy whooshed through him. His chest tightened, his shoulders weighed down by a swirling hurricane of emotions. Guilt. Lust. Shame.

The side of her mouth quirked up, unsure. "Hey."

"Hey." His voice cracked. He wiped his sweaty palms on his jeans.

After a few minutes of awkward silence, she unscrewed the cap on her ginger ale and took a sip.

Is she nauseous? Could she be . . .

Was she pregnant and afraid to tell him? Not that he would blame her. Everything had come out wrong that morning. Could morning sickness happen that quickly?

He sat straighter, turning towards her as he pointed to the drink. "Are you . . ." Link couldn't even say it out loud.

Her eyes darted between him and her ginger soda. She rolled her eyes and then narrowed them on him. "I thought you never wanted to speak of that again?"

He cleared his throat, checking the door for the lawyer they were expecting any minute. It remained closed. As he turned back to Emma, hurt flashed in her gaze before she closed off, erecting a wall between them, making her unreadable again.

"We may have to if you're . . ."

She huffed and shook her head, crossing her arms in front of her chest as she stared at the floor. "It doesn't happen that fast—the symptoms. I took the plan B pill that morning. I'll know for sure in the next few days."

"And then?" Link asked. Would she tell either way?

"And then we can continue never talking about it, or if I am pregnant, I'll make the choice that is best for me," she grit out.

He sighed and reached out for her hand before thinking better of it. The steady thrum of energy from their connection took him by surprise. "I'm sorry I was an asshole. This is my fault. I'll support whatever decision you make. I'm really sorry for putting you in a position to have to make a difficult choice."

Her eyes grew glassy before she nodded and rubbed her thumb over the soft flesh of his hand. "I have no plans for being a mother. I've never had the desire to have kids—at least, not anytime soon. I'm more auntie material, not mother." She blinked and looked away.

Fuck, he wanted to pull her into his arms and assure her everything would be okay. Instead, he'd caused her pain, and put her in a position to have to possibly make one of the toughest choices.

I'm a fucking asshole.

The door opened and he yanked his hand away. The hurt in her eyes was a spear through his gut.

"Ahh, there you are," the familiar voice of his auntie Yaa greeted.

He stood and turned to give her a hug, but she veered over to Emma first.

"How are you doing?" his auntie asked as she pulled him into a hug next. "Both of you look too thin. My brother would not want his children this sad. He's in a better place." She took the empty chair to his right as the door opened again.

"Thank you all for waiting. I had to get the original paperwork from the safe," Mike Driscoll said as he settled into his desk, spreading open a binder. After flipping through a few pages, he stopped, clasping his hands in front of him and glancing between his three guests. "First of all, I want to extend my condolences for Solomon's passing. He was quite an amazing man. A true loss to this town."

"Thank you," Aunt Yaa said.

Emma looked on numbly, not responding in any way.

Link nodded.

"Okay, did Solomon ever tell you what his final wishes were?"

"He wanted to be cremated. I know that much," Link supplied.

"Yes, he did. But as far as his remains are concerned, he left specific directions for his two children as to what he wants done with his ashes." Mike turned the page and pointed to the print.

"He said he'd spent his life living by one seacoast and he always wanted to see the other. He's left instructions, including a map, for you to both take the Chevelle and drive to California to lay his ashes to rest in the Pacific Ocean."

Huh? Panic seized Link. *A road trip alone with Emma?* "No." *Absolutely not. That's a bad idea. We can do it separately.* Why would he suggest that?

"Mr. Owusu was very specific. He said if his wishes were not fulfilled, all his estate, including what your aunt Yaa will inherit, is to be forfeited to the charities he's chosen. That includes the garage," Mike said.

Shit, I said that out loud? He turned towards Emma.

Her lips were flat on her otherwise blank face, but her eyes burned with anger. "I can do it. I'll have to talk to my manager and the band, to schedule some time off, so we can't do it right away, but I can make it happen."

Of course, she could. Because obviously being close to him wasn't as hard on her as it was on him.

Anger boiled, rage clawing at the edges of his sanity.

His father was dead. Gone so suddenly, just like his mother. And somehow the man was still pulling his strings from the grave. Link shook his head. His dad never had liked to give up control. Why would Link assume differently in his death? He loved his dad, but damn, he didn't like him very much right now. Shame and guilt crashed over him at the thought.

He's gone and I took him for granted all those years.

Link shook his head, emotion choking him. "I can't do this."

Emma gasped, turning her pain-filled gaze to his.

Link shot to his feet, ignoring his aunt's calls as he left the office.

Cold air nipped his face as he climbed into his car. As he turned on the ignition, the classic car roared to life. He sighed, raking his hands over his face. Everything was so fucked up. Emotions swirled inside him like a tornado, whipping him into dizzying circles until he didn't know which way was up or down, east or west. What he did know was anger.

"Fuck this." He shifted into gear.

He needed to get his hands dirty and his mind busy. Pushing on the gas, he pulled out onto the street and headed towards the garage. At least there he felt at peace. It was his. For now.

* * *

"Didn't think you'd be back in today," Reese, his best friend and second-in-command at the shop, said.

"Well, here I am. What needs to be done?"

Reese wiped his hands on his stained overalls. "Oil change for the Ford. New brakes and tires for the Chevy. And Matty Peterson said his car's electrical was shorting out."

Link pulled on his own set of overalls as he nodded. "I'll take Matty's car." He needed something challenging to distract him from the shit show that was his life.

"Keys are in it." Reese grabbed a thermos of coffee and lifted it to his lips. "How'd it go with the lawyer?"

Link grunted in frustration.

"That good, huh?" His friend laughed.

"In order for me to inherit the garage, I have to go on a

road trip with Emma to California to dump his ashes in the Pacific Ocean."

"That's all?"

Link crossed his arms over his chest. "What do you mean that's all? I'd have to leave you here alone for more than a week on some wild goose chase." Not to mention be alone with Emma.

"Do you have to go tomorrow?" Reese asked.

"No. We'd have to schedule it around Emma's concerts and stuff."

"Then we have plenty of time to enroll some more help for the time you'll be gone. You know I can handle things until you get back. Marissa would be happy to come in and do the books that your dad usually handled." Every time the man brought up his wife, his eyes flashed with adoration. High-school sweethearts, married sixteen years, and still happy as ever.

"I just hate that even now he's trying to control me."

Reese nodded, setting his drink down.

"What?"

"Nothing." His friend shrugged.

"Just say what you're gonna say," Link pressed.

"I know you and your dad have—had—your own relation-ship problems, but in all these years, I never saw him tell you to do something that wasn't good for you or this shop. Some-times you act as though you've been doing him a huge favor by working by his side to build this place from the ground up. Like he owed you."

Did he feel his father owed him? *Yes.* He should have the shop, no strings attached. He'd been the one here day in and day out, not Emma. Not that he blamed her; this was never her calling.

"Tell me how you really feel," Link grumbled.

He had put his sweat and blood into this place, just as much as his father had—more in these last ten years. It was because of his changes and ideas this place was thriving. It was why his father could have theoretically stepped back and worked less or even retired if he'd wished.

"So why are you being a whiny bitch about taking a vacation? You know who you sound like?"

"Shut the fuck up. It is *not* the same thing. My father was old enough to retire. I'm not. I'll take time off when everything slows down."

"Should I start looking for another job?" Reese asked.

Link met his gaze. *I'm being selfish.* "No. I won't let you and the guys lose your livelihoods." He turned and surveyed the large room. Memories of his life with his father were recorded in every scuff on the cement floor and each shiny tool they'd bought together. This place was the last thing left he had of his papa. Link would be devastated if he lost it.

"I'll do it." *And somehow manage to get my body under control around Emma.*

Something told him that was going to be much easier said than done.

7

EMMA

Emma leaned back in her chair by the window overlooking the incoming tide at The Lighthouse Inn. Her arm ached from holding her phone up for so long. She pulled her knees to her chest and rested her elbow on it.

"Okay, I have the next ten days cleared on your schedule, so you can have time for the funeral before you guys get back to your gigs." Callie's face took up most of the screen on Emma's phone.

"I appreciate it." Her manager might be new, but she did her job well.

"Most of the venues understood and were happy to reschedule. We had several magazines and reporters reach out for comment. I gave them news that you were dealing with a death in the family and that you ask them to respect your privacy while you grieve." Callie's gaze met hers through the screen.

Emma chewed on her nail, peeling chips of black polish

off while anxiety churned in her belly. This fame was all so new to her. "Will they show up here in Shattered Cove?"

"I mean, it's a possibility. Do you want me to hire a body-guard?" Callie asked.

Emma laughed, but her manager's silence meant she was serious. "No. I don't think that will be necessary."

"I'm sure there will be a bigger story in the rags tomorrow to draw some of the heat off you."

Emma sighed. "I don't see why anyone would want to know this much about my life."

"Welcome to fame." Callie grinned. "Are you okay?"

Emma forced a smile. "Of course. I'll be back after the funeral, and we'll get to work. I may have to take some time off again, but I'm not sure when. I have to find out what works for Link." *And if he will even go with me.*

She didn't want anything from her papa. But if his wish was to have his ashes scattered in the Pacific Ocean, she'd give him that.

Guilt settled over her shoulders like a heavy weight drawing them down. *Did I abandon Papa? Did I get too wrapped up in my life and the band?*

"Okay, well, I'm here if you need someone to talk to," Callie offered.

"Thanks. I'll be fine. If you really want to do me a favor, you could try to throw any media off my scent. I don't want people knowing I'm here." Emma sighed, imagining hordes of photographers climbing over the sand dunes leading to the inn.

"Okay. I'll spread a rumor you've been spotted somewhere far from Shattered Cove. You do what you have to, and I'll see you when you land in Austin."

"Thanks again." Emma nodded.

"No problem."

Emma ended the call and leaned her head against her knees.

Ping.

She opened the group message between her and her bandmates.

Asher: *You good, doll face? Callie said you won't be back for a bit.*

Nicky: *Her dad just died. Of course she needs some time, dumbass.*

Emma chuckled. Her guys weren't the most sensitive bunch, but they told it like it was and that was one of the reasons they worked so well together.

Emma: *I'm fine. Ghanaian culture takes a bit longer for funerals to happen. I'll meet you guys in Austin, and we'll give the show of a lifetime.*

Leo: *Working on new songs?*

Emma: *Maybe . . .*

Leo: *Sweet.*

Ravi: *You want us to come back for the funeral? We loved Mr. O too.*

A smile floated to her lips.

Nicky: *Remember when he came into the garage for one of our practices and told us we sounded like a cat being murdered?*

Emma laughed at the memory of her papa's face twisted in horror after listening to their song.

Asher: *He wasn't wrong . . .*

Ravi: *Speak for yourself, asshole.*

Leo: *He always pushed us to be better. Mr. O was our biggest supporter.*

Emma took a breath as tears prickled her eyes. *He was. And how did I repay him? By not being here when he needed me most.*

Ravi: *Em? When is it? Send us the deets. We'll be there.*

Emma: *I fucking love you guys. I'll send the info over once I get it settled with Link and my auntie Yaa.*

Leo: *Awwww. You're making me cry, sweet cheeks.*

Emma barked out a laugh.

Nicky: *She's so poetic. It's no wonder she writes songs that go platinum. LOL.*

Asher: *Em, be honest. You love me the most.*

Ravi: *Nah, she loves me more.*

Emma: *I take it back. I hate your ugly asses.*

Leo: *What did I do?!*

Asher: *Fickle woman.*

Ravi: *Ooooh, she gonna murder you now, son.*

Emma: *Okay, guys, I have to go. Try not to get into too much trouble while I'm gone.*

Nicky: *See? She still loves us. Why else would she care so much?*

Asher: *Don't worry. The only thing I plan on getting into is a few *peach emoji* *winky face emoji**

Emma gave a tired chuckle and tossed her phone onto the bed before walking over and falling on it herself. Curling into a ball, she closed her eyes. The desire to go to sleep and not wake up swallowed her whole. Her phone pinged again, but she didn't even have the energy to look at it. Dark emptiness settled over her.

Why did you have to leave me, Papa?

Did I disappoint you by not being there?

Will I ever be good enough?

Tears burned the back of her eyes. She clamped her eyes shut as a wave of grief overtook her. Her chest squeezed. It was all so heavy. Exhaustion stole her urge to cry. Fatigue like she'd never experienced crashed over her like a tidal wave. Each breath became a struggle. What if she just stopped breathing? Took a break from reality for a bit? What if she kept her eyes closed and never opened them again?

Sleep pulled her under, deeper into the darkness.

· · ·

Wind whipped across Emma's face, growing stronger. Cold water lapped at her feet as she stood in the shallow waters of the grey ocean. Her papa stood across from her on the shore. Next to him were her mother and Link.

"What are you doing here? You're dead." She glanced between her mother and Solomon.

Her mother shook her head. "I'm so sorry, Emma." She turned around and walked away.

"Mom? Wait!" Emma took a step forward, but the water was deeper somehow, coming up to her waist.

Her mother didn't listen. She kept walking, getting smaller and smaller in the distance. "Papa? How are you here?"

Her father gave her a sad smile. "I can't stay."

"Wait. Just . . . wait!" She took another step forward, only to be sucked under the water. She kicked and struggled to the surface, sucking in a gasp of air. "Help me, Papa!"

He frowned. "I can't. I'm not here anymore."

"Papa, please. I love you. I'm sorry. I'm so sorry I wasn't there."

Instead of replying, he turned and walked the same way her mother had. The only other person left on the beach was Link.

Her arms grew tired. No matter how hard she fought, the shore got farther and farther away. She screamed for Link. "Help me! Link, I can't get to shore."

Link just stared at her with sadness burning in his eyes.

"Link! Please!"

Her arms grew heavier than lead weights, sinking her lower. She screamed, but no sound came out. The last thing she saw before the darkness pulled her under was Link shaking his head and turning to walk away.

"Emma?" Jasmine's voice cut through her dreams.

Emma jolted upright, holding a hand to her racing chest.

Jasmine's brows drew together in concern. "Are you okay?"

Emma gathered her wits and nodded. "Just a bad dream." Her throat stung as if the saltwater she'd swallowed was real. Reaching for the bottle of water on the side table, she forced a shaky smile.

As she swallowed a few sips, Jasmine shifted next to her on the bed. "Dinner's ready. You haven't left the room all day, so I'm assuming you haven't eaten. Why don't you join us?"

The last thing Emma wanted to do was be around people and pretend she had it all together. But if sleeping led to more dreams like that, it was the better choice. "Sure. I'd like that."

Jasmine smiled and stood. "Okay, come down when you're ready. We'll wait for you."

Emma waited for her friend to leave before she went to relieve herself in the bathroom and splash some cold water on her face.

Ding!

She grabbed her phone, not expecting Link's name to flash on her screen.

Link: *What do you think about having the celebration of life at The Shipwreck?*

Her heart sunk. She hated that a part of her still held out hope that the other night had meant more to him too. All they had left between them was their shared grief now.

Emma: *He'd have loved that.*

Link: *Found this on his phone.* *Picture attachment*

Emma clicked the photo, and a younger version of herself appeared on the screen, laughing in Link's arms. Both of them were covered in mud from head to toe. Their dad had an unimpressed expression beside them with his arms crossed.

Emma stared at the picture, letting the memory wash over

her. Link had taken her mudding with a four-wheeler he'd restored. He wouldn't let her drive, so when he'd stopped to pee in the woods, Emma had climbed to the front and hit the gas.

Emma steered towards the field. I'll show him. *She peeked over her shoulder in time to catch Link's shocked expression morph into something a lot like disbelief tinged in anger.*

"Get back here!"

Emma ignored him and laughed as he chased her. She'd let off the gas just enough for him to catch up and then gunned it. Link kept hollering. She was laughing so hard, she could barely see in front of her.

"Emma, STOP!" Link's voice changed from protective-big-brother-who-was-pissed-he'd-been-outsmarted to actual fear.

But why—Emma gasped as the ATV dipped over an embankment she hadn't known was there, straight into a muddy trench. Cold splatters of mud splashed over her legs.

Her heart was racing, adrenaline surging in her veins. She was okay. A quick glance at her stepbrother with his hand clutched to his chest told her she'd scared him enough for the day.

She offered him the most innocent smile she could muster. "That was fun."

He shook his head. "Christ, Em, what were you thinking? You could have been hurt." Link climbed down the steep hill, the mud squishing under his shoes as he made his way to her.

"You'd never let me get injured." She slid back, letting him have control of the vehicle once again.

He moved in front of her. "Not on purpose. But you go off like a wild child and there isn't much I can do to stop it. You know if anything happened to you, Dad would kill me."

Wild child? Sure, she was wild, but only ever to get Link's attention. She liked having him look out for her. It made her belly flutter and tingles race through her body.

"Let's get out of this mess." Link pressed the gas and the ATV jolted

forward, only to stop. Thick, wet drops of mud splattered over them like rain.

Emma giggled and held her hands out as more landed in her hair.

"Fuck. You've really done it now," Link grumbled, standing and thrusting his weight as he hit the gas again. But the tires still spun in place.

"Get up front. Hit the gas when I tell you." Link climbed off.

"You're letting me drive again?" She slid to the front with a grin.

He positioned himself behind the four-wheeler. "When I say go, GO!"

Emma hit the gas. The ATV inched forward, so she kept the gas steady and steered towards the other side without mud. The machine jerked faster once the tires were clear. Emma let off the gas and parked it before turning around. Her mouth dropped open and her eyes widened before she burst into laughter. Link was completely covered in mud from head to toe.

His expression was unamused as he stalked towards her. Emma couldn't stop the giggles from pouring out of her. She clutched her stomach.

"You're going to get it now." Link reached out his arms for her.

She was giggling too hard to get away in time. He grabbed her and pulled her against his mud-soaked body, smearing it all over her as he embraced her.

"Link!"

He burst out laughing, joining her before he swiped his dirty hand across her cheek.

When they'd shown up at the shop looking like two swamp monsters, their father had just shaken his head and snapped the picture before teasing Link for being a bad influence. Link's eyes had widened as he pointed towards Emma accusingly. Emma had offered her dad an innocent smile. That was how it had gone with them. But that had been before. Before everything had changed.

Emma: *What happened to us?*

She waited a beat for the little response bubble to appear, but it never did.

Guess he got what he wanted and now he was done with her.

Emma bit the side of her cheek and set the phone down before glancing at herself in the mirror. She stared at her reflection. The ripped, vintage Rolling Stones T-shirt was looser than it had been when she arrived in Shattered Cove more than a week ago. Her white skinny jeans were just a tad easier to slip on and off. The bags under her eyes had only gotten worse. *I'm a fucking mess.* Her eyes darted to the shaver in the tub. The temptation of a temporary escape teased her.

I shouldn't. How many years had it been since the last time? She didn't want to throw all that away.

I thought I was over this. She fisted her hands, fingernails digging into the skin of her palms as she fought for control. The subtle pain of her nails against her skin doused her in painful temptation. Just a little more and she'd be free—at least for a little while.

Fuck it. She pulled open the plastic and separated the blades. As she took off her leather bracelet, the shiny white scars stared back at her. A reminder of all the other times she'd taken her pain into her own hands—seized back the control.

After grabbing an alcohol wipe from the first aid kit she'd found under the sink, she washed the area. Pressing the sharp metal to her wrist, she closed her eyes and took a deep breath, holding it in the space between the emotional pain keeping her captive and the blade that would set her free—even if it was only for a few moments. She exhaled and pressed it through the first layers of her skin. The bite of pain sent a welcome warm rush of endorphins rocking through her. All her thoughts cleared, the ache in her heart dissipating for a few perfect seconds when nothing else hurt except where she chose.

Opening her eyes, the crimson droplets dripped down her arm. The red was a beautiful contrast to her snow-white skin. Her body buzzed like she'd had a few drinks as a calm settled into her bones. She threw out the broken razor and wiped the blood from her arm before washing it down the sink. Next, she pressed a small piece of gauze against the cut. Once the bleeding stopped, she covered her mark with a Band-Aid and then slipped her wide leather bracelet back on to cover the evidence.

Now everything was going to be okay for a little while longer.

Dinner with Jasmine and Atlas went by with laughs and stories. She joked with her niece and complimented Atlas's new dish he planned on trying out at Atlantis. And all the while Emma was smiling, laughing, and conversing with her friends, she was simply going through the motions. An invisible wall kept her from truly connecting—lost in a haze of grey, while they stood in the light. It shone so brightly from them it was blinding. She had nothing but numbness.

Emma was the outsider, like she'd always been. No one would truly understand her struggles. How could they when she didn't understand why she was the way she was herself? Why wasn't she happy when she had everything she thought she wanted? What most people fought their whole lives to get? And here she was taking it for granted. Not only that, but she'd let down her father to get it.

Maybe it was time she accepted that she would be stuck here, forever in the grey. Light wasn't meant for her. But the darkness—sweet, tempting, black, churning, eclipsing darkness

—as much as it scared her, it also tempted her. Because the shadows were accepting and familiar. The cavern seemed impossible to resist, like it was fated. Was there any use fighting it anymore? Or should she just give in to the inevitable?

8

———

EMMA

Emma stared at the pregnancy test in her trembling hand. Three days late. Maybe it was stress? Or that pill had fucked up her cycle?

The blue dye helped her answer one question. She breathed a sigh of relief. At least Link wouldn't have something to resent her for. She tossed the test in the garbage and opened the door.

Jasmine and Remy, two of her best friends, sat on her bed, dressed in black. A stark reminder that today was the day of her father's celebration of life—what he'd wanted in place of a funeral.

Jasmine stood, holding out a garment bag. "This was delivered to you from your manager."

Emma reached her hand out, the plastic crinkling in her numb fingers. Her body moved without her permission, going through the motions like a zombie. Numb. Hollow. Separate.

"Shoes came too." Remy slid a box from behind her on the bed.

Emma lifted the material out of the bag. Inside was a

gorgeous sheer red-lace dress with cap sleeves. It cinched at the waist, and the bottom was trimmed in more lace that would come a few inches above her knee.

"It's gorgeous. But isn't it supposed to be black?" Jasmine asked.

"The shoes are." Remy opened the box, showing off the red-soled black stilettos.

Emma shook her head. "In the Ghanaian culture, people wear red and black to funerals."

"Well, you're going to look amazing." Jasmine smiled.

Why do people dress up at all to say goodbye to someone who can't even see them? Why bother?

She couldn't find the energy in her to fake it today.

"Come on. Let's help you get ready." Remy stood, taking the clothing from her. Emma stripped down to her underwear. Remy handed her the dress, and she stepped into it, slipping her arms in. She turned so Remy could zip it up as Jasmine set the shoes on the ground for Emma.

"Let's add some curls." Remy motioned to the side table where she had a straightener set up.

Emma sat, zoning out while her friends did her hair and makeup. How many times had they done this for each other? Prom, dances, Remy's wedding, Emma's first big concert. Her friends had always been there for her—as much as she'd let them. But they had their own families now. Their own lives to lead that didn't include Emma. How could they? She was on the road seven months out of the year.

Gratitude welled in her chest. No matter what, her girls were always there for her. True friends who didn't let her rising fame get between them.

Jasmine swished some mascara on her lashes and winked. "Don't worry, it's waterproof."

"You guys are the best, you know that?"

"We know." Remy laughed. She set the straightener down and unplugged it before setting the curls with hair spray. "Now, go look at yourself," Remy ordered.

Emma stood, adjusting to the too-high heels. She was used to Converse and Doc Martens—not stilettos. She'd have to remind Callie to tone it down next time.

The reflection in the mirror stole her breath. It was her, but she was stunning. Golden pink-and-blue-tipped hair flowed over her shoulders in waves. Smoldering makeup made her blue eyes stand out that much more. Her face was clean with highlights on her cheeks, her lips glossy. Emma ran her hands over the dress. It fit her like a glove.

"You guys made me so pretty."

They came either side of her and hugged her between them. "You are gorgeous even without all this. But sometimes a girl needs a little armor for days like today." Jasmine squeezed her tighter, her angular eyes meeting Emma's in the mirror.

Emma dipped her head, fighting off the urge to cry.

Remy lifted Emma's chin, her dark fingers contrasting with Emma's pale flesh. "You will get through this. It's gonna hurt for a while. You'll always have a missing piece where your dad should be. But it will get easier."

"He was so proud of you," Jasmine added.

Emma's eyes grew blurry with tears. "You guys are going to ruin my makeup." She laughed, blinking away the emotion.

Her friends chuckled with her and released her. "Let's go."

Big, fat snowflakes drifted from the grey heavens, floating on chilly air only to land on Emma's upturned face. She inhaled a shaky breath and walked through the doors of The Shipwreck. She scanned the faces, searching for Link. She needed to tell him about the test results. Though he hadn't asked, much less spoken to her since storming out of the lawyer's office. Auntie Yaa had communicated between them to arrange her father's requests for this event.

Several people had already gathered around the packed bar under a canopy of Edison-style string lights. A large blown-up picture of her father had been placed next to the wooden box that held her father's ashes on a separate table. The whole town seemed to be here. She swallowed as Remy bumped into her. Emma hadn't realized she'd stopped walking.

"Whoops. Sorry," Remy apologized.

"Go on ahead. I just need a minute." Emma waved.

"You sure you don't want us to stay with you?" Jasmine asked.

"Yeah. You guys go."

Remy searched her face and nodded before leading Jasmine to the bar.

Emma's lungs constricted as it hit her. She would never get to call her dad after a show again to tell him how it went. She'd never wake and see one of his random messages checking in on her. He'd never hold her in his arms. He'd never be able to give her advice or teach her something about cars. She'd never have another chance to tell him how much she loved him and know he'd heard it. There would never be a father—daughter dance at her wedding—if she ever got married. Her blood ran cold.

She gasped and took a step backwards. A couple of heads turned, their gazes filled with pity towards her. She needed a minute to gather herself before she broke down in front of all these people. Spinning, she left the main room, beelining along the hallway to the bathrooms. But she turned at the last moment, darting to the back room. It was darker in here, but the exit sign was lit up. She veered towards it, walking with purpose, and bumped into a solid chest of steel.

"Oomph."

Strong hands reached out to steady her. She tilted her head. The last person who would make her feel better frowned down at her in the shadows.

"Sorry," she said quickly.

Link just stared at her, his face an emotionless mask highlighted by the safety lights around the space.

"You needed a place to hide too?" She tried to lighten the tension, taking in the black and red kente he wore with all manner of ornate designs and patterns.

Link looked down and let her arm go. "I just can't believe he's really gone." He understood more than anyone else in here.

"Me either." She reached for his hand to comfort him.

He whipped his hand back, stepping away and clearing his throat. "We better get this over with."

She nodded, disappointed. Was he so disgusted with her he couldn't bear to touch her?

Tension thickened the air between them, making it hard to breathe. *Why can't he love me back?*

He stepped past her, but she wasn't ready to let him go. Grasping at anything to make him stay just a little longer, she blurted out, "I'm late."

Link stopped abruptly, turning around to face her, fear burning in his black eyes.

"I took a test . . ."

He ground his jaw and then snapped, "Are you——?"

She flinched from his outburst. "It was negative. I'm not pregnant."

He sighed in what seemed like relief, running a hand over his face as his shoulders relaxed. "It's for the best."

Emma nodded. "You're free of me for good now." She turned to pass him, but he gripped her arm, halting her steps. Emma's gaze met his.

Link stole a glance over his shoulders towards the crowd at the bar. He pulled her into the door marked office and flipped the light on before shutting them in. "I'm sorry I was a dick. I just . . . I don't know how to handle this."

Emma crossed her arms over her chest. "You need to be more specific. This as in the pregnancy scare or the fact that we fucked?"

He flinched. "Shhhh. Someone might hear you."

Emma huffed and shook her head. Anger boiled to the surface. Emma never should have slept with him. She cursed her drunk self; she should have known better. No more tequila in Link's presence—that was a new rule. Though this would probably be it. Their relationship had been strenuous these last several years without adding the complication of knocking boots. *I ruined the fragile thread of a relationship we had by giving in to a fantasy.*

"Is April good for a road trip?" Link asked, interrupting her despairing thoughts.

"What?" Her eyes widened.

"April will be better driving conditions than now to get to California." He said matter-of-fact, like he hadn't refused and stormed out of the lawyer's office a week ago.

"I can make that work."

"Don't know why Shattered Cove waters aren't good enough for him," he grumbled.

Emma laughed. "Papa never did anything according to what people expected." *Like taking in a young white girl to raise on his own.*

"He sure didn't." He chuckled. His smile was a carbon copy of their father's.

"Link?"

"Yeah?"

"You're still my family, even though Papa's gone. I know we haven't been close, except for . . . Regardless, I'd really love to have you stay in my life."

There. She'd said it, putting herself out there. No regrets.

His jaw twitched as he studied her. Brows drawn together, his gaze dropped to her mouth.

She licked her lips, and they burned under his intense focus. His throat bobbed as he swallowed, the vein in his neck pulsing. Link leaned in just a fraction. If she hadn't been studying him so closely, she would have missed it.

"You ready to do the song?" His voice was gruff.

"Always."

He brushed past her, leaving her alone in the dimness. She closed her eyes, fighting the pain tearing her heart to shreds. Taking a deep breath, she walked into the main room.

"Doll face, you look hot!" Asher picked her up in a bear hug, spinning her around before setting her back on her feet.

She wobbled and held on to his arm until she was steady. Emma smiled. "You came!"

"We all did," Nicky said, from her right.

Emma took in her four bandmates dressed in suits. "You guys actually wore suits?" Her hand covered her mouth in shock.

"Don't get used to it. We have a certain reputation to uphold, you know?" Leo loosened his tie and winked.

"Geo said he's sorry he couldn't be here," Nicky said, eyes flashing like he was hiding something.

Everyone grew quiet at the somber reminder of their missing bandmate.

"What would I do without you guys?"

"Probably a lot better." Asher shrugged.

She laughed, giving them each a hug and kiss on the cheek. Asher turned his head at the last minute, so she pecked his lips rather than his face.

Emma pulled away and smacked his chest and shook her head. "You are evil."

"Hey, a guy's gotta try." He shrugged.

"Really? I thought we already established I don't have the right equipment?"

"Maybe we should try again? Just to be sure I'm as gay as I think and not bisexual." He smirked.

She laughed.

Nicky shoved Asher playfully. "No more. We agreed no one fucks anyone involved in our band or business."

Asher held up his hands. "All right, all right. Geeze, you guys can't take a joke."

"Emma?" Link's voice cut through her bandmates' laughter.

She turned. His shoulders were tense, nearly at his ears. His jaw clenched as he looked between Asher and her.

Why is he pissed again? Unless . . . is he jealous? No. He couldn't be.

"Yeah?"

"We better get this over with." He motioned to the guitar in his hand.

Right. Papa had requested they play a song together.

"I can read the sheet music if you guys need me to play the keyboard?" Asher asked.

"No," Link snapped.

Asher nodded and shrugged, totally unfazed by Link's gruff behavior.

Emma followed Link over to the stage. He plugged the

guitar into the amp. They hadn't practiced at all, so it was possible this could suck. But if a performance was what her papa wanted, this was what he would get.

"Ready?" she asked as he strummed the guitar.

He nodded.

Link plucked the strings, the first chords of "You Are The Reason" by Calum Scott and Leona Lewis playing softly on repeat. Emma closed her eyes, drawing in a deep breath. When she opened them, dozens of friends and family stood under the blue lights of The Shipwreck bar, all gazes on her and Link. She scanned the room. This was the first place her band had played besides her dad's garage. It hadn't changed in all these years. Wood-paneled walls and circular fish tanks made it seem like they were underwater in the belly of a sunken ship.

Link leaned towards the microphone. "My dad had a lot of quirks."

Everyone laughed.

"He didn't always make sense to me, but everything he did eventually had a purpose. I won't ever know why he chose this song out of all his favorites, but I'm sure he had his reasons." Link looked towards the ceiling. "If you can hear us, Dad, I hope this makes you smile." Link backed away from the mic and strummed the guitar, nodding to Emma with glistening eyes.

His voice was deep and soft as the lyrics bled from him. Emma took a deep breath and sang the second line. Their voices melded together in a duet of love, loss, and heartbreak.

Link's eyes locked on to hers as she sang the beginning of the second verse. His deep timbre stirred her soul. His eyes lit up like they had the last time he'd sung in this very spot at Charli and Finn's vow renewal.

It seemed he put his heart and soul into the performance,

as was Emma. The world faded away as she sang from the depths of her being. It was just the two of them here in this bubble of chords and lyrics. A symphony of unspoken desire and forbidden affection twisted around them, swirling between them in a thick fog of lust and awareness and grief.

The song faded to an end. Link's chest rose and fell, as if he were just as moved as she. As if he felt as rocked to his core at the magnitude of the powerful exchange as she did.

The crowd clapped, breaking the moment. Link turned away, setting the guitar down and exiting the stage for the bar. Leaving her alone with the hurricane of emotions wreaking havoc inside her as always.

Unrequited. Unstable. And unlovable. It was time she accepted that what she wanted so badly would never be.

9

EMMA

1 MONTH LATER

Emma swiped her brow. Sweat trickled down her back under the hot stage lights casting her in red hues. Dark, pulsing music throbbed and vibrated from the speakers. She checked over her shoulder as the beat grew faster, nodding to Ravi picking the strings on his hot pink electric guitar. The beat dropped. Cymbals crashed as Leo thudded the drums to the chorus. A haunting melody flowed from the keys as Asher nodded his head to the beat on her right.

Stepping closer to the crowd, Emma gripped the microphone tighter, her black nails shining in the harsh bloodred lights. Her lips parted as she swayed seductively in her black romper, the front unbuttoned into a deep V, showing off almost half of the globes of her breasts. Thankfully the tape was holding up, even though she was covered in sweat, and she wasn't flashing a crowd of tens of thousands of people. Under the short romper, her ripped fishnet stockings ran down her long legs and disappeared into her black Doc Martens with decorative red roses on the side. This was her brand:

feminine and tough. Edgy and sexy. This was who she was to the world.

She inhaled a breath, filling her lungs with air. The music stopped only for the first line, her voice light and melodic.

"I gave you everything. And you took it all."

Electric notes and haunting chords intertwined as the bass thrummed.

"You played me for a fool. Should'a stayed behind the wall."

Drums crashed and built as Nicky and Asher sang backup, adding a deep contrast to her voice.

"But you're in my blood. Poisoning me from the inside out.

I'm your dirty little secret, 'cause you don't want to lose clout.

Depraved."

Emma inhaled sharply and screamed out the next word.

"Want!"

Her voice switched back to the raw, dark melody. She sang with attitude and all her heart, utilizing the one outlet that didn't leave scars.

"Obsessed savant.

Taboo lust and broken trust.

Giving in to the decadent darkness.

Thrumming in my veins like a violent sickness.

Maybe that's what this is.

Twisted fate.

Cursed love.

Call it what you want, but I'm helpless to this.

Unrequited motherfucker gonna kill me slowly.

Rip me open. Bleed me out.

Should have listened to the voice screaming in doubt.

Thought I couldn't hurt worse than this.

I gave you the gun. Should have known you wouldn't miss.

When I close my eyes, it's you I see.

Stuck in purgatory. Only you hold the key.

Maybe that's what this is.
Twisted fate.
Cursed love.
Call it what you want, but I'm helpless to this.
Unrequited motherfucker gonna kill me slowly."

Cheers erupted as the music faded, and Emma closed her eyes. Screams and shouts pierced the air, swallowing her up in an endorphin rush. Two sweaty arms wrapped around her, lifting her off her feet and spinning her around. Asher's wet lips met her cheek as the rest of her bandmates, except Geo, lined up beside her.

They took a bow as the audience chanted "Sirens!" over and over.

Emma gave a wave and followed Ravi off the stage. Callie was there to hand them each an ice-cold water. Emma downed hers, her hands trembling from adrenaline as she walked to the green room.

"Fuck, that was amazing. Did you hear them out there tonight? They loved it!" Leo said before splashing half his bottle over his hair and shaking his head like a wet dog.

Water droplets rained over her cheek as she held her hand in the way. "Damn you, Leo. That's disgusting. I don't want your sweat all over me."

He smirked, his lips shiny from water or sweat—both, most likely. "Aww, come on. Bet most those ladies and some of the guys would pay me to rub my sweaty ass all over them."

"It's not polite to force your kink on someone," she teased with a sly smile. The bus was small, and secrets weren't easily kept on the road.

Leo's eyes glittered in amusement. "I think we all know who the kinky one is here."

She rolled her eyes and settled onto a leather couch. Asher sat on the arm of the sofa next to her as the other guys took the spot across from her on the long couch. A platter with bottles of water and glasses of champagne in an ice bucket sat on a coffee table between them.

Callie picked up the bottle and popped the cork before pouring some into the glasses. "You guys, that was amazing. We have the car waiting to take you to the hotel for the night, and then we have to be back on the road by eight."

Emma took the flute Callie offered and cheered with her bandmates. The smile on her face faltered as she stared at the empty seat. Geo belonged here, not in prison.

Asher must have sensed her mood dampening. He looped his arm around her. "To Emma and her ability to persuade five guys to play music with her and call ourselves The Sirens."

Leo, Ravi, and Nicky laughed and clinked glasses with her before they all drank their champagne.

Emma couldn't hold back her smile. "You bastards know I wouldn't be here without you all," Emma admitted.

Callie's phone chimed again and again. She pulled it out while Emma poured herself another glass of bubbly. The adrenaline was fading, and melancholy once again swallowed her up, blocking out the light and happiness.

Ignoring the tiny bursts of air tickling her nose, she drank down the champagne until her glass was empty. Anything to fight the descent into numbness.

Emma grabbed the bottle of tequila, not bothering with a glass this time. She downed a mouthful and winced. The taste reminded her of *that* night. Of Link. Her hands scrambled for the container of clear liquid. Vodka it was, then. The alcohol was smooth and strong, slinking into her gut and heating her up from the inside out. Her veins buzzed with rich intoxication. It held off the cold, sinking numbness by replacing it with detached flames of liquor, trading the inevitable release of the blade for a momentary drunk illusion.

"Shit," Callie swore.

"What is it?" Ravi asked.

"Oh, some celebrity gossip site just published a picture of you all at the show just now and ran a story they must have had ready to go. It's nothing new." Callie waved them off.

Emma stood and walked over to grab her phone. She clicked on the first image of Asher holding her and kissing her cheek as the rest of the band members linked arms around them.

The Sirens are one big orgy.

Emma rolled her eyes and read on.

Emma, lead singer of The Sirens, was seen getting cozy with all four men of the band. Would it have been five if Geo was not behind bars for murder? She seems to like the taboo as her song suggests.

Is this really the role model parents want for their teenagers? A source close to the band says, "Emma has those boys on a leash. They have wild sex parties almost every night. Sometimes she takes them all at once."

Her anger boiled over. How the fuck could people write this garbage and get away with these blatant lies?

"Just ignore it." Nicky took her phone and slipped it into her back pocket.

"Can't we do something? They're printing lies," Emma asked.

"Any press is good press. You want exposure, and controversy does that." Callie waved her hand dismissively.

Emma's stomach swirled and knotted uneasily.

"Don't women go crazy for reverse harems? They probably think you're living the life." Asher wiggled his eyebrows up and down playfully.

Emma chuckled. "If I didn't see you all as my brothers, it might not be so gross."

"You want another?" Ravi asked, offering her a glass of vodka.

She accepted it before taking a gulp and relishing the smooth burn as the liquor slid to her belly, dulling the anxiety.

"They loved the new song," Ravi said, changing the subject.

"They sure did," Nicky agreed.

The lyrics had been torn from her soul and written in crimson ink from her bleeding heart. Link's face flashed in her mind's eye. The look of disgust in his expression after he'd realized what they'd done. She took another drink of the clear liquid. She'd need a lot more to drown out the pain. The last ember of her hope had died with the slam of his door. All this time she'd wasted pining and hoping he'd see her one day. She'd given him everything, shown every inch, and he'd found her lacking. Why wasn't she ever good enough? Why couldn't she stop wanting him?

The bottle clinked against her glass as Callie filled it up again. "Come on. Let's get back to the hotel. I figured we could share a room, since the guys doubled up already."

Emma nodded, noting the hopeful spark of lust in Callie's eyes. She drained the cup, relishing the burn as her insides lit in a liquor wildfire. The room tipped and swayed. Callie reached out her hand to steady Emma, wrapping her arms around her waist.

"Let's go." Emma grabbed the vodka, taking it with her. If she drank, the pain dulled. And maybe if she got drunk enough, she'd get lucky and forget for a little while. Emma could escape into a bottle and soft sheets and forget that the man she loved didn't want her.

Unrequited love was a motherfucker.

10

LINK
2 MONTHS LATER

The vibration from the engine rumbled through Link's body as he idled outside Remy and Mikel's house. Emma pulled out of Remy's hug, wheeling a suitcase down the steps and holding her guitar case in the other. Those jeans hugged her ass like they were painted on. The black T-shirt she wore lifted to show a sliver of her back as she leaned over and tied her Converse shoes.

How am I going to survive this?

Emma stood and adjusted the baseball cap on her head.

Fuck, I need to cool off.

Link got out of the car, the spring rain dusting over him like a fine mist as he walked to meet her. His hand grazed hers as he took the suitcase handle from her. He ignored the buzz of energy shooting up his arm. She looked at him, her pink mouth parting as a tiny gasp escaped her.

"Is this everything?" His voice came out gruff. It was the first words he'd spoken to her since his father's celebration of life at The Shipwreck three months ago. A few texts about scheduling this trip were all they'd exchanged.

"Yeah." She opened the passenger door and climbed in while he put her things next to his in the trunk before settling into the driver's side.

After shifting into gear, he pulled onto the road. Emma tucked her knees under her and leaned against the door, her eyes aimed out the watery window.

"I figured we'd take route eighty and see how far into Pennsylvania we can get before we need to rest for the night." His plan was to make it just about nine hours today. The sooner they could get this road trip over, the better.

Emma nodded.

After another few minutes of silence, Link switched the radio on.

Guess this is how it's gonna be.

Hours went by with nothing but the radio and the on-again, off-again April rain showers making sound. Emma had drifted off at one point, her head lolling to the side as he shifted lanes. He reached over, gently pushing her neck to a better angle.

A sign for food and restrooms whizzed by on the right side of the highway. He flicked the blinker on and pulled off the exit. Following the signs, he turned into a diner as his stomach rumbled. Shutting the engine off, he nudged her shoulder.

Emma stirred and sat, her big blue eyes blinking as if trying to make sense of her surroundings. The dark circles under her eyes seemed worse than they had been after their dad passed. A pang of concern lanced his chest—the urge to pull her into his arms, inhale a lungful of that strawberry scent that had teased him this whole ride, and give her . . . What exactly? What could he possibly give her that she didn't already have? Nothing without crossing a very fine line.

"Figured we could stop for some lunch." He grabbed his wallet from the visor.

Instead of answering, she swiped a few strands that had gotten loose from her braid behind her ear and lowered her ball cap. Emma opened her door and climbed out, stretching her arms wide before crossing them in front of her and walking into the diner. Link jogged to catch up, holding the door open for the man coming in behind them. Emma chose a booth in the far back corner, keeping her head dipped low as she slid in.

"Gonna hit the head."

She nodded.

Damn, he'd really fucked up. She was just as alone as he was. He needed to fix things between them.

After relieving himself and washing his hands, he returned to the table. Two coffees had been poured. Emma dumped a packet of sugar into hers and stirred.

He slid into his seat and plucked a menu from the table, scanning the items. "Did you already order?"

She shook her head. "Not hungry."

He frowned, looking at her over the menu. Her cheeks were more hollow than usual, and her T-shirt seemed baggier than she generally wore it. Was she eating enough? "Do you usually skip meals?"

Her gaze cut to his. She lifted the arm with the leather bracelet that had become a permanent staple since high school and gave him the middle finger.

He chuckled. "Same old Emma."

"What's that supposed to mean?" She sat straighter, eyes narrowed.

"Deflecting with attitude."

She rolled her eyes. "Like you're one to talk."

He sighed. "Yeah, guess we're two of a kind, huh?"

Her gaze cut to his as if surprised by his honest admission.

A couple walked by, drawing her attention. She tugged her hat down and angled her face away.

"You afraid someone is going to recognize you in here?"

She chewed on her lip, a show of vulnerability as she met his eyes once again. "Yeah. Lately it's been a little . . . much."

"No one will think the lead singer of The Sirens would be in this Podunk town. I'd bet my car you're safe." He smirked.

Her shoulders lowered, relief evident on her face.

Without thinking, Link reached across the table and grabbed her hand. "Hey, you know I won't let anything happen to you, right?"

Something flashed in her eyes, some unnamed emotion masked in hurt. "I know."

The waitress, with a name tag that announced her name as being Betty, walked over to their table, pen in hand. "What can I get you two?"

Link glanced back at the menu he'd abandoned, pulling his hand away. "You still serve breakfast?"

"All day, every day." She gave him a warm smile.

"I'll have two orders of pancakes, bacon, sausage, some fried eggs, and whipped cream on the side, please."

"Is that it?" Betty eyed Emma.

"Yup," Emma answered.

"Be right out." The waitress turned and left them alone once more.

"Guess you're hungry enough for the both of us," Emma teased.

Link patted his hard stomach. He'd done a lot more working out at the Tidal Gym since his father had passed.

"One of those pancakes is for you. That's why I ordered the whipped cream."

"I told you I'm not hungry."

"And I told you I'm gonna take care of you," he teased.

"I believe you said you wouldn't let anything happen to me. That's different," Emma argued.

He shrugged. "Same difference. Both ways you get taken care of."

"Why do you *care* so much all of a sudden?" Emma's voice sounded bitter.

Jesus, he'd really done a number on her. He understood sometimes it was easier to be angry than face those uncomfortable facts and feelings. "You're family. And real family takes care of each other."

She winced. Right. Her family of origin had abandoned her. That was a sore spot, understandably.

"How's work?" He sipped his coffee. It was a little weak, but it would do.

She tugged her bottom lip into her mouth, and his cock jumped to attention. He pressed his hand down, trying to get his dick under control.

"It's fine."

"I saw the spread you guys had in *Rolling Stone*. That was pretty sweet."

She shrugged before taking another drink of her coffee.

"It's gotta be nice to have it all like you've always wanted," he pressed. Having a conversation with her was like pulling teeth. Usually, she was the one jabbering on.

Then I had to go and put my dick in her and complicate everything.

Her gaze flicked to his, vulnerability flashing in those aqua pools. "It's not all it's cracked up to be."

"Living the actual dream isn't all you'd hoped?" Disbelief coated his words.

Her flinch was so microscopic that if he hadn't been studying her, he would have missed it. Any vulnerability in her gaze was gone, replaced with steel walls. She laughed a moment later, a far too bright smile showing her teeth. "You're right. What could a woman like me be lacking?"

Something about the way she said it made the hair on the back of his neck stand on end. Was she in over her head? Was life on the road too much for her? Was this just the grief talking?

Before he could voice any of his concerns, Betty returned and emptied her tray of food onto the table.

"Thanks," Link said.

"Let me know if you need anything else." She filled up their coffees once more before she left.

Link pushed a plate of pancakes towards Emma, throwing on a couple pieces of bacon. "Eat up, buttercup."

"I told you I'm not hungry." Just as she finished speaking, her stomach rumbled, betraying her.

He chuckled and nudged the bowl of whipped cream towards her. "Come on. Just a little taste. We can't stop again until we get to Clarion, Pennsylvania, if we want to get some decent sleep tonight before getting back on the road."

She sighed and gave in, picking up her fork. His chest puffed up triumphantly as she poured the syrup over the pancakes and added a dollop of the sweet cream. He'd won this battle. But something told him this was just the beginning and the war of his life was coming.

11

EMMA

Emma rolled her neck from side to side as Link carried their bags to the front desk of the hotel.

A young woman with dark hair greeted them with a bored expression, seemingly annoyed they'd pulled her attention from the phone in her hand. "Do you have a reservation?"

Link shook his head and set the bags down. "No."

The girl's eyes roamed between the two of them, lingering on Emma. Her name tag glinted in the florescent lights. *Stacia.*

Emma tugged her hat lower and dipped her head, pretending to be interested in something on the ground.

"Do you have a reservation, ma'am?" Stacia asked.

"No, I'm with him," Emma answered without looking up. The last thing she needed was to be spotted and have the paparazzi following her on this journey. They were bad enough in the cities they stopped at for the concerts. It seemed everyone wanted to know all about the mysterious lead singer of The Sirens. Was she dating one of her band members or all of them? Where was her family? Who was she really?

"Would you like a king or double beds?"

"*Two* rooms." Link put a little more emphasis on the number of rooms than necessary, causing both Emma and Stacia to dart their attention to him.

"Uh, doesn't matter what beds. Just having them on the same floor would be best." Link rubbed the back of his head.

"Okay, you guys can have rooms three-sixteen and three-eighteen. They're right next to each other. What card will you be using?" Stacia popped her gum.

Link went for his wallet at the same time Emma dug into her pocket. He cut her a glance. "Don't even think about it."

Emma didn't bother to argue. This was just night one of what was sure to prove a very long trip. It was pure torture to be so close to what she wanted most and not be able to have him. *At least he's talking to me again.* Why did she still want him even after he'd acted like such an asshole to her? *I wish he'd let me fuck him into a better mood.* Although that hadn't seemed to help last time. It had made it worse. If he wanted to pretend nothing happened, she'd go with it. A piece of him was better than nothing.

She tried not to let her gaze linger on his toned arms as he collected his card from the girl and signed the paperwork in exchange for the rooms. He'd bulked up since January. He'd always been lean and muscular, but this was another level.

"Do you spend all your free time at the gym now?"

He shrugged. "Going to The Shipwreck after work for beers with Dad had been our routine. Doing it without him . . . just didn't feel right."

A pang of grief twisted in her heart. He probably felt the same way she did whenever she picked up the phone to call her dad before a show, only to remember he wouldn't ever answer: lonely.

"I signed up for MMA classes at Tidal Gym."

Images of his lean, muscular body in nothing but a pair of long shorts flit through her mind—sweat dripping down his chiseled abs and catching the lighting just right, so he looked like a bronze Adonis. She forced her eyes away from him and swallowed hard. This was going to be a very long road trip.

Why did you do this to us, Papa?

The hollow pain of knowing she'd never have the answer tore a little more at her damaged heart. These past three months, she'd thrown herself into her music. Working, barely sleeping, getting lost in her craft, and fighting the urge to mutilate her body.

She exhaled the breath she hadn't realized she was holding as Link took the keys from Stacia and handed one out to Emma. She took it, swallowing the ball of emotion that caught in her throat every time he touched her. Even the subtle graze of his fingertips on her palm sent a shiver tumbling through her. It was the only time she felt anything anymore.

She picked up her guitar case and headed towards the elevators. Link followed, slipping beside her and hitting the number for their floor.

Silence swallowed them as the metal box rose. Tension thickened, making it hard to draw in oxygen. The doors opened, and she followed the signs to their rooms. After taking out her key, she opened the door and walked in, setting her instrument on the ground to the side of the hall. The room was outdated, with weird swirly wallpaper and a picture of flowers on the far wall. A small TV, king bed, dresser, and a chair took up the tiny space.

Link set her bag at the foot of her mattress, eyeing the bed and then turning to face her, his eyes shifting to the door behind her. "You wanna get some dinner delivered?"

Emma glanced at the digital clock by the bed. *Seven thirty-*

two. "I'm pretty tired. I think I'll just head to sleep." She pulled her ball cap off and flipped the bathroom light on, illuminating the dim hallway.

Link opened his mouth as if to argue, his eyes drawn to her face. His brows drew together in concern as he nodded. "I'd like to get on the road by eight if that's good with you. Maybe get to Illinois tomorrow?"

"Sounds like a plan." She undid her braid, running her fingers through it.

His eyes darted to the action. Licking his lips, he clenched his open fist by his side. "See you then. We'll get breakfast at the diner next door and then gas up before we head out." Link didn't wait for her response. He left, the click of the door following him.

Needing to wash off the day, Emma stripped and climbed into the shower. The warm water sluiced over her skin. She blinked slowly. Her heart tore just a little more—an ache she'd grown used to. A hole she'd tried to fill with almost everything she could think of throughout her life except the one thing she'd never touch—what had killed her mother. In moments like this, she could almost sympathize with her mother for turning to heroin. Loving someone only to have them use you and leave, carved lasting scars . . . *Why can't I just shut it off?* Her mother had chosen drugs, and in turn they'd taken her life. *But they took her from me long before that.* Or had she ever really had her mother's love?

There was a few sacred memories Emma held locked away, with skinned knees and butterfly kisses. Moments where she was sure her mother had loved her. But that was *before.* Before her dad had left, taking the piece of her mother that destroyed her. *And then she did the same to me.* Anger quickly replaced the sympathy, merging with shame.

A buzzing sound filled her head as her body trembled.

Somehow, she'd lost track of time. *How long have I been in this freezing water?* She shut the shower off and grabbed a thin towel to dry off. After shuffling to the bedroom, she opened her suitcase and quickly changed into the pajama shorts and T-shirt she'd packed. Then she ran a brush through her hair before twisting it into a messy bun on her head.

After tossing and turning for an hour in bed with no luck, she sat and pulled open her guitar case and collected the notebook and pen she kept inside. Settling on the edge of the bed, she took a deep breath.

She strummed a few chords that had been stuck in her head this past week as she prepared for her journey west. Emma hummed, closing her eyes and letting the music surround her, flow through her. She opened herself up, mind and spirit. This was her safe place, free of judgment, where the lyrics could flow through her. The one place she could truly speak what was in her heart. If it was too vulnerable, no one ever had to see it. But this way she could let the pain out. Let it bleed from her soul into words and music notes.

This struggle seems all too familiar.
   This path overworn.
   These lungs gasping for air.
   This heart shattered yet again.
   To love is not to breathe.
   To give in is to die in darkness.
   To quench this thirst is to starve my soul.

They tell me breathe. Just breathe.
   When the flood comes and darkness reigns.
   Hold on just a little longer.

Go a little farther.

Escape cuts just a little deeper until the ecstasy flows over, drowning me with endorphins coated in red.
  Sick of all these disguises.
  Time to get off my stage.
  Got to channel this rage.
  Who am I really?
  A shell, numb and hollow.
  Darkness pulling me under.
  Suffocating in the open.
  Alone in a crowd.
  Silent screams swallowed by a fake smile.

They tell me breathe. Just breathe.
  When the flood comes and darkness reigns.
  Hold on just a little longer.
  Go a little farther.

But, in the end, what's the point? Why keep going when it hurts too much?

Emma underlined the last line twice. Why indeed?

She pulled off her bracelets and rubbed the raised scars. The urge to add another mark rose. Closing her eyes, Emma pinched the skin. *No.* It had been three months since the last time she'd given in to temptation. Her father's weathered brown face flashed in her mind. Disappointment and worry marred his kind expression.

He'd never brought it up with her directly. One day, he'd eyed her wrist and told her she was the most precious woman in his life and then made an appointment with a therapist. She'd gone for more than a year. He'd driven her there every time but never directly spoken to her about it.

It was in those therapy sessions she'd learned some coping techniques. But nothing ever worked for long. Five years were down the drain from her relapse back in January. Sometimes music wasn't enough. Sometimes, when the pain was too much and nothing helped, cutting kept her alive. Life was drowning her, and the blade gave her a gasp of fresh oxygen before she was pulled under again.

It wasn't that Emma wanted to die. No, she very much wanted to live. She'd never do that to her friends. It was just that sometimes it was all too much. This was her way of hanging on just a little longer. Her way to breathe.

LINK

Link turned the radio down before he cracked his neck to the side. They'd been driving for four hours already. He angled towards Emma. Her golden hair fanned out over her face, the pink and blue ends matching her pastel hoodie. Her legs were tucked under her, covered in black leggings with mesh that crisscrossed in strips running down each side. He returned his attention to the road ahead, rolling down the window in an attempt to cool the heat that rushed through him at the slightest peek of her skin.

Damn, what is wrong with me?

A light snore came from his passenger. He couldn't help the smile that tugged on the side of his mouth. He'd heard that damn guitar through the wall until two in the morning. No wonder she was exhausted today. Memories flicked through his mind. It was just like old times, when they'd both lived with his dad.

Link was the one who'd taught her to play in the first place.

"Hey! Why did you shut my music off?" Emma asked, her face flaming red as her eyes burned with anger.

Link stepped away from the CD player on her shelf and surveyed her room. She sat and crossed her arms in front of her chest. He stepped towards her bed and pulled the guitar from behind his back before shoving it in her hands.

Today was a hard day for her. She'd gotten news her mother had died, and Link understood what that was like. She needed an outlet, a way to express herself.

Emma's eyes widened, her mouth dropping open as she took in the instrument. She didn't reach for it, timid as she'd always been. Her eyes curiously flicked back and forth between him and the instrument.

"I figure if you learn to play, your taste in music will improve," he teased.

Disbelief flashed in her cautious gaze. "You got this for me?"

"I thought it was about time you had your own."

She smiled, eyes lighting up as she cradled the guitar in her arms like it was the most precious thing. Her eyes grew watery, but she didn't cry. Emma had never cried as long as he'd known her.

"Link, this is the best gift ever." She reached out and wrapped her arms around him. "Why did you get it for me?"

"Because I love you, little bird."

When she pulled back, pure adoration reflected in her baby blues, and it was all aimed at him.

Every week, he'd taught her a few chords. She'd never complained about the pain in her fingers. She had done everything he'd told her, memorizing them and stringing together songs on her own in no time. They'd have weekend jam sessions, learning the covers to his favorite songs. Even Dad had given her a few to learn.

That duet they'd sung at his celebration of life was one of them. Did she still have that old Gibson?

She'd fucking worshipped his attention. And he'd protected her like the good big brother he was. When had everything changed between them? When had they grown apart?

When I started noticing her in unbrotherly ways.

He'd needed the distance to get his deviant desires in check. His father would have killed him if he'd known the feelings for Emma that had risen in Link.

Link rubbed the back of his neck and sighed. And now it was worse. His lust left unchecked. After that night, some of the memories had returned in flashes. Enough that his cock would twitch with the reminder. And God, did they like to come at the most inconvenient times. Like when he tried to take someone home or when he was rubbing one out. No matter what buxom beauty he pulled up on his phone, the only woman who was forefront in his fantasies was the one person he couldn't have. He'd had to stop masturbating because the shame of who he envisioned sucking him off had become too much.

This infatuation would end once he found someone else to set his sights on, just like it had with Rachel. Well, at least he thought it had worked.

Emma stirred beside him, sitting and rubbing her eyes. "Where are we?"

"Almost to the Indiana border."

She reached for the bottle of water and drank it before yawning.

"Have a good nap?" he asked.

"Yes. The vibration of this beast always lulls me to sleep." She laughed.

Or the fact that you didn't get much last night.

"I can take a turn driving, you know?"

An image of her blond hair flowing behind her from the open window as she had her hands wrapped around the steering wheel, a confident hungry smile on her lips, popped into his mind. He gripped the wheel harder and shook his head. The last thing he needed was her having even more control over him. "Nah, I'd rather not crash."

"Hey!" She punched his arm playfully. "I'll have you know I'm a great driver. You should know. You taught me."

"Maybe if you're a good girl." The words left his mouth in jest, but panic quickly riddled his body as silence descended upon the car. Damn it. He'd just made things awkward again.

"It's way more fun to be bad these days." Her voice was sultry, like a sex vixen had taken over her body.

Fuck, he wanted to pull this car over and teach her a lesson. He adjusted himself in his seat, hoping she wouldn't see how hard his dick was. "What happened to the good little angel you used to be? Back when you and Remy thought going out to the backyard for a midnight snack of gummy worms counted as sneaking out. You went from that to a hellion pretty quick," he said, trying to turn the conversation back to anything but sex.

"Hmmm. Well, for starters, I'm not fourteen anymore." She laughed. "And you really don't know me at all if you thought those were regular gummies."

His gaze snapped to hers and then back to the road, his mouth hanging open. "No way . . . at fourteen?"

She burst out laughing. "Just the one time. And Remy had no idea what I was feeding her. I hated how out of control it made me feel. I quickly found I'd much rather relax in *other* ways."

Images of grown-up Emma touching herself burned in his brain. Her hair splayed out over her perfect perky tits. His mouth watered, wanting to lick and suck them. Her hand would glide down her smooth stomach to the triangle between her thighs. One finger would dip inside as her eyes would flutter close. Her lips would part as she sucked in a gasp.

"Link, you're too close!"

He snapped to reality and hit his brakes so as not to rearend the slow driver in front of him. He checked his blind spots and switched lanes, passing them easily enough.

Link risked a quick glance towards Emma. A small smile split her pink lips like she knew why he'd been so distracted. He was fucked. She'd always been crass and blunt with sexual innuendo, and never in a million years had it affected him like this. He'd been grossed out when he happened to hear about her escapades, like any older brother should be.

"I heard the guitar last night," Link said, hoping to steer the conversation back to safe ground.

Emma's face paled. "You did?"

He checked his mirrors. "Couldn't make out the words, but the music sounded good. New song?"

She swallowed and exhaled, her shoulders relaxing with the action. "Yeah, just something I'm playing around with."

"You remember when I gave you your first guitar?"

He caught her smile from the corner of his eye. "Of course. I couldn't ever forget that. All the nights spent practicing until my fingers screamed at me to stop. Dad loved it when we would play for him."

"He sure did."

Silence descended in the car once more. The only sound was the wind whistling through the cracked window and the rumble of the V-8 engine.

"Link?"

"Yeah?"

"What changed between us? We used to be so close, and

then . . ."

He took a deep breath, holding it for a few seconds before letting it out. *I started to have unbrotherly feelings for you.* "We grew up. I had more responsibilities at the shop, and you went to chase your dream."

Her head turned as her shoulders drooped. "I'm sorry I wasn't present more. If I'd known he needed me, I would have dropped everything to be there." Her voice sounded so small —nothing like the Emma he knew.

He reached out and took her hand in his, giving it a squeeze as he navigated them on the highway. Energy buzzed from the connection, swirling heat stirring him up inside. He cleared his throat. "Look, it wasn't your fault. What happened to Dad was out of the blue. We didn't see it coming. You were here for him. I know you guys talked almost every day. He wanted you to chase your dreams."

After another moment of silence, she squeezed his hand back. "He wanted that for you too, you know?"

A ball of emotion clogged his throat. He swallowed. Music had been a dream of his once upon a time, but that wasn't uncommon for a young kid. When he'd gotten into his twenties, he realized his dad needed his help at the shop, and Link had found his groove. Restoring classics was his passion. Besides, the old man had been slowing down, and the pain from his arthritis was way worse than Solomon Owusu would ever admit. The garage had become Link's life. Knowing how hard his dad had worked to build the company from the ground up, Link had gotten a degree in business. As a child of an immigrant, education was paramount.

"Why don't you take a few of those music classes too?" his dad asked as they poured over the class sign-up page.

"I don't need them for business. I'll take some marketing classes instead," Link insisted, wanting to make his dad proud and show him how committed he was to continuing his legacy.

And now the garage was all Link had left of his dad. That and his father's house and the belongings he and Emma had yet to go through. Once this road trip was over, they'd tackle that.

He risked another glance in her direction. Her eyes met his, understanding flashing there. Desire mixed with something more swirled in their deep blue depths. For the first time in a long time, Link was seen.

He focused back on the road, resisting the pull, shoving down the lust that twisted up his spine. Holding his breath, he suffocated the rising feral desires coursing through him. His body burned as if he were soaked in gasoline and her touch was the spark. He ripped his hand away, fisting it on his thigh before returning it to the wheel.

"Check the glove box." His voice was hoarse with unbidden wants. His body trembled from this violent depraved sickness.

Emma obeyed. Her smile fed his soul as she pulled out the bag of gummy worms. "Oh my God! My favorite." She opened the bag, and he forced his eyes to remain ahead as she plucked a few out and slipped them into her mouth. She moaned, and his cock twitched. Fucking traitor.

"Want some?"

Wasn't that a loaded question? He shook his head, grinding his teeth, shifting his thoughts to rebuilding an engine piece by piece in an attempt to get his body under control. Hard to do when he was stuck in a car for seven hours with the very definition of temptation.

I'm so fucked.

13

EMMA

Today was a good day. The sun shone on her face, thawing some of the numbness. Today, Link was relaxed and joking with her like he had when they were younger. God she'd missed his banter and sarcastic quips.

Emma belted out the lyrics to the song on the radio. She shoved Link's shoulder. "Come on. I know you know this one."

Something had shifted between them yesterday. Emma wasn't sure exactly what had done it, but she'd take the easy-going, teasing version of her stepbrother over the grumpy asshole any day.

He laughed and gave in, his voice melding with the music. They sang of love and heartbreak, and two people who wanted each other but couldn't find their happily ever after.

Ironic. But she'd steal these memories and lock them away to keep them safe for when the dark moments became too much.

The grey T-shirt he wore rippled in the breeze, showing off his muscled torso. His strong, veiny forearms flexed as he gripped the steering wheel. Her panties had been in a perpetual state of dampness since they'd started this trip. She'd had to make sure to consume enough water just to stay hydrated. Was it possible to dehydrate from too much arousal?

She let her eyes drink in the rest of his body, memorizing every detail for when she was alone in her hotel room later tonight. She needed to take the edge off. And after he'd mentioned hearing her guitar through the walls, she was pretty sure the hum from her powerful vibrator might also be heard at the next cheap place they stayed. A wicked smile played on her lips. *Maybe if he heard me getting off next door, he'd come join me.*

She shook her head, trying to rid the thoughts. *Look how well that turned out last time.* No, she couldn't ruin what they had now. She couldn't lose him.

Ding!

Emma picked up her phone and smiled.

Leo: *How's the drive going with Mister Grumpy Pants?*

Emma: *Better than expected.*

Ravi: *You dirty ho.*

She chuckled.

Emma: *Not THAT good.*

Nicky: *Have fun, but don't do anything I wouldn't do.*

Emma: *That doesn't leave much.*

"Who's got you smiling so much?" Link asked, his voice tinged with a hard edge.

She cast a quick glance towards him. His fists were nearly strangling the wheel as his jaw clenched.

Emma's brows drew together. He almost looked jealous, but that was impossible. Link didn't think of her like that.

Ding!

"Just the guys." She focused on her phone screen.

Nicky: *Ouch!*

Ravi: *She's got you pegged. LOL.*

Asher: *Hey! The only one doing any pegging will be me. Understood?*

Leo: *Em, we need you to come back soon. There are way too many dicks up here. We need our leading lady.*

Asher: *There can never be too many dicks. *winky face* *eggplant emoji**

Emma: *I'll be back in a couple weeks. You can all survive that long without my kitty.*

Asher: *Meow.*

Emma: *How's Geo this week?*

Ravi: *. . .*

Worry cinched her gut.

Emma: *What?*

Asher: *I'm sure he's okay.*

Emma: *But you don't know?*

Nicky: *Look, babe, you've got enough to worry about right now. We'll talk when you get back.*

She sighed in frustration.

Emma: *Just tell me! Is he okay?*

Ravi: *He's fine. He's safe. He's just being a stubborn asshole.*

Nicky: *Gotta go.*

Leo: *Me too.*

Emma: *No, you don't! Tell me what is going on.*

Asher: *Same. Dog trainer just got here.*

Emma: *You don't even have a dog . . .*

Ravi: *Geo is safe. You focus on this trip and saying goodbye to your dad. We've got this. Talk to you later.*

Emma shoved her phone in the bag at her feet. Geo was safe, and that was the least she could hope for. When this trip was over, she'd go visit him.

"Figured you guys would enjoy the break from each other.

Doesn't it get old being stuck with them for long periods of time?" Link asked.

"We're like a family. We fight and make up, but at the end of the day, we love each other." It was sort of how she felt about Link, only that ran oceans deeper.

He nodded. "You ever been with any of them?"

She turned towards him as he kept his gaze steady on the road. "You really want to know?"

"Fuck. That's a yes," he growled.

He *was* jealous. But that only added a ton of confusion to this messed-up situation they were in.

"Asher and I shared one awkward sexual encounter in high school. I knew he was questioning his sexuality and offered to help him see if he really was attracted to women at all."

A growl ripped from his chest.

"Why do you even care?" she pressed.

Link remained focused on the road. His shoulders tensed near his ears and his arm muscles flexed as he strangled the steering wheel. And they'd been doing so well.

She needed to get them back to a lighter topic. "I was thinking that maybe when we hit Denver on the way back, we could get a tattoo in memory of Dad. I have a friend there who's really good."

His brow creased in confusion. "You have a tattoo?"

She smirked. "A few."

His eyes narrowed like he was trying to remember. "Birds on your collarbone."

She nodded. "And a couple others."

"Where?"

She shrugged. "Perhaps I'll show you someday—if you're lucky," she teased.

"You can't shut that off, can you?" he grumbled.

"Shut what off?"

"That sass."

She chuckled. "I'm taking it easy on you."

"Oh really?"

"You couldn't handle all of me." She bit her bottom lip.

"Fuck, I don't remember you being this . . ."

"This smart? This confident? This beautiful? This charming? You'll have to be a bit more specific." Emma laughed.

He grumbled something under his breath that sounded like *"Need your ass spanked."* He grabbed his water and brought it to his lips.

A thrill of molten desire rocketed through her. She'd push him a little further. "Not everyone can keep up with me. It's okay—happens to the best of them. Takes a firm hand and a very good tongue to get my mouth under control."

Water spewed from his mouth, dribbling down his shirt as he choked. He set the bottle in the cup holder and coughed a few times.

After he'd caught his breath, she shrugged. "See? Not everyone can rise to the challenge."

He reached out and grabbed her wrist. She gasped at the sudden connection.

"Trust me. Rising isn't the problem." His gaze darted to her leather bracelet hiding her scars and tugged at it. "I bet one tat is under here. Is it so bad you keep it hidden?"

Panic seized her chest as she ripped her arm away. "How about your love life? Seeing anyone?"

"No."

Has he been with anyone since me? Not that it really mattered, because they were not together.

The air in the car grew thick despite his window being down. They'd done a great job of avoiding talking about that night, but today's conversation had brought the awkwardness to the forefront. Maybe she should bring it up and put it all out there. Why couldn't she try and enjoy her time with him to the fullest? The best way to do that was to get rid of the elephant in the room.

"How do you think Dad would feel knowing his ashes were in the trunk for this road trip?" Emma asked.

"Do you think we should bring him up front with us?" Link's voice held a hint of humor. It had worked.

"Just the back seat. You know he'd hate that." She laughed.

Solomon had only ever sat in the driver's seat, except for the one time Link had had to drive him home after his cataract surgery. He'd never let them hear the end of that either.

"Serves him right for sending us on this wild goose chase," Link added.

Emma turned towards the window. Trees and flat open farmland whipped by. "I don't know. I think this might have been a good idea, after all."

After a beat of silence, Link sighed. "Yeah, maybe it's not so bad."

Emma smiled. A warmth surged, filling her chest with liquid sunshine. Perhaps her dad had known all along that they needed this trip to make things right. And just maybe Solomon had a few more surprises up his sleeve.

14

LINK

Link balanced the bag of takeout and drinks in one hand and knocked on Emma's door with the other. He surveyed the mostly empty parking lot around them, somewhere in bumfuck Nebraska.

"Come in!"

Come in? What the fuck—?

He twisted the knob and frowned. She hadn't locked it. He stormed inside and set the food on the small dresser holding the old TV. "Why the fuck isn't the door locked?"

"I knew you were coming over and didn't want to make you wait if I was still in the shower," she huffed.

He turned to face her, his mouth dropping open. Emma's wet hair stuck to her face on the sides. Water dripped, pooling in the cleft under her chin. Nothing but a tiny, cheap motel towel was wrapped around her, not leaving much to his imagination. Her perky tits were squished together, overflowing from the top of the white terry cloth.

His hands itched to pull it away from her, exposing every

delectable inch for him to explore with his tongue. He licked his lips as his cock stood to attention.

"Like what you see?"

Emma's voice snapped him out of his forbidden fantasy. He whipped around, putting his back to her. "Jesus! Put some clothes on."

"It's not like you haven't seen it all before."

The sound of fabric falling to the ground made his dick throb. *Engines. Check main bearing clearances. Pull the main bolts off. Clean the bore, solder walls, and threads. Clean crank shaft and caps . . .*

"I forgot. You don't want to talk about the elephant in the room," Emma continued.

He shook his head, balling his fists at his sides as anger and guilt rose at the reminder of how badly he'd fucked up.

"It's safe to turn around."

He grabbed the bag of food and pulled out the Styrofoam containers and plastic utensils before handing Emma hers and taking a seat on the only available place in the almost-bare motel room: the bed. She took a spot next to him, laying his bottle of Pepsi between them by her iced tea.

"You know why I don't want to talk about it. It's sick. You're my little sister. It was just the alcohol and grief. We were both going through a lot and . . . sought comfort and escape."

Emma moved the fork around the lo mein noodles without speaking.

He reached out and grasped her face gently, turning it towards him until she met his gaze. "Wasn't it the same for you?"

Emma opened her mouth and closed it. Her usually bright blue eyes dimmed. Biting her bottom lip, she looked away and nodded. "It was just a fuck."

She always looked to the left when she lied. But there was

no way he was going to continue this uncomfortable conversation.

"If I could take it back, I would." He'd take back the pain he'd caused her in an instant.

She winced.

"We good?" he asked before shoving a bite of his sweet and sour chicken into his mouth.

Emma nodded and stuffed a big bite of her own food in her mouth.

Link tapped the remote, turning the TV on, flipping channels until he found some mindless action movie.

They finished the food. He ate the half of Emma's that she didn't want. After cleaning up the containers, he stood.

"The movie isn't over," Emma pointed out.

He hesitated. He should go. Their earlier conversation was still fresh in his mind.

"Stay?" She patted the spot next to her on the bed. "I promise to keep my hands to myself." She winked, but her smile didn't reach her eyes.

Always with the sass. He really shouldn't.

"Please?" The vulnerability in her voice made his knees go weak. His chest tightened as sadness swirled in those baby blues.

"Alright. Just for a little while." He climbed onto the bed, sitting against the creaky headboard.

Emma lay down with her head on his thigh, facing the TV.

He closed his eyes and took a deep breath, letting it out as if that would lessen the energy thrumming in his veins from the closeness. He sat as still as possible, hoping she didn't move too much and become aware of the tent forming in his jeans.

After half an hour, light snores drifted from her sleeping form. He smiled and took the time to admire her. Spreading his fingers through her fine hair, he brushed a few strands that had fallen in front of her angelic face. The lights from the TV reflected against her porcelain skin, her blond eyelashes fluttering in her deep sleep.

Link dragged a knuckle over her cheek, ignoring the lurch in his heart. Touching her silky skin was the closest thing to heaven—and that was a problem.

No, they weren't really related, genetically or legally. What if he gave in to this pull? What if she wanted him back? What if he could hold her like this every night? Kiss her when he wanted?

He shook his head. He'd never know. Everyone in Shattered Cove saw them as brother and sister. If they found out and the media got a hold of it, she'd become a pariah. The couple everyone laughed at behind closed doors, and some in their faces. He'd be the cause of her name being smeared and possibly losing her contract. Not to mention, what would his father think of this?

"Watch out for her, son. She doesn't have anybody else who loves her like us." His father's words took hold in his mind, digging in and cementing the truth that he and Emma could never be.

15

EMMA

Emma rolled over, breathing in sandalwood and fir. She opened her eyes, searching for the man that scent belonged to. But she was alone in the dark motel room. The TV was off, and their takeout containers overflowed in the tiny garbage bin.

She closed her eyes and drew in a shaky breath as exhaustion hit her like a wall. Emma should get up and shower before they got back on the road, but she didn't have the energy. She just wanted to lie here and sleep. At least in her dreams Link stayed and held her—wanted her. She'd taken a chance last night by lying against him. Starved for loving touch, Emma had taken what she could. Even if it wasn't real. Even if it wouldn't last. He'd made it clear to her that night didn't mean anything to him.

Tears burned the back of her eyes at the hopelessness of her situation. "He'll never love me like that. Move on."

For now, she'd shove all of it down. She needed to focus on getting her father's ashes to the Pacific Ocean. Then, after they got everything in order in Shattered Cove, she'd leave and never look back. At least not for a while. It was the only way to get over Link once and for all.

Knock. Knock.

"Going to get us breakfast and then we can head out. Can you be ready in twenty?" Link asked through the closed door.

She didn't even bother rising from the bed as she shouted her answer. "As ready as I'll ever be."

* * *

Several hours and the next state over, Emma swiped some lip gloss over her lips in the car mirror. Checking her mascara one more time, she put the makeup back in her bag. "Take a left here and park over there." She pointed to Link.

He found a parking space and backed in before cutting the engine. "A karaoke bar?" His eyes narrowed on the blinking neon sign.

"They have the best burgers. Trust me." She opened the door and climbed out, stretching her muscles after the long drive.

Link followed her into the building, stopping to glance at the autographed pictures of several popular musicians.

A brunette woman met them with a smile, holding up menus. "Party of two?"

"Yes. Could we have a table in the corner, please?" Emma asked, tugging down her baseball cap.

"Of course. Right this way."

Link's hand rested on the small of Emma's back protectively as they followed the woman to a small table with a simple candle in a mason jar at the center. It was in the far back corner and more dimly lit than the rest of the room. Several square tables were scattered around the restaurant, most of them filled with patrons facing the stage where a man belted out Celine Dion's "My Heart Will Go On."

A bar was situated directly opposite the stage, on the other side of the room, with two mixologists working their way down the line. Both of them had handlebar mustaches that put the man on the Pringles can to shame.

The hostess set the menus in front of them. "Your server will be along shortly. Can I get you started with a cocktail?"

"Rum and Coke, please." If Emma was going to get through the rest of the trip, she could use a little help.

"Do you have Sand Dune Brewery IPA here?" Link asked.

"We do."

"That would be perfect," Link said.

The hostess left them alone.

Emma smiled and shook her head.

"What?" Link questioned.

"Can take the man out of Shattered Cove but can't take the Shattered Cove out of the man," she teased.

He chuckled. "I like what I like."

"You sound just like Dad." She laughed.

His smile dimmed just a little before he scanned the room. "Think he would have liked this place?"

"It does have his favorite beer," she noted, tugging Link's menu from his hand.

His eyebrows drew together in question.

"Trust me and let me order for you. Promise you won't regret it," she said.

He shrugged. "Okay."

A moment later, a young man appeared with their drinks. "Here you go. I'm Will, and I'll be your server tonight. Did you decide what you want to order?"

She handed over the menus. "We'll have two of the house special burgers with fries and a side of ranch, please."

"Coming right up." Will turned and left.

Emma stood. "I'm gonna use the bathroom. Be right back."

She didn't wait for his acknowledgement before she wove through the tables towards the restrooms. After doing her business and washing her hands, she set out for the one woman she wanted to see.

"Delia?"

The bronze beauty turned around, her nose ring flashing in the overhead lights. "Emma? I didn't know you were in town." Delia hugged her.

"Just passing through. I wondered if you could do me a favor?"

Delia smirked, tracing her bottom lip with her tongue. "Well, I do owe you for that night with Tony. Is it the same kind of favor? 'Cause I gotta tell ya, girl, I've been itching for another threesome."

Emma laughed. "Nothing like that. I was hoping you could hook me and Link up with some timeslots." She nodded towards the stage.

Delia's smile grew. "Abso-fuckin'-lutely. Am I announcing you by your name or are you going incognito?" She flicked Emma's cap.

"I'd like to try to stay anonymous if possible."

"You got it, girl. Give me a little bit."

Emma gave her friend another hug before darting out to the car and grabbing her guitar. She handed it over to Delia before making her way back to Link. If he'd seen her little detour, he didn't mention it. Half his beer was gone. She had some catching up to do.

"Get lost?" Link teased as she sat down.

"Ran into an old friend." She winked.

Link's jaw tightened as he took a look around the room.

Emma gulped her cocktail, welcoming the warmth that spread from her throat to her stomach.

Will delivered their meals, and after a suspicious glance at the fried egg on his burger, Link bit into it before moaning his approval. Another round of drinks had conversation flowing about the shop and them getting caught up on movies, current events, and all the news from Shattered Cove that she'd missed these past three months.

"Want another?" She pointed to the empty beer bottle in his hand.

He shook his head.

"We can take a cab to the hotel if you want to let loose?" she offered.

"Nah, I'm good."

Did he not want to get drunk with her because of what happened last time?

She plucked her glass from the table, swallowing the last of the dark liquid. The warm buzzing of the rum filled her veins, relaxing her.

After a woman doing a cover of a popular country song finished, Delia walked onto the stage. "It is with great honor I invite my friend up here to entertain you all with something special."

"Be right back," Emma said, heading straight for the stage. She grabbed her guitar from Delia and adjusted the mic just a couple of inches higher. Keeping her head tilted, she spoke into the mic. "Hello, Denver. How are you all tonight?"

A few claps and shouts were her response. It was hard to make out Link on the far side of the room, but his body shifted towards her.

"This song is dedicated to my dad, who passed recently." She strummed the first chords of "My Girl" by Elvie Shane. Country was not her usual genre of choice, but the lyrics summed up exactly the relationship she'd had with her father, Solomon Owusu. She'd never gotten to sing it to him. She hoped, somehow, somewhere, he was looking down with a smile as she sang about a man falling in love with a daughter who wasn't biologically his.

"Thank you, Papa."

Applause and whistles came from the crowd as several of them got to their feet. Her eyes flicked to Link, who stood in the back, his fingers going to his mouth before an ear-piercing whistle sounded in the room.

Her emotion was so thick, it was hard to breathe. She pinched the bridge of her nose and took a deep inhale. "Now I'd like to invite Link up here for this next song."

Link shook his head vigorously and slammed into his seat.

"Looks like he might need some encouragement, Denver."

Heads turned to where she pointed. Link crossed his arms in front of him.

"Come on, Link. Don't be a chicken."

Several people in the audience began to make clucking sounds before Link held up his hands and got to his feet once more. He stalked towards her, shaking his head. "You owe me for this," he grumbled.

"Whatever you say." She smirked.

She pointed to her song choice on the screen to the side and asked him, "Think you can keep up, old man?"

"It's only six years difference. If I'm old, so are you."

Emma nodded to Delia, who played the soundtrack to "Love Me Harder" by Ariana Grande and The Weekend.

Emma closed her eyes and let the music flow over her as she sang into the mic, facing Link. She knew how to put on a show for an audience, and that was what she did. As she sang about asking the man she loved to let her into his space, she pretended they weren't the words from her heart to Link. But it was all bullshit.

When it was his turn, he leaned into the mic, his deep voice softening. His eyes locked on hers, darkening as he sang the sensual lyrics. She joined back on the chorus, each of them on one side of the mic, breaths mingling. Eyes connecting. Voices syncing. He was the missing piece of her, and he made her whole for a few seconds in time.

Did he understand what she was telling him through the song?

The last notes faded as the room erupted in applause again. She backed away and took a bow, motioning for Link to do the same. Instead, he tapped the bill of her hat and led her down the stage stairs to her guitar case.

"You didn't tell me you still had that old thing." He pointed to the turquoise Gibson he'd gotten her years ago.

She set the instrument down and locked the case before standing and meeting his eyes. "It's the most valuable thing I own. Of course I still use it. All my songs are written with it."

He blinked as if he hadn't been expecting it to mean that much to her. Did he not remember how much time they'd pored over this very guitar? How special he'd made her feel—like she was the only person in the world? *I've never told him how much he means to me.*

She wrapped her free arm around him, hugging him close. Soft lips brushed her forehead as he hugged her back. She waited for him to pull away first. If she could suspend a moment in time, she would. Just to be in his arms—whole, despite the lingering pain of grief.

He pulled away to meet her gaze, and what reflected in his eyes—it looked a lot like lust. "Em—"

"Hey, you look just like Emma Sterling."

Emma pulled out of his embrace and faced the young woman. "I get that a lot."

Link took the guitar from her hand. His body tensed beside her.

"You sound just like her too." The woman squinted her eyes at Emma. "Oh my God!" she squealed. "Can I have your autograph?"

Emma scanned the room. A few more people turned their heads in her direction. It was better to sign the paper and get out of there before causing a scene if they could manage it. "Sure."

But in her life, nothing usually went according to plan.

16

LINK

Link adjusted the guitar case in his hand as Emma signed a piece of paper for the young girl. He'd already settled their tab while Emma had been singing her first song, so making a clean getaway wouldn't be a problem.

Two more girls approached, whispering to each other.

"Are you her?" the blonde asked.

Emma offered a smile and nod, reaching out to accept the hat the girl wanted signed. Link surveyed the room, anxiety snaking around his spine as more heads turned and a loud group of frat boys approached.

"Oh my God! Emma Sterling!"

"Are your bandmates here?"

"Is Ravi here too?"

The crowd surrounded them quicker than he thought possible. Emma offered him a panicked glance as she signed things and answered questions as fast as she could. She adjusted her cap. It hadn't been much use after she'd gone on the stage. Her voice was unique and notable, no matter which type of music she sang.

After she posed for what seemed like the twentieth selfie, she said, "Okay, guys, we have to get going."

"You up for some fun later? Here's my number," the six-foot guy with a university emblem on his shirt said, slipping a piece of folded paper in Emma's back pocket.

Emma jolted and smacked his hand away.

Link got into the guy's face, stepping so they were chest to chest, eye to eye. "Don't fucking touch her," Link growled, balling his fists in anticipation for a fight.

Fear reflected in the guy's eyes before he cocked his head to the side in challenge. "Who are you? Her bodyguard?"

"Link, let's go." Emma placed her hand on his arm.

"We can hold them off, so you guys can get to your car, but you'd better hurry," a female voice said, barely audible above the loud crowd.

"Thanks, Delia," Emma called, before pulling him towards the door.

Link went with Emma, all his senses on alert in case someone broke through the small line of security the bar had.

Once they were outside, Emma ran to the car. He whipped open his door and pushed the guitar case into the back seat before climbing in and slamming them inside. He twisted the key in the ignition, the engine roaring to life just as people poured out of the bar entrance and headed their way. Link flicked on the high beams and revved the engine, causing the mob to hesitate as he shifted into gear and tore out of the parking lot.

Chest heaving, he checked his mirrors, making sure no one was stupid enough to follow them. He continued a few blocks and doubled back before turning into a hotel with the vacancy sign lit. Link found a parking spot in the almost-full lot and cut the engine. He turned, needing to make sure Emma was alright. She burst out laughing. Link swallowed as her mirth got even more out of control. Emma tipped her head back and held her belly as her hysterical laughter grew silent, she was laughing so hard.

He shook his head and chuckled along with her. Her joy was contagious. Those bright blue eyes sparkled with life. They'd seemed so dull lately.

"Oh my God." Emma took a few deep breaths as if to calm herself.

The moonlight filtered into the windows, glinting off her golden hair. Her chest rose and fell rapidly, her cheeks flushed from the excursion. Flashes of that pink spreading over her chest as she'd ridden him came back with a vengeance.

His cock jumped as fire burned his veins. She licked her lips, teasing him with that pink tongue. It tasted like strawberries if he remembered correctly. Her gaze held his in a trance, sucking him into the depths of temptation.

He leaned forward just a fraction, giving in to the magnetic pull between them. His mind swirled, warring with right and wrong, fear and want. Desire pooled over his skin like liquid fire. He was going to burn alive for this woman.

Emma's mouth parted, her eyes dropping to his lips. Fuuuuuck he wanted her with every cell in his body. To climb over the gear shift and peel those tight pants down her thighs. To pull her on top of him and test the suspension in the car. He'd bury himself inside her and finally be able to release this built-up need. Nerves frayed, every muscle tensed, and sweat dotted his brow. His heart raced, pounding in his ears. Anger welled at the amount of control this woman had stripped from him. At his weakness to her.

Her head dipped, leaning in as if to kiss him.

Link bolted upright and snapped, "What the fuck were you thinking?"

Emma winced before staring out the window blankly.

"Getting on that stage . . . Why not hang a neon sign that says, 'I'm Emma Sterling, rock star and lead singer of The Sirens'?"

She lowered her head and sighed.

"Has that happened before?" His tone softened just a little.

"A couple times."

"You could have been hurt. Maybe you should hire some protection."

"You sound like Callie," she scoffed.

"Why are you not taking this seriously?" he growled in frustration.

Emma sat back, her head tipped to the ceiling, her arms crossed over her chest. "Look, I needed to do this tonight, okay? You're not in charge of me. You are not my boyfriend. You don't get to avoid me for years only to fuck me one night, make it clear I am nothing to you, and then speak to me like you care a damn thing about me." She opened the door in a huff and slammed it closed before running towards the hotel entrance.

"Fuck!" Link punched the seat. The fuck he didn't care about her. His hands itched to grab her and throw her over his knee. Then he'd edge her until she yielded. Until she understood the problem wasn't that he didn't care, but that he cared too much.

He took another minute to compose himself. After grabbing their bags from the trunk, he locked the car.

He stepped inside the automatic double doors and Emma's panicked voice put him on edge.

"What do you mean you only have one room?"

The flustered concierge pointed to the flyer on the counter. "I'm sorry, miss, but there is a music festival in town along with some university events. We're booked except for the one room we just had a cancelation for."

"Then we'll go somewhere else." Emma turned, but Link held out his hand to her arm to stop her.

"It's unlikely there'll be any vacancies anywhere else, except maybe the hourly motel outside of town; and trust me, your car would be a better option," the young guy, Ralph, according to his name tag, said.

"We'll take it," Link said, setting down the bags and pulling out his wallet.

"It's one room," Emma repeated as if he hadn't heard.

Ralph took the card and typed on his computer as Link sighed, exhausted from this tug-of-war between the two of them. "Look, I'm tired, you're tired, and they have a room. Let's just call a truce tonight, okay? We can go back to battle tomorrow."

Emma's eyes searched his, sympathy painting her expression before she nodded her silent approval.

"Sign here, sir." Ralph pointed to the digital pen and pad. Link signed and accepted the two keys for their room.

"Room three ten. The pool closes at eleven and opens at eight. The bar to your right is open until midnight. Breakfast is from six to ten. And checkout is eleven." Ralph smiled.

"Thanks."

Emma grabbed the handle of her suitcase and rolled it to the elevator. They rode to the third floor in silence. He slid his card against the lock in the door. The light turned green, and he stepped in. Cool air blasted from the air conditioner. The room was simple but clean. Better than anywhere else they'd stayed so far. His eyes zoned in on the one queen bed in the center of the room against the wall. One—as in singular. He searched the rest of the room for a couch or something besides the floor, but he had no such luck. Just one small chair that would surely be torture for his neck.

He closed his eyes and sighed. *Fuck my life.*

Emma placed her suitcase on said chair before pulling out a few items of clothing and a small bag. She closed herself in the bathroom and then the shower turned on.

He sat on the bed, pulling off his shoes. Relaxing on the mattress, he stared at the ceiling. But thoughts of the water rushing over every sleek exposed dip and curve of Emma with just a thin wall to separate them was giving him an erection of steel. He flicked the TV on for a distraction.

As the minutes ticked by, he had to press his hand down on his cock. He groaned in part pain and part sexual frustration.

The water shut off, and he tried to calm his racing heart. Another five minutes later, Emma came out with a burst of hot, moist air that smelled like strawberries. Her hair was pulled into a messy bun, and she wore a baggy men's T-shirt over a pair of tiny shorts. She bent over to place the dirty clothes into a bag in her suitcase. The bottom half of her ass stuck out of her shorts. He bit his lip until he tasted blood.

"Isn't that my shirt?" he ground out.

Emma spun around; her face flushed. She cocked an eyebrow, picking up the hem of her top to expose her pierced belly button. "Yeah. You want it back?"

The sass ran so deep with this one. Instead of answering, he bolted into the bathroom and locked the door, for her sake just as much as his. He stripped and turned the water on. His dick was so hard, it nearly slapped his stomach once it was freed. Stepping into the scalding water, he gripped the base, squeezing tight. He braced one arm against the tub, leaning his forehead on the cold tiles. Closing his eyes, he rubbed up and down his shaft and imagined a woman on her knees. *Toned thighs, squeezing from the pleasure of sucking him off. Her tits hard enough to cut diamonds. Her fingers pinching and pulling as her straw-berry-colored lips wrapped around him, sucking him deep into her throat.*

Link groaned, working himself up, continuing the fantasy. *He'd reach down and cup her jaw, thrusting his hips forward until he hit the back of her throat. She'd hum, the vibration tickling his balls, sending a thrill of desire shooting up his spine.*

His mouth parted, panting as he pumped faster, squeezing harder. *Golden hair wrapped around his fist as he fucked her mouth.* So close. He was almost there. Pleasure gathered at the base of his tingling spine. His balls drew up.

She pulled away, her hands replacing her mouth, continuing the rhythm. Her blue eyes opened and stared up at him, a wily smirk crossing her face. Fuck, it was *Emma.* Emma was the woman in his fantasy. *"Come on me. Mark me. Make me yours."*

He couldn't hold back, exploding all over the side of the shower. He groaned into his arm, trying to muffle the sound of coming the hardest he'd ever orgasmed by himself—and with any woman. It didn't help the whole bathroom smelled like her and whatever strawberry shampoo she used. That fruity scent saturated the air, making it impossible to think of anyone else.

His chest heaved as he caught his breath. He waited for the shame to come, but it didn't.

Cleaning up, he finished his shower and wrapped a towel around his waist. Staring into the foggy mirror, he shook his head at his reflection.

I need to get laid—and not by Emma.

17

EMMA

The last two days, Link had barely said a word to Emma. He'd been quiet and broody through Colorado and past the Nevada border.

"You work on any fun projects recently?" Emma asked, turning down the alternative rock station playing.

"Not really," Link said before he flicked the radio back up, effectively ending the conversation as he steered them along the Las Vegas strip.

"Right here," Emma yelled over the music.

Link followed her directions into the front of a large casino and hotel. She shut the music off as a man in a uniform opened her door and another walked around to Link's side.

"Valet parking." She winked and climbed out. Speaking to the concierge, she pointed to the trunk. "We have two bags and a guitar. Take extra care of that, please."

"Yes, ma'am."

"There's also a mesh bag with dirty laundry. Please see

that it's taken care of and returned to our room. The reservation is under Emma Sterling."

"As you wish, Miss Sterling." He gave her a little bow before attending to her instructions. When she turned, Link was staring at her, slack-jawed.

"Come on. Let's make use of the perks of being famous." She led him inside as his eyes widened, taking in the large, elegant lobby. There were fancy white couches and opulence in every direction you looked. Gold embellishments adorned the walls and marble pillars in the grand entryway. Men were dressed in expensive suits and women in fancy dresses with heels that clacked on the shiny marble floors as they passed them.

She was far out of her element, but she'd gotten used to the snubs from her travels. From the side-eyes and noses upturned at her simple Converse, the other patrons wanted her to know she didn't belong.

Emma approached the woman at the counter. The lady's smile didn't waver as her eyes skimmed over their plain-clothes appearance. "Welcome to the Glass Castle Hotel and Casino. Can I help you, miss?"

Emma smiled. "I hope so. I have a reservation under Emma Sterling. Should be two suites."

Her eyes scanned the computer as she clicked keys. "Of course, Miss Sterling, we have you all set with the specifics you requested. Here are your keys. Do you need a list of the amenities?"

"No, thanks." Emma accepted the black cards from her hand before giving one to Link.

"Okay, well, the concierge will have your bags delivered to rooms ten thirty and ten thirty-two. Is there anything else you need?"

"Nope."

"I'll charge the card on file for any of your other needs or damages." The woman's eyes focused on Link as she spoke the last.

Emma grit her teeth.

"Let me pay," Link said, touching her arm.

Emma pulled away, leading them towards the elevators. "You've paid for every other hotel on this trip. Let me get this one."

"Let me at least pay my half."

She entered the otherwise empty elevator and pressed the button for the tenth floor. The only button higher was the penthouse suite. "Just drop it, Link."

"How much?" he growled.

"Eight." She sighed.

"Eight hundred? A night?"

His shock made her smile. "No, eight thousand, per room, per night."

His mouth dropped open as the elevator doors opened on the sixth floor and another couple entered, effectively ending the conversation.

Emma inched closer to Link and whispered, "Enjoy the perks. Let's live it up in Vegas. We'll order room service, unless you want to take advantage of the personal chef offered with each of our rooms. We can drink fine champagne and get a massage. Dad wanted us to have fun on this trip. So, let loose and swallow that pride."

The door opened on the tenth floor, and they filed out before turning down the hall to their respective doors. Emma used the first key card and opened the door. There was a room service table with a six-pack of Sand Dune's IPA chilling in the mini fridge, as per her request, along with a plate of chocolate-covered strawberries—a little something special she had prepared for him. "This room is yours."

Link stepped in, taking in the large space. Next to the door was a vase with fresh flowers. Farther down was the sitting room with overstuffed couches and pillows with a few fuzzy throw blankets. A mirrored table holding more arranged flowers sat between the couch and a couple of matching chairs. The walls looking out over the city were all reflective, coated glass from floor to ceiling, so guests could see out, but no one could see in.

"It's huge."

Emma snorted. "That's what she said."

Link gave her an unimpressed look.

"Through that door is your giant room, fit for a king, and an equally embarrassing fancy closet and bathroom. If you get lost, just call me," she teased.

Knock. Knock.

"That would be your luggage, your highness." She walked to the door, but Link beat her to it.

He opened it, positioning his body in front of it, blocking her view to whomever was there as if to protect her. A pang of gratitude flit through her. Link widened the door and accepted the baggage from the bellhop.

After getting their luggage settled, Emma walked past him and across the hall. She opened her door and turned to lean against the entrance of her room. He mirrored her actions, crossing his arms and waiting expectantly.

"Let's go out tonight. See the town."

"Is that a good idea, Miss Famous?" He arched one perfect eyebrow.

She smiled. "It's much easier to hide here."

"I don't think it's a good idea for you to be out alone. We should stick together. Where do you want to go?"

"Hmmm, strip club?"

He shook his head. "No way in hell am I going to a strip club with my sister."

So, they were back to this: Link pushing her away and making it clear she was completely off his radar.

"When in Rome." She shrugged.

He rubbed a hand over his face. "How about a club?"

"I can do that. Enjoy your massage, order some dinner, and we'll meet up at eight?"

"Massage?"

"They'll be here in an hour." She gave him a wink and shut the door before he could protest.

Several hours later, her belly was full and every muscle relaxed and loose. She'd taken a long, luxurious bath. She'd primped and pressed. Her makeup was flawless, close to what she did for shows—smoky eyes with black and silver shadow, drawing out the blue in her sapphire orbs. Emma had curled her hair and then teased it to get that tousled she'd-just-snuck-into-the-closet-and-had-a-quickie look. Puckering her bloodred lips, she blew herself a kiss in the mirror.

Emma pulled the zipper up on the side of her little black dress. The corset top made her breasts look bigger than they actually were, and the lace bottom came just below the globes of her ass. Adding a pair of fishnet stockings and leather boots that laced up and reached under her knees made her look like a real-life rock goddess.

Her body buzzed from the bottle of champagne she'd already finished; she was ready for a good time out on the town. Hopefully Link would relax a little and they could have fun.

Knock. Knock.

Emma gave herself one more glance before she made her way to the door and opened it.

Link stood there. His sandalwood scent drifted into her space, wrapping around her and winding her up. His obsidian eyes raked over her body slowly. She took in the fitted black dress shirt that hugged his large, muscled torso to perfection. It tapered in at his waist and was tucked into a pair of dark washed jeans held up by a black belt. His black and red Converse were the perfect addition.

"Go change."

Her smiled dropped. "Wh-what?"

He shook his head. "You can't go out wearing that."

Gritting her teeth, she said, "There is nothing wrong with my outfit. You're not my daddy, and I'm not a child. I'll wear whatever the fuck I want. Sexist much?"

His jaw clenched. "Can't you just listen to me one goddamned time without argument?"

"There is only one place I submit to anyone, and you've made it clear we are never going there again." She stood straighter, meeting his eyes in challenge.

"Fuck." He swore under his breath. "Here." He dug his wallet out of his pocket and handed her a couple of twenties in cash.

"What's this for?" she asked, confused.

"In case we get separated, or if we don't come back to the hotel together tonight. You need cash for a cab." Link looked away as he said it.

Meaning he was planning to go home with someone else. *Or bring someone back to his room.* Pain tore at her already shredded heart. She'd had to endure Link with other women for years, but that had been before. Before she'd had him to herself. Even if it was only for one drunken night of intoxicated pleasure that still had black spots from unrecovered memory.

A violent sickness churned in her belly. Jealousy reared its ugly head like a dragon spewing green fire through her veins. He wanted to fuck someone else? Fine. She could too. She'd show him she'd moved on as well. And maybe one day it would be true.

18

———

LINK

Link tipped the glass to his lips, taking another sip of the dark, expensive whiskey. Loud, pulsing music pounded through the speakers below the VIP area cordoned off for Emma and her guests, along with a few other high rollers. Women sat on either side of him on the blue velvet couch. His gaze flicked through the glass balcony to the pulsing bodies and the two dancers in the cages on either side of the stage, one male and one female.

"Do you need another drink, handsome?" the waitress in a barely there pink cocktail dress asked.

He nodded.

"Shots!" Emma yelled over the music. "Tequila!"

The waitress turned to go back through the velvet rope and down the stairs to the main bar.

The women next to him were wearing some pretty powerful perfume, neither of which complemented the other.

"So, what is it you do?" the blonde to his right asked. *Carla? Carly? Carol?*

"Mechanic."

She ran her red-painted nails over his biceps, giving them a squeeze. "That's sexy."

"You work on bikes or cars?" the brunette to his left asked. He was pretty sure her name was Amanda.

"Cars mostly. But sometimes a hog or two."

Emma's laugh drew his attention to her once more. Her hands were wrapped around a pink-haired vixen covered in tattoos and leather. Violet had been the first one up here, introducing herself before they'd even made it through the rope.

Violet spread her hand on Emma's thigh, inching it higher as the sensual music pulsed and throbbed.

"I bet you're good with your hands," Carly, or whatever her name was, said.

"Mm-hmm."

The waitress returned, handing him a fresh glass of bourbon. He set his empty on her tray as she passed the tequila shots around.

Violet set her shot glass in between Emma's breasts. Link's grip tightened on his cup as the two women in his ears rattled on. Emma gave Violet a sultry smile and held the lime wedge between her lips. Violet flicked her tongue over the pale flesh of Emma's neck before shaking some salt on it. Emma tipped her head for Violet to lick her again, as Violet took longer than needed to lap up the granules. Jealousy roared like a hungry lion.

Her pink-haired head dipped as she dove between Emma's tits, removing the shot with her mouth. A growl emanated from Link's chest. Violet's mouth captured Emma's, only the lime between them. Every muscle pulled taut in his body, his chest heaving. Anger roiled in his gut like a whirlpool of hot lava, melting his insides and all rational thought. His self-control was frayed and raw. *Mine! Fuck! No, she isn't.*

His eyes remained glued to the pair as the music switched to "In My Bed" by Rotimi and Wale. Violet stood, taking Emma's hand and leading her towards an open space under the flashing red lights of the club. Emma hadn't looked his way once, and yet he couldn't keep his eyes off her.

"Do you want to dance?" Carly asked, seemingly mistaking his interest for the few couples grinding and writhing against one another as a desire to join them.

"Sure." He tipped back the rest of his bourbon, enjoying the burn as he got to his feet.

Both women encased him, one behind him and one in front. He was normally a one-woman-at-a-time kind of guy, but this was Vegas. Like Emma had said, when in Rome. He tried to get into it, focusing on Carly grinding herself against him, but when he looked at the beautiful woman, she didn't hold a candle to his little spitfire. He shook his head. *I don't have to like her, just fuck her.* Damn, when had he become this brand of asshole?

Emma spun around with a smile on her face as Violet grabbed her hips, holding her close to her own body. Emma's eyes closed as she tipped her head back to her partner's shoulder. Violet dipped her nose to Emma's exposed neck, peppering kisses down to Emma's shoulder.

Amanda wrapped her hands around his waist, coming to the front with Carly. Four sets of hands molested his chest as they rubbed against him like two cats in heat. His body reacted, but not to them—to the sight of the beauty before him. Emma's lips parted as Violet's hands moved to her breasts as she said something in Emma's ear.

Emma's eyes popped open, indecision sparking as she looked right at him for the first time since they'd arrived at the club. Her gaze roamed over the girls attached to him, disappointment flashing in her eyes. He couldn't hear her over the music, but he could read her lips and the nod of her head. "Back" and "hotel." She was taking Violet back to her room. His heart lurched. Pain lanced his rib cage, slicing like a knife, leaving damage unseen and unspoken.

Emma cast him one more look with a roiling mix of emotions before resignation rose like a wall between them. She took Violet's hand and led her down the stairs and out of the club.

Link's chest burned, his lungs squeezing tight as he tried to suck in oxygen. His shoulder muscles bunched as every cell in his body screamed at him to go after her. But what then? Rage flushed through his veins, mixed with lust. His control frayed. Each second ticked by seeming like an eternity as he waged war between his mind and his body. He couldn't have her—not really. But he couldn't let her go either.

His feet were moving before he knew what was happening. One thing was clear—he didn't want Emma to fuck someone else.

He rushed to the door, weaving between the bodies to the exit. Hot, stale air blew in his face as he made it to the street. Emma opened a yellow cab door. His gaze grew hazy, his lungs burning. Desire radiated through him, the last of his self-restraint snapping. He ran over to Emma and grabbed her arm before she could join Violet in the cab. Energy zinged up his arm.

Emma gasped, turning towards him with wide eyes. "Link?"

"Don't go with her." His voice was pure gravel, rough and raw.

Emma's brows drew together in confusion before anger pinked her cheeks. "Why not? Looks like you were going to be occupied for the night."

Violet turned towards them, casting a curious glance between Link and Emma.

"You're not going with her." His command was gruff, leaving no room for argument.

Emma pulled her arm free from his and stood straighter in challenge, her eyes burning blue flames of indignation. "Why not?"

He took a step closer, so they were chest to chest, and growled, "Are you going to make me say it?"

"Say what?" Her eyebrows lifted coyly.

Link glanced around at the other people passing by and giving them a wide berth, as if even they could sense the thick tension roiling between them. An invisible storm raged. Right and wrong. Temptation and fate. A war he wasn't sure who had started, but he sure as fuck was going to end once and for all.

He bent to growl into her ear. "That I don't want to see anyone's hands on you but my own."

She let out a small gasp.

"That even though it's wrong on so many levels, I want to fuck you out of my system. Make you mine, even if it's just temporary."

She panted, her chest heaving against his. "What happens in Vegas, stays?"

"Exactly." Even if it killed him to let her go after. Because his little bird deserved the room to fly. And he'd only drag her down.

"He could join us," Violet interrupted, reminding them they weren't alone.

Link reached out, wrapping Emma's hair around his fist at the base of her neck and tugging so her chin tipped. "I don't share what's mine." His voice came out harsher than intended.

The blue in Emma's eyes disappeared until all that was left were two dark pits of desire and lust matching his own.

That's my girl.

"Take me, then. *Now.*"

He motioned for Violet to get out.

"At least take my number in case you come to town again." Violet slipped a business card into Emma's cleavage as she exited the cab. Link released Emma to climb into the taxi before closing the door after he'd joined her.

"Where to?" the cab driver asked.

"The Glass Palace." Link pulled out his wallet and handed over a fifty. "This is all yours if you get us there in less than ten minutes."

Link turned to Emma. Her dress had risen higher on her parted thighs, exposing the black lace panties underneath.

He plucked the paper from between her breasts. The soft swell of her skin blistered his fingers before he crumpled the note and tossed it to the floor. "You won't be needing this."

Fuck, he was going to die in anticipation. In this moment, it didn't matter if he was going to fuck the woman everyone thought of as his sister. Here, in this cab, no one knew them. Here they could be anyone. Tonight he was just Link, and she was just Emma. A man and a woman with matching needs and burning lust.

This was the city of sin, after all. And Emma was definitely no angel—just the way he liked it.

19

EMMA

Emma walked ahead of Link into his large suite. The walls seemed to close in as she shut the door with a click. The lock engaged, echoing through the hall. Her heartbeat thudded in her ears. The tiny hairs on her arm stood on end as goose bumps rushed over her flesh, prickling her with awareness. Breathing became difficult, as if she were in a smoky room. Each second lingering in his presence only tainted the air more, replacing it with a haze of lust curling around her limbs, tickling her nerve endings in anticipation.

"You ready for me to fuck you?" he asked.

Butterflies tumbled in her belly, but his deep voice cut through the fog. *Is this really happening? Link actually wants me?*

Calloused fingers wrapped around her arm, jerking her against the wall roughly. Link stepped into her space, tilting his chin to look in her eyes. His hard brows were drawn together. Droplets of sweat dusted his forehead as if it was taking everything in him to hold back from tearing her clothes off. Power rushed through her veins, drowning her in adrenaline. Lust burned her from the inside out. Sandalwood and pine saturated her every breath.

"Answer me, little bird." The rumble of his voice vibrated in his chest against her body pressed into him. Tingles raced down her spine. Bursts of color exploded through her grey world.

"Yes." Her voice was all breath.

He intertwined his fingers through her hair, holding her firmly in place as his black eyes searched her face—for what, she didn't know.

"Just until we get back. You hear me? This is only ever temporary. I'm gonna fuck you until we get back, and then we move on. This isn't forever. This isn't even a relationship. This is sex."

She tried not to let him see how much his words tore her apart. She knew better than to hope. He meant every rough, calloused, promise. Link was nothing if not honest. If this was all she could have of him, she'd take it. She'd cherish the pieces he gave her for as long as she could have them.

She licked her lips, drawing his attention to them. Wetness seeped into her panties at the control she elicited over him. "Under one condition."

His jaw clenched.

"After all this is over, you don't push me away. I need you in my life. You're the only family I have left."

"Done."

She breathed a sigh of relief and smirked. "You think you can handle me?"

"I should be asking you that."

She'd bring this man to his knees, even if it was just for tonight.

The corner of his mouth turned up. "Didn't you say you liked to submit?"

"You have to earn my submission."

Obsidian eyes transformed into dark pools of lust as he growled, "Challenge accepted."

His mouth crashed against hers, soft lips tangling and merging, sending explosions rocketing through her consciousness. *Yes! Finally!* The tension at the back of her head increased, prickling tingles of pain morphed with desire. Her body propelled from her grey existence into technicolor as her senses burst awake.

She raked her teeth over his bottom lip—hard.

He groaned, picking her up and walking her into the bedroom. "You like to play rough, huh?"

"I told you, you couldn't handle me," she teased, catching her breath.

His hands released her, and she free-fell for a second, gasping before she landed on the soft comforter of the four-poster bed.

He whipped off his shirt, his rich umber skin glistening in the low light of the room. Tattoos wound around his defined pecs and along each arm into sleeves with a mixture of gears, machinery, and car parts in dark ink.

His eyes raked over her, making her skin burn with the fire of a thousand suns. Suddenly the short dress and fishnet stockings were too much clothing. She wanted them off, needed his gaze worshipping her flesh.

Link unbuckled his belt, letting it hang open in invitation as if he had all the time in the world. He bit his bottom lip, reaching for the zipper on the side of her knee to her laced-up boots. The sound of the zipper was somehow erotic and he slowly slipped the boot off her leg. Cool air rushed over the newly exposed skin. He repeated the motion with the other shoe before climbing onto the bed, crawling towards her.

"Get closer to the headboard," he directed.

She turned around on all fours, giving him a nice view of her exposed panties as she obeyed.

Smack!

The sting on her ass made her inhale a sharp breath.

"Get on your back." His low voice, with barely held control, made her thighs clench.

She wiggled her ass in challenge. If he wanted her to do as he said, he'd have to make her. She was the cat in this scenario, and he the mouse. He just didn't know it yet. Emma needed the control—it was the only way to protect her heart.

Large hands massaged her ass, kneading it roughly. Emma whimpered. She'd have fingerprint bruises tomorrow, and she'd proudly carry his mark for as long as it lasted.

Another zipper undone—this time it was the one to her dress. The fabric pooled onto the bed before he dragged it down her legs. He straddled her calves. Arching her back, she pressed into him. His hard arousal rubbed against the spot she needed it most.

She moaned.

Smack! Smack! Smack!

Pain burned her backside, arousal pooling in her soaked panties. She fisted the soft bedsheets.

"You like that, you dirty girl?" Link asked, sounding surprised and pleased.

"Yes. I can take whatever you want to give me."

He spun her around on her back, one hand on her throat, pressing her into the bed.

"Be careful what you ask for." The bass of his voice tickled her ear.

There was a sound of metal clanking and a whizz of fabric before her hands were pulled above her head. Leather bit around her wrists. She gasped as he tied her to the bed with his belt.

"Say the word and this stops." Link searched her eyes once more.

"More."

The hunger in his gaze grew. "You ready to submit to me? You ready to be a good girl?"

"No."

His lips hovered over her. His breath, kissing her mouth, taunted her. "I'm gonna make you beg for my cock."

She swallowed, holding back the moan she wanted to release at his dirty words. No—he'd need to earn each and every one.

Featherlight touches skimmed down her neck, massaging her breasts. Her nipples were painfully hard, yearning for attention. But Link seemed to know what she wanted and purposely didn't give it to her. She bit her lip as he caressed her soft flesh, dipping his head to lick and suck everywhere but the dark pink buds.

She pulled at her restraints, needing to shove his mouth onto her.

He chuckled. "What do you need?"

"Your mouth."

"Gotta be a bit more specific. You want me to use my mouth to tell you just how I'm going to break this tight body until you're putty in my hands? Or do you want me to suck on these candy tits?"

She couldn't help the moan that escaped. Needing to reclaim back the power, she challenged, "Who said anything about sucking? Bite me."

His grin turned wolfish as he bent and raked his teeth over her nipples. She arched her back, pressing herself farther into his mouth. Wrapping her legs around his waist, she squeezed him closer.

His hot, wet mouth clamped over her nipple, sending a

shockwave of pain and pleasure mingling together in a firestorm of lust. Desire pooled in her center, spinning out of control. Needy, she keened for more.

The soft flick of his tongue over her throbbing nipple was the perfect contrast to soothe one ache and stoke another. He moved over her body, pressing kisses to her ribs and stomach, trailing lower—taking his time to map every inch of her like he was memorizing it.

He pulled off the fishnets and her panties until she was left completely exposed and at his mercy. His teeth grated over the music notes tattooed on her hip bone before he spread her thighs. As he kissed a trail from her knee to the edge of her pussy lips, she squirmed, yearning for more.

"Something you want?" Link asked, inhaling at the juncture of her thighs and groaning.

"Make me come."

"Say please," he commanded.

She shook her head.

He smirked. "Do you know what edging is, sweetheart?"

Emma blinked; a violent burst of lust overflowed the dam within her. *He wouldn't.*

"Yes, I would. Just how long do you think you can last?" he asked, reading her mind.

Spreading her legs as wide as she could, she raised one eyebrow. "I guess we'll have to see."

"Fuck, you are a bad girl."

"Life is more fun that way." She winked.

Two fingers thrust inside her without warning. She sucked in a breath as he finger-fucked her.

"I'm gonna shut that sassy mouth of yours with my cock. How would you like that?" Curling his digits, he hit her G-spot inside, creating a build-up of pressure in her womb. She squeezed her inner walls around him, biting down. The hollow ache grew in hunger for the erection pressed against her thigh.

She was so close. But it was as if he could sense it. He pulled back as she groaned in frustration before he began teasing her again.

"So wet. Bet you taste sweet too."

Her eyes rolled back in her head at the thought of his mouth on her.

"That fucking dress you wore, showing off almost every delectable inch like you wanted me to punish you for not obeying me."

"You're not the boss of me." She could barely form a sentence as pleasure built. The urgency to come sunk its claws into her as he swirled his thumb all around the spot she needed it most, never even grazing her clit.

Link crawled over her, adding another finger inside her, stretching her more as he kissed her lips. He intoxicated her with his mouth while spinning her in a web of desire with his hand.

His kiss was tender, his fingers determined, and his teeth rough as they pulled at her bottom lip. "No, I'm not. I'm just the man who is gonna fuck you the best you've ever had. The one who's gonna make you beg for more."

Her ears rang as her impending orgasm clouded the edge of her vision.

Link pulled his fingers out of her and lifted them to his mouth. He sucked all but one finger clean. "Taste yourself." He lowered his finger, glistening with her juices, and dragged it over her mouth to her chin before licking it off her, ending in a kiss with her essence melding with the taste of bourbon and man. "You ready to beg?"

Was she? She wanted to come, needed him buried deep inside her. But she wasn't quite ready to submit to him. She didn't want this to be over. "You giving up already?" Her voice wasn't as strong as she'd hoped, wavering with her own sexual hunger.

Link got off the bed and dropped his pants and boxers in a pile. He pulled his cock out, rubbing it as his gaze wandered over her body. "Maybe I'll leave you tied up here, fuck those perfect tits, and come all over you as punishment."

She clenched her thighs together. The sight of this beautiful man pleasuring himself was almost enough to make her come without touch.

"Open your mouth."

Emma's lips parted without hesitation. Link leaned over her, his thick dick brushing against her lips. Her tongue darted out, licking the drop of precum. He groaned and untied her wrists, releasing her.

He lay next to her. Her eyebrows drew together in question as she rubbed the red rings at the base of her palms.

"Suck my cock."

Emma smiled and sat before bending to his erect perfection.

Some people might think that a blow job was the ultimate act of submission. But Emma held all the power here. It was her mouth sucking him in until he hit the back of her throat, giving him pleasure, or taking it away. It was her teeth that raked over the soft, vulnerable flesh of his cock. It was Emma causing the groans of pleasure pouring from his lips. In this way, it was Link who submitted to her.

Two large hands grasped her hips, picking her up and pulling her pussy onto Link's face. He didn't even ask—he just took. His hot tongue lapped up her juices, flicking over her clit until her moans melded with his in a symphony of depraved lust and carnal desire. He sucked hard on her clit before his soft tongue lashed in a steady pace, driving her closer and closer to the edge.

She hummed her approval around his cock.

Pressure built. Need tangled and spun. Her hand wrapped around the base of his cock in frenzied strokes. She was almost there—

Link pushed her onto the mattress, pulling out of her mouth. He sat, leaning over her, thrusting his fingers back inside her. "Say it. Say please like a good girl and you can come," he ordered.

Her body burned with the need for release, her sex pulsing from the exquisite torture. The look in his eyes is what finally broke her. Like he needed this just as much as she did.

"Please." She conceded.

"Say it again."

"Please? Make me come," she begged.

He flew off the bed and grabbed his pants from the floor. After pulling a foil packet from the back pocket, he ripped it open with his teeth and put the condom on before climbing on top of her.

He spoke against her lips. "Hold on to me. I've got you."

Link kissed her once more. She wrapped her arms around him, hanging on as she prepared to shatter.

He lined up at her entrance, pulling back to gaze into her eyes as he thrust inside her.

She inhaled sharply, eyes widening at the delicious stretch. "Link!"

He gasped, surprise flickering in his smoky gaze. His body trembled against hers with the intensity as they became one for this brief moment in time. His exhale became her inhale. He drove his hips into her. Wrapping her legs around him, she dug her nails into his back as he thrust in and out. Shockwaves of pleasure sent her soaring. Sparks and shimmers clouded her vision. All-encompassing desire weaved her in a warm blanket of euphoria as she came on his cock. Pleasure crashed over her like a rogue wave, drowning her in a boiling frenzy of delirium-inducing rapture.

"That's it, baby. Come. Come for me." Focus and self-restraint were etched across the hard lines and contours of Link's chiseled features.

The sound of skin slapping against skin, moans, and primal grunts became the erotic soundtrack to their carnal rhapsody.

"Fuck!" Emma screamed, clawing at his back, needing something to ground her as she rocketed into other planes of ecstasy.

Link's hand clamped on the sides of her throat. "Come!"

Blinding white light filled her vision as her body shook from the intensity of her orgasm decimating everything in its path.

Link grunted, rocking her harder. "Emma!" he roared her name as his own climax caught up to him. He bit her shoulder before darkness filled the edge of her vision.

Silence descended on the room with the exception of their sated breaths. His hand released her throat before he made a move to pull out of her. But she held on tighter.

Just one more minute. Sixty seconds of pausing the moment and experiencing technicolor. Of living in a fantasy where she loved Link and he loved her back. Where she'd just experienced the best sex of her life, and it didn't have to end.

Just one more moment where she was whole.

20

LINK

Link's eyes fluttered open to the dawn light peering through the tinted windows. He ran a hand over his abs and turned his head towards the soft body lying on his arm. Emma's golden hair fanned out over the pillow, the pink and blue ends wrapping around his arm. He waited for the shame to come after what they'd done—after the dirty words he'd spoken, and how roughly he'd handled her. It didn't. Shouldn't he feel like this was wrong? His body was ready to go again, to explore her nakedness, to find the bruises his handling of her had left. Maybe that meant he was surely depraved—to be turned on by his marks.

His gaze roamed over her profile to the tiny diamond stud in her little button nose and the Cupid's bow above her full lips. Her smooth, porcelain cheeks had a slight pink blush. That tint had darkened and spread over her chest when she'd fallen apart in his arms last night. Her coming had been one of the most beautiful things he'd ever seen. He had to witness it again.

After dragging the sheets over her body, he climbed

between her thighs as she stirred. Lifting her thighs over his shoulder, he spread her wide open as a small gasp left her mouth.

Dipping his tongue inside her pussy, he tasted her. She was sweet like ripe strawberries. Emma moaned, digging her heels into his back. Link licked her clit, up and down, side to side, and back again. He tested out which pattern and rhythm had her stomach muscles clenching.

"Link," Emma whimpered.

"I know, baby. Just relax. Let me enjoy my breakfast." He scanned the bruised flesh on her hip where he'd bitten her and the fingerprint-sized marks on her thighs. His cock twitched as he slipped a finger over the spot between her clit and the tight hole he wanted to bury his dick in again.

She jackknifed off the bed, hands pulling the short dreads on top of his head until pain prickled his scalp.

"Mmmmm," he moaned into her clit as he sucked it into his mouth. She was close. He reached out with one hand to pinch her nipple. Arousal shot out of her pussy, squirting all over his mouth and beard, running down his chin.

"Fuuuuuuck!" she screamed.

His cock throbbed against the mattress, begging for release. He'd never been so turned on before.

He dove into her pussy, drinking in the sweet nectar as her body vibrated and clenched around him. Link looked up just in time as she fell apart. A red flush spread over her neck and between her breasts.

Link gentled the assault on her clit from his tongue to soft strokes as she came down. Her legs were still quaking as he licked his lips and crawled up the bed to lie next to her.

Her glazed eyes were only half open as she sucked in heavy breaths.

He smiled. "Good morning."

"I'd say so." She gave a soft laugh.

"You squirted all over the bed. Wonder what house-cleaning will think."

She turned towards him, a dreamy smile on her lips, her blue eyes sparking with humor. "That you might know your way around the female anatomy and left one woman very satisfied."

"You've squirted before?" he asked, curious.

"Only with women."

There was no use getting jealous. They both had a past. And this wasn't even a relationship. He needed to remember that.

Link dragged his knuckle down her cheek. She shivered. His chest tightened, affection battering in his ribs like a caged bird trying to get out.

"What's the plan for today? Back on the road?" she asked.

Their little bubble had to pop at some point, but it didn't mean they had to rush it. This was the best sex of his life. Maybe it was the shared experience of loss and the journey of healing they were undertaking together, but he wanted to stay wrapped up in her just a little longer. He'd worry about the consequences later. "No. Let's stay another day. How about we hit up the casino? Walk down the strip? Unless you think you'd be recognized."

She smiled, joy sparking to life in her eyes. "Let's order room service, take a shower, and I take care of this." She wrapped her hand over his hard cock.

Link groaned his approval.

"Then we check out the blackjack table downstairs?"

"Sounds like a plan. Call it in."

Emma didn't hesitate. After grabbing the phone by the bed, she put in an order for a feast. "Twenty minutes."

He rolled over her to the other side of the mattress as she

laughed. He scooped her into his arms and carried her to the bathroom.

She clung to his neck as he leaned over to turn the shower on, not waiting for it to get warm. Screaming, she slapped his chest as he lifted her under the cold spray. "Asshole!"

He laughed, setting her onto her feet. Emma shivered, her teeth chattering. He leaned in, melding his mouth against hers, sucking the anger from her. Their tongues twisted together, soft lips brushing and teasing. She gripped the back of his head, pulling him closer as if his kiss was giving her life, like it was more important than oxygen.

She pulled away, dropping a couple inches as if she'd been on her tiptoes. Emma dragged her hands over his chest, flicking her tongue across his nipple, kissing her way down his body as she kneeled before him. The sight of this beautiful creature on her knees as hot water rained over them, steam fogging up the glass doors, created the illusion of the world falling away until it was just him and her.

Every muscle tensed in anticipation as her mouth parted. This tryst was temporary, but he'd bear her mark on his heart forever. He'd never be the same after this. Emma might be the one on her knees, but he was the one at her mercy. Sooner or later, everyone fell under her spell.

After the best blow job of his life and a hearty breakfast that probably cost way too much, they threw on some clothes. Emma grabbed her baseball cap and tied her hair into a braid running down her back. She traded her usual skinny jeans in for some white shorts that made her legs look like they went on for days and a black Breaking Benjamin T-shirt. Her leather bracelet and a pair of Doc Martens completed the look. She was effortlessly beautiful. Low maintenance and yet sexy as hell. His cock had a taste and instead of moving on, wanted more.

They headed down to the main floor, following the signs for the casino. After cashing in their money for chips, Emma wrapped her arm around his waist and tucked her palm in his back pocket like it was the most natural thing in the world. He rested his arm over her shoulders, guiding her towards the blackjack table with two empty seats.

"Good afternoon, ladies and gents. I'm Robert, your dealer. Go ahead and place your bets," the young man in the dealer seat directed.

Emma took the seat to Link's right, setting two red chips into the betting circle. He followed suit.

After the other players were done, the dealer laid out the first two cards for everyone faceup, and his own, with one facing down. It was Emma's turn to decide what to do; she had a deuce and an eight. She tapped the table, hitting. Robert flipped over another card, revealing a queen. She was at twenty.

"Not bad, sweetheart." Link winked.

She waved her hand over her card, letting the dealer know she was standing.

Link had a six of hearts and a seven of clubs. He tapped the table before the dealer gave him another card. A king of spades ended his turn, losing him the bet. "Damn it."

Robert collected his chips, completing his turn. After the other players had gone, the dealer flipped his card, revealing an eight to join his ten.

"You won, ma'am." Robert pushed the chips from his bet over into her pile.

Emma beamed. "This is so fun."

God, that smile did things to him that he wasn't entirely ready to face. "Because you won."

"Do you need me to teach you how to play?" She smirked.

"Beginner's luck."

"Mm-hmm."

After a few more rounds, Emma cleared out the table with her winning blackjack, and Link couldn't help the grin on his face despite his wounded pride. "Alright, we'd better give up our seats before I go broke."

She collected her chips and followed him to cash them out before they headed to the main doors of the lobby.

"Where do you want to go now?"

Emma tapped her lips, her eyes lighting up with mischief. "I have the perfect activity."

"No strip clubs," he grumbled.

She shook her head. "Not quite the excitement I was going for. Do you trust me?"

He took a breath, studying her face for any clue. She seemed more relaxed than he'd seen her in a while. And he liked to think the orgasms he'd given her had something to do with that. "I guess so."

"Don't look so excited," she deadpanned.

"Alright, let's go. Lead me to this exciting activity that is definitely not a strip club." He grabbed her hand, telling himself it was so he didn't lose her in the crowd on the strip, to keep her safe as they navigated the city of Las Vegas—not because it felt like the most natural thing in the world.

"You do have a living will all drawn up, right?" Emma asked.

"Emma," he growled her name.

"Just kidding. Trust me. You'll be fine . . . probably." She laughed, and damn if it didn't stir up the moths in his gut. They flickered around and hit the walls like insects attracted to a light at night. And he had a feeling he was just as done for as the lot of them.

21

LINK

"No fucking way. Nah-uh. This is some crazy white-people shit. Nope." Link shook his head and held up his hands.

"Come on. It's perfectly safe," Emma argued, crossing her arms over her chest with a teasing smile on her lips.

"Haven't you ever seen Final Destination? No way am I trusting a tiny rope to carry my two-hundred-and-sixty-pound body mass eleven stories above ground." He shook his head again.

"The weight limit is three hundred pounds. You'll be fine."

"Not happening." He crossed his own arms to match her stance.

"I mean, if you're too scared, there is a shorter one only two stories up." She raised her eyebrow in challenge.

"Fear is the body's natural response to perceived danger to keep us alive," he defended.

She shrugged. "Sometimes fear can keep you from really living too."

He sighed. "I can't believe you want to do this."

"I can do it alone." She turned and got into the ticket line.

He shifted his weight from foot to foot. His heart raced. This was foolish. Reckless. But so was everything else he'd been doing with her lately. What was one more risk?

He stood next to her as she ordered her ticket.

"Make it two."

Emma spun towards him, surprise painted on her features before a wide, triumphant smile split her face. His belly flipped. He'd put that there.

Once they'd gotten their tickets and made their way to the mouth of the giant slot machine they would zip-line out of, Link focused on taking deep breaths. A couple of employees strapped harnesses around them and connected them to the zip line so that they were lying belly down, supposedly to fly over the city below like superheroes.

"Why the fuck did I agree to this?" he grumbled, nerves twisting him up.

Emma giggled next to him, her eyes glittering with excitement and anticipation. How had he not noticed how expressive those turquoise eyes of hers were before?

"Ready to have your world shook?" Emma asked.

He gazed back at her, a smirk displaying more confidence than he felt. "I think I can handle anything you dish out, sweetheart."

"Challenge excepted." She winked.

Fuck, that sass—that life that bled from her like the brightest star. Her light touched everyone around her until they had no choice but to fall in love with her. From his dad to the other people in Shattered Cove, and the thousands of screaming fans, Emma was a force to be reckoned with. A tornado, spinning him up, sucking everything in her path into her beautiful chaos. He'd resisted her for as long as possible, but she was right. After this was over, they were still family. All they had was each other. A pang of grief constricted his rib cage.

"Ready to fly?" one of the employees asked.

"Yes!" Emma answered.

Link nodded despite his stomach roiling. Somehow, he'd ended up vulnerable, eleven stories high on a wire rope, about to risk his life all for the girl with the big blue eyes and golden hair who'd showed up in his home one day with her mom. The girl who'd grown into a woman with a body that tempted his sanity and desolated his restraint. That was the thing about tornados—their force was unmatched. But they also destroyed everything in their path. If he wasn't careful, she'd leave him ruined. He had to remember this was just sex. Just a temporary escape from their grief. Tomorrow they'd drive to California, dip their toes in the Pacific Ocean, and spread his father's ashes in the waves after they said their final goodbye.

An ache burned in his chest. These three months without his father had been hard. Every tool held a memory. Every Post-it note scribbled in his father's writing along the office wall in the shop was one more reminder his papa wasn't coming back. After they'd fulfilled his father's final wishes, he'd drive them back to Shattered Cove, and they'd return to their normal lives: she a rock star, and he a mechanic. Like the African proverb said, *"A fish and bird may fall in love, but the two cannot build a home together."* After this trip, they'd move on with life . . . somehow.

Emma reached over and squeezed his hand as if she could sense his inner turmoil. "I got you."

He might have staggered back if he was standing. Her understanding gaze held his as the employee counted down.

"Three. Two. One. Fly!"

His body was jerked forward along the metal cable before the hot city wind hit his face. Lights glowed below them as his stomach rose to his throat. Adrenaline coursed through his veins before a feeling of part terror and part awe swallowed him.

"Weeeee!" Emma squealed beside him, holding tight to his hand, never letting go. She had the same look in her eyes she got when she sang. Like a caged bird let out to fly towards the heavens, free of her chains.

He laughed. *I'm an idiot.* What kind of chains could hold his little bird back? She was a rock star for Christ's sake. All the amazing sex was making him delusional. The city below whizzed by as neon lights surrounded them in a tunnel.

For the first time in a long time, he let go. Let go of expectations and his plans and agenda. He just *was*—living the moment to the fullest. Just like his little bird.

22

EMMA

The sun was setting by the time they reached the California coast. The ride was mostly silent with Hozier on the radio. The windows were down; the wind whipped Emma's hair free. She closed her eyes, leaning her head towards the door, scenery passing in a blur as Link drove them along the highway through Malibu towards Topanga Beach.

A heaviness descended like a cloud with the reality of what they were here to do—say a final goodbye to their papa. Link's sinewy forearms had remained tense the last hour of the journey, his shoulders rising to his ears. She was sure he'd have a headache from all the jaw clenching he'd done on the last leg of the journey.

As long as she'd stayed busy, she had been able to keep the grief at bay. But now it was staring her in the face, bearing down on her with the silence.

She reached over and took one of his hands from the wheel before resting it on her thigh and wrapping hers on top protectively. If she cared for him and focused on his pain, she could push hers further away. He needed her to be strong for him. It seemed he was teetering on the edge of a breakdown, barely holding it together. Emma would be there to pick up the pieces, hold him up, and support him. She'd always loved him. Maybe he'd see that after this trip. Maybe he'd see that she was good for him. That no one on earth could love him like she did.

He flicked the blinker on and pulled into Mastros Ocean Club, off to the left. Waves crashed against the beach to the side of the restaurant. Inhaling the salty ocean breeze, she shoved thoughts of what they were about to do out of her mind.

Turning to Link, she asked, "Ready?"

"Let's grab dinner first."

Was he delaying the inevitable just a little longer? *I don't want to say goodbye either—don't want this to be the end.*

She rolled up the window and followed him inside. He asked for a table overlooking the beach below. They were seated by a giant window. The server came and took their order.

Their drinks and food were brought, all with silence between them. Her gaze snagged on him. His face turned towards the setting sun. Red and pink light cast him in burned sunset shadows. The edges on his face, sharp and somber. The deep tone of his skin seemed more bronze under the soft light. One would think black eyes couldn't be that expressive, but his were—like the night of a new moon. They had a powerful energy that drew her in. There were a million shades of emotions swimming in those raven pools. Pain. Anger. Guilt. Sorrow. *Grief.*

What she wouldn't give to take a fraction of his pain away. She pushed the pasta around on her plate before taking a long gulp of the expensive wine she'd ordered. "You should eat." She motioned to his meal.

Link flinched as if just realizing he wasn't alone. After lifting the fork and knife, he cut into the steak before putting it into his mouth and grimacing as if it tasted like sawdust. "Why do you think he sent us on this trip?" he asked before draining the last of his beer.

She took a deep breath. It was her turn to gaze out the window as the last sliver of pink disappeared into a monochrome dark blue sky. "Maybe it was his way of trying to bring us together."

He scoffed. "I doubt he would be very happy with just how *close* we got on this trip."

She opened her mouth and closed it. *So that's where the guilt in his eyes comes from.* Emma could tell him that his father was more perceptive than he was.

"You deserve to be seen, baby girl. Don't settle for anything less." Her father's words after finding her in one of the rare times her emotions had got the best of her returned, and the tears came. Hearing Link with his girlfriend from college, Rachel, talking about moving in together had torn the fantasy she had built in her head.

It was impossible to tell him that his papa had known something was there between them—at least on her part— without admitting she'd always had a thing for Link. Emma wasn't ready to confess this had always been more to her. That she was willing to agree to temporary because she'd take the table scraps of his attention. *And here I am settling.*

"Maybe he knew we needed each other," she offered instead.

"You think he'd hate me for what we did?" Link asked, looking directly at her.

She swallowed and shook her head. "He could never hate

you. You are his son. Everything he did was for you—for us. Sometimes, I think he knew me better than I did."

"I guess we'll never know." He sighed and waved over the server. "We'll take the check."

Link paid and then they went back to the car.

She climbed into the back seat, unbuckled the wooden box containing the urn, and held it close to her chest as she walked down the rocky shore to the sandy beach. A gust of warm salt air blew against them, sending their clothing rippling over their skin. Link wrapped his arm around her, pulling her close, with only their father's ashes between them.

He kissed the top of her head. Her face turned upwards as stars began to peek out from the darkness. The half-moon provided just enough light to see Link's face. Dark waters rushed the beach before receding. Back and forth. Over and over in an unbreakable cycle.

"Do you believe in an afterlife?" Emma asked. Their father had been religious, but he'd never pushed those beliefs on his kids.

"I don't know. I'd like to think he's in a better place. But there's also a part of me terrified he can look down and see what I've done." Link's shoulders drooped.

"Hey." She lifted her hand to his cheek, making him meet her eyes. "Papa was proud of you. He understood more than you know. And if this is what brings us happiness, he would be our biggest supporter."

Link's doubt-filled gaze shifted back to the black waves. "So how do we do this?"

"Why don't we start by saying something?"

"You go first," he directed.

Emma swallowed and peered out to the vast ocean and luminescent sky above her. Only at the edge of the world could one feel so insignificant. "Papa? I'll always love you and carry you in my heart . . . I *am* because you rescued me. Thank you for taking me in, for loving me . . . for seeing me . . . I'll never forget you. Wherever you are, I hope you've found peace." Her throat caught, a ball of emotions clogging her voice. She blinked back the tears that wanted to fall. Link squeezed her shoulder, bringing her comfort. She leaned into his touch, savoring his reassurance.

"Uh, I guess . . . I don't know what to say except . . . I miss you." His voice was a rasp, as raw as his confession. "I wish you were still here. I wish I'd cherished our time more. I don't know what I'm going to do without you giving me a hard time and telling me what I should do, just so I can go out and do the opposite and learn the hard way." Link chuckled, a self-deprecating laugh.

Emma rubbed his back in encouragement.

"I-I'm sorry, Papa. I'm so sorry." Link's voice broke as he stumbled, falling to his knees. Emma crashed into the sand with him, wrapping her arms around him.

"I've got you. I'm here," she soothed as a sob was wrenched from him. "I'll be here as long as you need me." *As long as you'll let me.*

She held him, rocking back and forth as he let out his grief. Her heart ached right alongside his.

Once his breathing slowed, he wiped his eyes with the back of his hands and picked up the wooden box. After opening it, he pulled out the urn. Link plucked the bag of their father's remains and held out his hand for hers. She wrapped her fingers in between his as they walked towards the water. His chest rose and fell as if he were summoning the strength to say goodbye. She squeezed his hand, letting him know she was with him, tethering him to her as their shared grief pounded against her ears like a relentless push and pull of the waves.

A gust of warm wind blew at their backs before he dumped the ashes, the tide carrying them out to sea. His body trembled and jerked as a sob broke free.

Emma's heart tugged, a string pulling her towards the dark water. She wanted to chase the wind, swim until her muscles gave up and the cool waters pulled her under into blackness. Maybe there, in the darkness, she could find the other piece of her soul. Maybe then it would stop hurting.

Link took her hand, pulling her away, anchoring her to reality. They gathered the things they'd brought, and he led her to the car.

The drive back into the city was silent.

She rolled her suitcase into the hotel room they'd booked —just one this time. The door clicked shut as she approached the king-sized bed. She stripped off her clothes and left them in a pile on the floor before she turned to face him. "Get naked."

She needed to feel something besides this pain. Needed a little bit of his magic touch. Wanted to feel loved for just a little while, even if it was pretend.

Link hesitated, guilt in his eyes eating away at him.

"Please?" The plea rose from the deepest depths of her soul. *Please love me. Please see me.*

Link's eyes darkened. He removed his clothing until nothing lay between them but air saturated with sandalwood, fir, and arousal. She lay on the bed as he followed, climbing on top of her. They fused their mouths together as the first bursts of color painted her world. His tongue teased the seam of her lips. She parted her mouth, letting him inside—like she had any other choice. She was utterly powerless to this man. He owned her heart, soul, and body—and he didn't even know it. All she could do was give him everything and hope he didn't destroy her in the end.

Rough hands slid over her body gently, exploring. This time, he seemed to take care, treating her like she was precious—laving at her breasts, worshipping between her thighs, bringing her to the brink of pleasure. He built the pressure in her womb until her body burned brighter than the sun. Liquid lust shot through her veins, tangling her in desire, drowning out the grief. Their mingling breaths became pants. Their murmurs became moans and groans of pleasure.

He pulled away only to grab a condom, sheathing himself before he slid the first inch into her pussy.

"Look at me, little bird."

A flush crept over her cheeks, burning in her chest, at the endearment. Her gaze met his as he lowered his weight over her.

"I want to see you when you come. Keep your eyes on me."

Emma obeyed as he thrust into her, stealing her breath.

His brows drew together. Sweat beaded on his forehead. "God, you feel so fucking good. So wet and tight. All for me."

"Yes. It's yours. I'm yours." She uttered the words in the throes of pleasure as he rocked her body back and forth, sending ripples and shivers of ecstasy coursing through her. Her need coiled tight, threatening to snap. He drove his hips slow, steady, and hard, drawing out her pleasure in exquisite torture. Skin slapped against skin. His abs flexed with each powerful thrust. His back muscles bunched under her hands. He palmed her thighs that were wrapped tightly around him to her ass, squeezing tight.

Pushing his hand between them, he rubbed her throbbing clit and sent an avalanche of overwhelming sensation crashing over her as the first orgasm splintered through her body with a vengeance.

The hold of his gaze never wavered from hers. "That's it, little bird. Fly free."

"Link!"

He rubbed his mouth against her sensitive lips, the gentleness a contrast to the rough force of his cock. Link moved his hand away and drove into her harder. Her body clenched around his, holding on as if her life depended on it, completely powerless to do anything but experience the ruthless pleasure as if she were in a trance.

He growled her name, his muscles locking up as his forehead pinched in focused bliss. Link leaned in, kissing her nose, her forehead, both cheeks, and then her lips. Her heart fluttered, hope sparking.

Maybe he did see her after all.

23

LINK

Link nursed his second beer at the hotel bar. Flipping through the messages on his phone, he checked in with Reese to make sure everything was okay at the shop.

Reese: *All good here. Marissa has your accounting up to date.*

Link: *Can't thank you enough, man.*

Reese: *I'd do anything for you, bro.*

Link's chest squeezed. He'd been at the shop since he was a toddler, but Reese hadn't been that far behind him. Reese had gotten caught stealing at the general store while Solomon shopped, and his dad had talked the owner into letting him work it off. After Reese had finished at the store, Solomon had brought him to the shop, giving both him and his dad work until his dad eventually ended up in prison, leaving Reese's mom to raise him and his brother alone. Reese stayed at the shop. He became part of their family—misfits who fit together.

Maybe it wasn't just Emma that Papa had a soft spot for.

His father had been a good man—the best. A single father,

taking on a young girl and other strays who needed a helping hand, or just someone to believe in them. He'd have given a stranger the shirt off his back.

I miss you, Papa.

He wished his father was still here, so he could talk to him about this situation with Emma. How could a woman feel so right when it was so wrong? His father would be able to make sense of it. His thumb hovered over his dad's contact name on the screen of his phone. He couldn't bring himself to close Solomon's mobile account. Sometimes he just needed to hear that voice on the other end of the answering machine. His shoulders slumped as his phone vibrated in his hand.

Reese: *Oh, wanted to give you a heads-up. Rachel's back in town. Came by the shop looking for you.*

Rachel? The only woman he'd ever loved. They'd lived together after college, but she'd gotten a job in Texas, and he couldn't leave his father and the garage.

Link: *She just visiting?*

Reese: *No idea. I told her you'd be back in a week.*

Link: *Thanks for letting me know.*

Reese: *No problem.*

What was Rachel doing back in Shattered Cove? Did he want to see her? Her leaving had broken his heart, but he'd never wanted to hold her back from her dream job.

He sighed in frustration. He had enough to deal with without adding his ex to the mix. Nothing had made sense since his dad died. *Fuck. He's dead.* It still didn't feel real. He needed a distraction. Something to take his attention away from the fact that everything was spinning out of control in his life.

Link took a gulp of his warm beer, his eyes flicking to the digital clock.

Where the hell is Emma? She had left him to "run a few

errands" hours ago. *Maybe she was discovered and got hurt?* Anxiety snaked in his belly.

A woman brushed against him as she took a seat on the stool beside him. Her sweet, musky perfume teased his senses. Her shoulder-length black hair came to the white silk blouse she wore, see-through enough to hint at her dark undergarments matching the short leather skirt that ended just before a peek of flesh between her garter and stockings.

"Like what you see?" Her voice was deep and sultry.

Link's cock twitched. Damn, he needed to get that under control. *Wait!* Someone else was getting him excited for the first time in months besides Emma? He should be ecstatic. Maybe he had fucked her out of his system. His relief was quickly clouded by guilt. They hadn't said anything about exclusivity during their tryst. And maybe he should end this with Emma before he got any deeper.

"Cat got your tongue?" she purred.

"Uh, sorry, I was just . . ."

"I have better uses for a mouth like that than talking anyways." She kept her head angled away so that the dark hair covered her face, only hinting at her profile as she slipped a black and gold room key over the bar top.

"Penthouse suite. Ten grand for the night."

His eyes widened as she stood, turning her back to him.

"I don't—I'm sorry—I'm with someone." Fuck. What was he doing? Was he turned on? Abso-fucking-lutely. But going with someone else besides Emma while they were doing whatever it was they were doing felt . . . wrong. Not to mention the fact that this woman was apparently a high-class prostitute. He'd never paid for sex before. Seemed his dick wanted a walk on the taboo side lately. *Fuck my life.*

She leaned over his shoulder and laid her hand on his

thigh as she spoke in his ear with a sultry voice. "I don't think she'd mind if you came with me."

Her hand drifted over his cock straining beneath his jeans. Temptation curled up his spine as his dick throbbed with arousal.

It was one night. *No one would know.* His hand shot out, grasping her wrist and pulling it away. The familiar leather band made his breath catch as he turned to look at the face of his temptress. "Emma?"

"Not tonight. Tonight I'm just an expensive hooker, who goes by the name of Candy." She winked.

He gripped a strand of raven hair.

"It's a wig, so don't pull too hard." She smiled.

"What is this? Were you testing me?" His anger sparked.

She ran one red nail up his chest to his chin, tipping it towards her. Emma leaned in so that her lips barely brushed his as she explained, "This is called role play. It's a chance for you to be whoever you want tonight. And I'm here to be whatever you need. Yours to do with as you please—*anything* you want. My safe word is poison."

"Safe word? What the hell—?"

She silenced him with a kiss, dipping her tongue in his mouth. "Give me five minutes and then come on up."

She walked away; his eyes glued to the sway of her hips in the skirt that clung to her ass. *Holy shit.* His little bird was kinky as fuck.

He glanced at the clock, his leg jumping up and down as he waited for the time to change. "Fuck it." He drained the rest of his beer before tossing a twenty on the bar top and making his way to the elevators, black and gold key card in hand. He had to slide his card into a reader on the elevator panel after pushing the button for the penthouse suite. He didn't even want to know how much a place like this cost for the night.

The elevator opened to the suite itself. He walked in. It was somewhat similar to the one they'd stayed in before, with white marble floors and white walls, but this one had high ceilings and the room was huge, seemingly taking up the entire top floor. Expensive-looking pictures and furnishings decorated the huge lounge area. Past the plush white carpet and black couches with gold pillows stood the silhouette of a goddess—or fallen angel. She turned around, her hands on the buttons of her blouse.

Link stepped forward, holding out his palm to halt her movements.

Emma—or *Candy*—tilted her head to the side in question.

"You're mine for the night, huh?" he asked.

"Yours."

"To do whatever I want with?"

She gave him a sultry smile, her eyes flaming with lust. "Anything . . . except I don't do the whole peeing-on-each-other thing—I'm not into that kind of humiliation." Her nose wrinkled in disgust.

He barked out a burst of laughter at the cute expression. "Got it. No piss. But if there's anything you don't like, just tell me to stop or slow down. 'Kay?"

She bit her lip, giving him a once-over. "I can take whatever you have to give me. I mean it. Use me."

God. Fucking. Damn it. This woman was trying to kill him.

24

EMMA

Emma held her breath, waiting as the air between them grew thick with anticipation.

Link's eyes lit up with dark hunger. The intensity of his stare was unnerving.

Since yesterday, she'd sensed a chaos of grief inside him. A violent energy raged like a storm in his every inhale. Pain bled from his gaze. She recognized it because it was the same inside her. And she knew the temporary cure—control. He needed just a piece of escape, and she could give that to him. Giving him dominance over her body would give him some relief, and in return, she could shove her pain down just a little longer. She'd deal with it later . . . someday. Right now, she couldn't afford to feel anything but his wicked perusal lashing the exposed skin of her neck and cleavage. She'd stuff it all back into the dam around her heart and hope it held just a little longer.

Link gripped the soft fabric of her shirt and ripped it apart, sending buttons scattering across the floor. Emma gasped, the swell of her breasts rising and falling as heat rose in her neck. Her nipples instantly hardened at his savage treatment.

His gaze never left hers, searching her face as if to continually seek consent.

"Don't stop now." She gave him a sly smile.

His chest heaved up and down as he growled, "I bet if I slipped my fingers inside you right now, you'd be wet for me. Wouldn't you, you little slut?"

A thrill shot through her, seeping moisture into her panties. She swallowed hard. "Yes."

He traced the webbed leather bondage bra—though it could hardly be called that—wrapped around her breasts, covering nothing. His eyes traveled down her waist to the tiny skirt she'd picked out from one of the many stores she'd visited, all in preparation for this moment.

"Such a bad girl. Wonder what I'm gonna find under here." His voice was like honeyed lava—sweet and hot—building her desire with every rough syllable.

"Why don't you find out?" she challenged.

Link gripped her hips and spun her around roughly. Her hands reached out and pressed into the cool glass. The whole city was laid out before them on the other side. The people below had no idea what they were doing. But a part of her wished they did. Wished some might even see them. *God, I'm fucked up.*

He pulled down the zipper and let the skirt fall to the ground. Cool air rushed over her ass, exposing the pair of crotchless, red lace panties and a matching leather garter with silver rings and straps tightening to her hips. The reflection in the window showed the dainty stockings tied with a red ribbon to the silver hoops on her thighs.

"This look suits you. A contest of edgy"—he dragged his

knuckle over the leather garter to the red bows—"and feminine."

Her mouth watered as his gaze savored her in the reflection like she was a glorious sight before him. Like he didn't know where to start.

He licked his lips. "Candy is a fitting name."

"Why?" Her voice was breathy.

"Because you look delicious." His hand snaked up her spine.

She shivered.

"So responsive," he hummed. Grabbing on to her hips, he ground his rock-hard dick through the constricting jeans into her ass.

She couldn't hold back the moan.

Next, his hands wound around her breasts, pinching her nipples.

She whimpered, pleasure sparking as her tits grew heavy with his ministrations.

"Think I should take you against the window? Fuck that pretty cunt hard until you can't even scream anymore?"

Oh, God. Oh, God. Yes! Emma moaned in response.

"Or maybe lay you on that table in the living room and eat you out, edging you until you cry pretty tears and I let you come?"

Her hands fisted against the window, clenching in anticipation. Her body throbbed for his rough touch.

He bit on her neck, hard enough to leave a mark, and she gasped. Using his tongue, he soothed the sore spot—a warning of what was to come. A preview of what she was getting into. Of course, if she said the word, he'd stop. She was safe with Link. And she wanted to see just how dark his tastes went. Or how far she could pull him into hers. Excitement and adrenaline coursed through her at the possibility.

His eyes burned with lust, as if he was enraptured by her for one stolen minute in time. She was fed by dominance and submission. Control and trust. His touch spoke to her. It was like he knew her down to her soul. What she needed. What she craved.

"I left some surprises in the bedroom too," Emma offered, her voice nothing but breath.

He ground his cock into her ass. "You're just full of them tonight, *Candy*."

Her body trembled beneath his.

"What's in there?"

"Why don't you go see?"

He pinched her nipple harder, making her cry out. "When I ask you a question, I expect an answer."

"Paddles, clamps, rope, lube, plugs, a dildo, and vibrators . . . Just the basics." She gasped as he massaged the angry red skin around the buds, sore from his handiwork.

"You raid a sex store?"

"Yes, sir."

"God fucking damn it." He leaned his head against her spine, shuddering as if trying to get a hold of himself. His whole body vibrated with a hum of satisfaction. "What are you doing to me?" He said it so low she barely heard him.

God, she loved that she had this effect on him.

"Get on your knees," he ordered.

She quickly obeyed. The cold, hard marble bit into her soft skin. She'd have bruises tomorrow. But she hoped those would be tame compared to what he planned to do to her. She wanted more—everything.

I can't have everything. He only wants to fuck.

She pushed the disappointment from her mind, burying it deeper. What was one more thing in the cesspool of pain locked in the dam?

He whipped off his shirt, his muscles rippling and bunching as he breathed hard, chest heaving.

His thumb pressed against her chin. "I could come just from the erotic sight of you, mouth open, eyes hungry, ready to please me."

A rush of liquid heat collected in her pussy and slid down her leg.

"Take my dick out."

She unfastened his jeans and pulled them down along with his boxers, far enough for access.

"Now suck my cock." He gripped the back of her head, guiding her lips over his shaft, groaning as she slipped her hot wet mouth over his perfect, veined cock. "Good girl."

She clenched her thighs together, staving off her want just a little longer, eager to please him.

Her tongue danced over the ridges, swirling at the tip, tracing the veins of his erection before she swallowed him down until he hit the back of her throat.

His hand tightened around her head, holding her there until the count of five before pulling out. She sucked in a breath before he thrust back inside, waiting until the count of ten this time before continuing to fuck her mouth. "Fuck, you feel so good. Such a good girl. So beautiful on your knees like this."

She moaned around his cock. He trembled as if shivers of pleasure vibrated up his spine. She continued to suck, reaching her hand up to grip his balls and rolling them before pressing along his perineum.

His balls drew up. "Fuck, you're gonna make me come," he grit out through a clenched jaw, his forehead furrowed. "You don't know how bad I want to come in your mouth and watch you swallow me down."

Do it! She sucked harder.

He pulled out of her mouth, roaring like a hungry lion, panting as sweat glistened off his body.

Her brows drew together in confusion. "Why—?"

"I have one rule. My woman always comes first." His voice was raw with need.

My woman. A part of her knew he meant whichever woman he was with. But she'd pretend this once he meant she belonged to him—this was a fantasy, after all.

"Get on that table. Lie on your back." He pointed.

Emma scrambled to her feet, clearing off the decorations with frayed nerves. But it must not have been quick enough. Impatiently, Link pushed the vase filled with flowers onto the ground—the rug between the couches the only thing saving it from breaking.

"Play with yourself. But don't come. I'll be right back." Link pulled his clothes the rest of the way off before jogging to the bedroom.

She spread herself out on the table, not hesitating to obey him. The hard nub of her clit throbbed from his touch and dirty words. She closed her eyes, tipping her head back as she sought relief, picturing his naked body, repeating the order in her head.

Play with yourself. But don't come.

Link's sharp inhale of breath had her opening her eyes to find his mouth parted, his gaze glued to her fingers rubbing her clit. Pleasure curled her toes, gathering to her center. She was so close.

"Good girl. You listened. Do you want your reward?"

"Yes."

"Spread your legs apart, so I can see all of you."

Emma drew her knees farther from one another, moving her hand from her glistening pussy to the table to keep her balance. He grabbed the red lace panties and ripped them off her as she hissed, sucking in a breath.

The clink of metal sounded on the glass as he set down whatever toys he'd grabbed, the butt plug catching her eye. He cracked open a bottle of lube.

Fuck yes.

He squirted some on the plug before adding a small glob to his finger. The cold gel on her asshole made her hiss. He teased her puckered hole with his finger, going in a little at a time and then drawing out. "Do you want this? Want me to fill you up, prepare this sweet ass for my cock?"

"Yes!" She didn't hesitate.

The second his finger exited her, the cold steel of the plug pushed inside her. She jolted onto her elbows.

"Shhhh. Relax," he coaxed. "Christ, you're beautiful. I can't wait to sink my cock into you."

She breathed out as he leaned forward and stroked the sensitive bundle of nerves of her sex, easing the plug the rest of the way in.

"Fuck! Yes!" The only two words left in her vocabulary repeated on a loop as he sucked her clit into his mouth, draining the pleasure from her. She was so close.

"Ask me. Ask me if you can come." He drew back, her climax receding and frustration growing.

"Make me come. Please? Please make me come," she begged.

He gave her one long lick and backed away. "Make yourself come."

Wait—what?

He walked to her side, kneeling to lick and suck hard on one breast as he caressed the other gently.

"Do what I said." He slapped her breast—hard.

She sucked in a surprised breath. Link's eyes searched hers as if to make sure this was still okay.

She bit her lip and nodded her silent consent.

Thwack! Thwack! He did it again. Heat and pleasured pain blossomed in her breasts, her nipples tight and more sensitive than ever before. Her breathing grew shallow. She was close.

"Told you to finger yourself, beautiful. Are you gonna play with that pretty pink cunt or do I need to punish you some more?"

Her body trembled with excitement as her hands remained on her open thighs, her nails digging into flesh with anticipation. "More."

He leaned closer, the bulk of his shoulders clouding the light from the setting glowing orb, hovering over her like a dark, powerful god. Potent and powerful, he eclipsed even the sun. Her own Hades, sent to cleanse her with fire and bring her darkest fantasies to life. Tension throbbed between them as he made her wait. His cock bulged and throbbed against her arm. She trembled from the overwhelming need only this man stirred in her. She'd never wanted someone more in her life. His hand moved to her breast.

She closed her eyes, anticipating a slap. Instead, her nipple pinched with pain. Emma cried out. "Link!"

He gave her a wolfish smile as he clipped a clamp onto her other nipple.

She let loose another hiss of pain. It was too much. "Link! Please."

"Play with yourself."

Her hand moved immediately, needing to find the balance between the hurt and the bliss.

"That's it, baby. Come for me. Imagine it's my fingers fucking you."

She tensed. Her eyes slammed shut as she broke apart, spinning and shattering into a million pieces until nothing existed but pure unchained and unbound euphoria. Her body burned white hot as he placed his hand over hers, continuing to use her finger to extend the orgasm, giving her back the power to set herself free.

Tears gathered in her eyes. Only here, where she was the most out of control, could the emotion bleed from her eyes. He'd given her this gift of reclaiming her power, taking her pleasure into her own hands—literally.

"Now taste yourself."

Her hazy eyes focused on him as she lifted her wet fingers to her mouth and licked the remaining arousal off her digits.

Link leaned over her, capturing her mouth in a sinful kiss —sharing her essence. He pulled away, breathless. "My turn." He reached for the gold foil packet.

"I'm on the pill."

His eyes darted to hers, brows drawn together in a hard line as if thinking through what she'd offered. "I'm still clean. Haven't . . . there hasn't been anyone since the first time we . . ."

"Fucked? Come on. Don't go getting shy on me now, Lincoln." She hoped her voice didn't betray how vulnerable she was inside.

"And you? You let anyone else inside this cunt since you've been away?" His voice turned dark and possessive.

Only my vibrator.

"Just my highest-paying clientele. I am an escort, after all." She winked playfully, easing her way back into her role as Candy. Because Candy wouldn't get hurt. Candy knew this was a one-time affair. Candy's heart wasn't on the line.

A shadow crossed Link's gaze. Was that disappointment?

He didn't waste any more time. He moved between her thighs like a man of desperation. He sunk his cock inside her with one thrust, filling her so completely she couldn't draw breath at first. With each thrust, his balls slapped against the butt plug, tipping her over the edge again and again.

She cried out.

Link flicked one of her clamped nipples before he drew out of her. The hollow ache inside her immediately caused her to protest. Next, he pulled the plug from her ass. The cap of the lube clicked open again before he rubbed it over his glistening cock. "I'm gonna take that sweet ass now. You ready, little bird?"

Words were not possible at the erotic sight of him pleasuring himself, his dark gaze flashing with depraved lust that matched her own. Too spent with her orgasms, too overcome with violent need, Emma nodded.

He inched into her ass slowly before bringing his body on top of her as a vibrating sensation entered her pussy.

"What?"

The pink silicone in his hand drove into her until it reached her G-spot.

"Oh, God!"

"Yes, baby, that's it." He rocked inside, filling her ass at the same time the vibrating dildo fucked her pussy.

It was mere seconds before she came again, her thighs wrapped tight around him, keeping them both locked in a prison of pleasure. Liquid splashed onto the table as she ejaculated. Her orgasm ripped through her like a tsunami, leaving devastating rapture in its wake. Tears ran over her face. She was unable to contain the emotion he was fucking out of her. Emma scraped her nails over his back to his ass, needing to hold on to something as she spun so out of control. Her gaze focused on his. "Please?"

"You want me to give it to you? Fill you up with my cum?"

"Give me everything."

And he did. Link gave until it seemed he'd left nothing behind. He drove into her with a force only matched by Mother Nature. He rocked back and forth. Her body had gone limp at the sheer force of the orgasms tearing through her, ruining her for any other person.

Link removed one clamp as Emma screamed with a mix of pain and pleasure blooming from her bruised nipple. He continued to fuck her as her mouth opened in a silent wail, no sound escaping this time. Tears fell over her slick cheeks. He pulled out and slid his cock between her tender breasts, fucking her tits as he came. His control finally splintered, and his hips bucked. Boiling hot cum shot out all over her neck and chest, some of it landing on her chin and mouth.

He hunched over her, unfocused eyes trailing hers.

She tried to smile, but her muscles were too spent to make the full expression. Her ears rang. His heart thundered in his heaving chest against hers like a war drum.

Emma licked his cum off her lips before dragging her finger over the bit on her chin and lifting it to his mouth. "Taste yourself," she instructed, throwing his own words back at him.

A look of astonishment and awe crossed his features before he sucked her finger.

How was she ever supposed to go back to normal life after this?

25

LINK

aste yourself. Link ran Emma's words through his head on repeat as they coasted down the highway towards the East Coast. He'd tasted himself for the first time in his life. *Apparently, yesterday was a whole day of firsts.* He'd never done half that shit with another woman. Who would have guessed his little bird was a sexual deviant? It might have been his cum painted across her body, but it was Emma who'd left a mark on him—in more ways than one. He'd never been that turned on in his life. Never desired another woman the way he craved her.

Emma tossed her phone into her bag and focused out the window.

"Was that the band?"

"No. Remy and the girls were just checking in with me."

He glanced to the rearview mirror before flicking his gaze towards her.

She switched the radio on, alternative rock bleeding through the speakers over the rumble of the engine. Their trip was more than half over. Soon they'd be back in Shattered Cove. Back to normal life. A pang vibrated in his chest.

He focused on the road, not ready to examine that feeling too closely. "You stay in touch with them pretty often while you're on tour?"

"They're my sisters. Even if we don't talk for a month, they know all they have to do is pick up the phone and I'm there." She scratched her arm above the ever-present leather wrap bracelet.

"It's nice you didn't forget about us little guys and let all that fame go to your head," he joked.

"I'm not a total shallow bitch," she snapped.

Whoa. "I didn't mean to imply you were."

She sighed, tucking her knees closer to herself, leaning against the door, and gazing out the window. "Sometimes it feels like no one knows the real me. All they see is Emma, lead singer of The Sirens. The woman with no filter and a string of failed relationships. And in Shattered Cove, they still see me as . . ."

As the white daughter of Solomon Owusu? "As what?"

She licked her lips and faced him.

He took one look at those blue, soulful eyes and fixed his gaze back on the white lines, chest tight. In that brief glance, it was as if he could see all of her for the first time. Overwhelming grief, vulnerability, and fear darkened her cerulean spheres. That image imprinted in his mind. The pleading in her eyes that screamed, *see me!* But what could a woman like her possibly need from a man like him? Nothing. Emma was always happy, the life of the party. She was the one solving problems for her friends, not needing help.

Ask her. He shook his head. No. He was reading way too much into this. If there was grief, it was because their father had passed and the knowledge she had that like him, she was an orphan now.

"As the small-town girl who made it big? They're just jealous." He reached for her hand and gave it a squeeze.

Her eyes shuttered for a moment, and then, as if it had been a figment of his imagination, the overwhelming sadness in her gaze was gone. She gave him a smile, nothing like the ones he'd seen the rest of the trip. This one wasn't flirty or genuine but forced. "Right."

His gut pitched and twisted uncomfortably at the sudden change. He didn't like the pretending, or Emma walling herself off from him. *But isn't that exactly how this has to go?* This wasn't a relationship. This was . . . this was fucking. He cringed. It was, but it wasn't. Because at the end of the day, she was still his family. He cared about her and wanted the best for her.

"Check the glove box." He dropped Emma's hand to motion in front of her.

The handle clicked open before the crinkle of plastic and Emma's chuckle became music to his ears. He took his eyes off the road one more time just to capture the image of her lips splitting into an authentic smile of glee. "You got me more gummy worms?" She tore open the package and popped three into her mouth.

"Gotta keep my little bird happy."

"Why do you call me that?" she asked around a mouthful of candy.

Because you were always meant to fly. To climb to heights most of us mortals only dream of. He shrugged, not wanting to dig too deep into the motivation behind the endearment. "Because you like gummy worms, duh."

"Oh my God. Did you just say 'duh'? What, are you a twelve-year-old boy all over again?" She laughed, and that sound split through his defenses, digging into his chest, taking root.

His heart warmed with the tinkling sound. "I never said duh. That was you," he argued with a laugh of his own.

"Where do you think I got it? I learned everything from you. Don't you remember how I'd follow you around?"

Like the lost bird in the book his father used to read him. The little thing kept going to creatures and inanimate objects asking, "Are you my mother?" Until finally at the end, it was reunited with the mother bird. Of course, that wasn't why he called her that. No, that was coincidence. Her mother was long gone, just like his.

"That must have bothered you so much. You never showed it though. Having a kid follow you and your teenage friends around couldn't have been easy," she mused, stuffing another worm into her waiting mouth.

Link switched into the left lane, quickly passing a slower-moving car. "It wasn't always easy. Remember that time you came into my room when Finn was over? We were so busy with the dirty magazine we didn't even hear you until it was too late."

"That's the moment I realized I liked women, actually."

He whipped around to look at her before returning his gaze to the gas station ahead of him. "Seriously?"

She burst out laughing. "No, but you should have seen your face!"

He shook his head, grumbling under his breath. "At least you never told Dad about it."

"Your secrets have always been safe with me." She sighed.

There were many times she'd caught him sneaking out or getting into things he probably shouldn't have been. When she'd gotten older, she'd begged him to take her with him. They'd been thick as thieves at one point. And not once had she ever told his papa on him. "I don't think I ever said thank you."

"For not snitching?" she clarified.

"Yeah. Some of the shit I got into would have had me whooped for good if Dad found out." If his papa knew some of the antics he and his friends had gotten into, he would have been grounded for life, especially the drag racing.

"You know I got your back. That still hasn't changed. Besides, snitches get stitches, right?" she teased, laughing it off. "Anyway, it meant I got to go along."

He'd always made sure to protect her from other guys' wandering hands. They all knew if they messed with her, they'd have to deal with him. His chest tightened. *But when was the last time I looked out for her?* "I remember this one time, we were at a race and Ricky Emerson put his arm around you." He shook his head.

"He was harmless." She waved her hand away.

"I had just gotten Lucy Albright to talk to me. Well, I'd just convinced her to go somewhere a little more . . . private. And when I turned around to check on you and saw that, I nearly lost it."

"So, I was a cockblock too? Hope I'm making up for that now." She smirked. And damn, if it wasn't the cutest thing.

"I don't know." He shrugged playfully. "I mean, we're talking about my entire high-school experience here. That's a lot of missed sloppy kisses and fumbling tit grabs. You think a few days of hot sex can make up for that?"

She giggled. "You think it's been hot?"

"You know it has." He grinned.

"Well, I suppose I can think of a way to make it up to you." The click of her unbuckling resounded like a shot through his system.

"What are you doing?" He checked his mirror before

switching to the right lane. The highway was mostly empty today—not too much traffic.

"You know I've had this fantasy ever since those drag races. I wondered what it would be like . . ." She crawled over, reaching for the button on his jeans.

His hand shot out to stop her. "Em—"

"Are you really going to deny me my fantasy?" Her breathy words slithered through him, making his muscles tense in anticipation and longing. His cock hardened with the erotic ideas playing through his head. This was stupid—and dangerous. But wasn't everything between them?

He put his hand back on the steering wheel in silent consent.

She unzipped his pants and pulled his erection into her hands. Sweat beaded on his brow as he focused on the horizon ahead of them.

Her soft hands seared his skin, burning him alive with her touch. She'd wanted to do this since his drag-racing days? To whom? Surely, it wasn't him. So, which motherfucker had she fantasized about giving road head to? He gritted his teeth. It didn't matter. Because right now, he was the one benefitting from it.

Her hot, wet mouth enveloped him. Biting his lip, he jerked the steering wheel to stay on the road as her head bobbed up and down, sucking the pleasure and the self-restraint from his body.

His chest heaved as he tried to maintain control of the car while she gave him the best blow job of his life. The risky danger element only added to the fucking perfection of this experience. Just like at the penthouse, it was as if she knew what he wanted, what he craved even before he did. Or were they that perfectly matched? She was like a drug, getting him high off her lips and forcing him to live in the here and now.

"What the fuck are you doing to me?" he gasped as his cock hit the back of her throat, squeezing the steering wheel as he used all his effort to keep the car straight and the speed even.

She pulled back, swirling her tongue over the tip of his dick before saying, "I hope it's the same thing you're doing to me."

26

EMMA

A chime rang as Emma pushed open the glass door to the Denver Colorado's Rocky Mountain tattoo parlor. The floors and walls were real pine. A black leather C-shaped couch was to their right in a waiting area. Books of tattoo art were scattered across an iron and glass coffee table. On the wall to their left were images of fully naked bodies inked in detailed and realistic designs, posed to keep it erotic but tasteful.

Link was right behind her as they greeted the man at the front desk. A blue-haired guy with gauged ears, a spike coming out of the space between his chin and bottom lip, and a septum ring smiled. He reached out his arms, covered in intricate tattoo sleeves, to her.

"Roy!" she greeted excitedly, jumping into his big, waiting arms.

A low growl came from behind her. *Link?*

"Hey, wildcat! Been too long. You stayin' out of trouble?" he joked in his thick Irish accent. He set her back on her feet and gave Link a quick once-over.

"Oh, you know me." She waved her hand.

"Right. So, getting into mischief as usual, I see." Roy winked with a gleam in his eyes before his attention darted to Link once more.

"This is Link. He's my . . . um, he's Link." She certainly wasn't going to ruin things and remind Link they had been raised as brother and sister. Friend didn't seem right either. He was just Link.

"Right. Well, nice to meet ya, mate." Roy held out a fist to bump with Link. When Link hesitated, she elbowed him in the stomach.

Link's fist met Roy's. "So, how do you two know each other?"

"Oh, we go way back. Dinna we, wildcat?" Roy smirked.

"Roy is Geo's cousin. He helped us get some gigs here in Denver," Emma explained. "How is Geo? Have you heard anything?"

"He's cut me off too, lass. Your boys called here last week askin' if I'd been able to get through to him. No such luck." Roy sighed.

Emma crossed her arms in front of her and looked away. *What is going on with Geo? Why is he closing everyone out?*

Link's palm pressed against her lower back, bringing her to the moment. She swallowed. "After we get home, I'll see what I can do. Maybe if I show up at the prison, they'll let me see him."

"Worth a shot," Roy agreed, flicking the lock on the front door.

Link shot her a questioning glance.

"He's closing his shop for us."

"Of course. Celebrity treatment for my rock star and her . . . Link." Roy winked before turning away to the hall to the tattoo rooms in the back.

Link's hand gripped her waist, walking by her side, seemingly in ownership. But that couldn't be, because Link had made it very clear what this was and what this wasn't. Maybe he'd changed his mind?

"Alright, Link, you'll be with Tessa here. Her bedside manner is shite, but her lines are true. She's got an eye for detail and knows how to make the color really pop on darker skin." Roy motioned to the first area partitioned off with the gorgeous Black woman she'd met a handful of times. Tessa had done the music notes tattooed on her hip.

Tessa smirked. "Just admit it. I'm the better tattoo artist."

"For fuck's sake, I'll never hear the end o' this." Roy rubbed a hand over his face in frustration. He walked away down the hallway, under the exposed wooden beams, before disappearing through the next doorway.

Tessa's eyes followed him, glowing with humor. And was that attraction?

"All right, Link, was it? Where are we doing the design?" Tessa asked.

"Well, I wasn't sure what—"

"Actually," Emma interrupted Link. "I had Roy draw up my idea. I thought if you liked it, we could get matching ones in honor of Dad?" She held her breath, searching his face.

"What did you have in mind?" Link asked.

Tessa pulled out the image they'd sketched and printed. "I can size it to wherever you choose to get it. Or we can change something or add more details."

Emma's gaze traced over the image that Roy had emailed her this morning, hoping Link would love it too. The colorful red, yellow, and green with a lone black star of the Ghanaian flag took the shape of a wrench outlined in black.

Link's swallow was audible. He nodded. "It's perfect. I'll do it here." He pointed to the spot over his heart.

"Alright. Take your shirt off, and let's get this stencil on you."

Link tugged the hem of his shirt over his head, exposing the intricate gears and cogs and car parts inked into his skin. His abs clenched as he dropped his hands to his sides once again. Was there ever a more perfectly designed man? Her gaze snagged on the deep V leading into his light denim jeans.

"Where are you getting yours?" Link asked, drawing her attention to his knowing smile.

"Uh . . . guess you'll have to wait and see," she teased, needing to get her emotions back in check, and by emotions, her lady parts.

"Ready when you are, lass," Roy called from next door.

"See ya soon." Emma turned and headed towards the room Roy had all set up for her as Link's deep chuckle sent butterflies skittering in her belly.

Roy held up the stencil in black-gloved hands. "Sit your arse up here and take off those shoes."

Emma climbed onto the table and removed her Converse and sock from her right foot. Roy prepared the area and held up the guide. "Right here?"

"Yeah. That's perfect."

He smoothed the stencil over her skin before peeling it away. He had the petroleum jelly, ink cups, and the tattoo gun all ready. "Lie back and bend your knee. Keep that foot still now, like a good lass," Roy instructed.

A smile teased her lips as she did as he instructed.

The buzz of the gun started, and his chair wheeled closer. "You ready?"

"Yes." She closed her eyes, anticipating the bite of pain as the gun broke the skin. A prickling sensation of needles curled up from her foot, winding above her leg and unfurling until it reached the tip of her head. She relaxed into it, welcoming the warm sting. Roy knew she preferred to be tattooed in silence, and she was grateful he didn't try to make small talk with her. This was as close as she could get to the relief the blade offered while still not technically self-harming. She deepened her breath as the tattoo gun made the outline of the wrench, savoring the itch of the burning sensation as her synapses fired and endorphins flooded her veins. Emma was forced into her body, held prisoner by pain to feel only the hurt she chose. The burning vibration took center stage and drowned out all other sensations and emotions. Everything else inside quieted.

Just like when I'm fucking Link.

Roy pulled the gun away and switched heads to a thicker needle. "Ready for the color?"

She nodded, needing to have the biting soreness back to distract her from her thoughts already.

The steady buzz filled the room again, and she closed her eyes, sinking deep into the darkness behind her eyelids, adrenaline coursing through her veins. She relished the silence inside that the prickling fire brought. Time ceased to exist; there was only this heady, weightless feeling, as if she were in a cloud. Relief washed over her like a comforting warm wave.

"All done. Take a look," Roy said, wheeling his chair back as he wiped her tattoo with the paper towel, clearing the ink and blood.

Emma sat, staring at the swollen red-tinged skin. The colorful wrench on the outside of her right foot was exactly like she'd envisioned. "I love it." Tears burned the back of her eyes, but she blinked them away. The only time those bastards had managed to escape was when Link had shattered her apart, making her come so completely undone that she'd not been able to hold anything back. A crack in her well-made dam. It wouldn't happen again though—it couldn't.

Roy slathered some more jelly over it and prepared the dressing. "I get the symbolism of the wrench and Ghanaian flag. But, why the foot of all places?"

"So I can take a piece of him with me everywhere I travel," she answered. *So I won't be alone.*

"Ahhh, I see. Your Da would love it," Roy agreed.

The thought made her laugh out loud. Her father had never been a fan of tattoos. He'd probably hate to see more ink marring her body, but also love it at the same time because she'd done it for him.

"So, who's the lad really?" Roy asked, taping the black gauze pad onto her foot carefully.

Emma gazed towards the only wall separating Link and her. The steady buzz of Tessa's tattoo gun was still going. His tattoo was larger, made to cover his pec, so naturally it would take more time than hers.

"He's my father's son," she answered honestly.

"He sure doesn't look at you in a brotherly way," Roy pointed out.

Emma cut her gaze to him. "Are you suggesting there's something more going on between Link and me?"

Roy's expression grew serious, one brow quirking in concern. "I'm telling ya, that lad is more than halfway in luv wit ya."

A soft gasp escaped her lips. *No. Could he be?*

Warm hope bubbled in her belly, sending butterflies of possibility fluttering through her. Maybe she was doing the same thing to him as he'd been doing to her. Maybe Link was falling in love with her too. And just maybe she'd let herself believe that for once he would finally see her. *And love me back.*

27

EMMA

Emma crashed forward onto the bed in the hotel room, exhausted. Her mind swirled with questions. Roy had planted a seed she was terrified to hope for. Could Link be falling for her?

Smack!

Her ass stung, surprising her and sending a warm rush to her core. She smiled and turned on her side to face him. Link was smirking as he stretched out beside her.

"Do I get to see it now?" she asked.

"What do I get in exchange?" he teased.

"I'll show you mine if you show me yours." She winked.

He chuckled and gripped the end of his T-shirt, raising it over his head. His ab muscles tensed and flexed as he rid himself of the top. Her hand traced the defined ripples on his abdomen, up over his ribs to the black piece of gauze taped to his pec. Her eyes searched his for permission.

"Go ahead." His low voice rumbled, his hot breath tickling the shell of her ear.

Emma peeled the tape, slowly revealing the work of art

underneath. The raised skin in the shape of a wrench stood out in vivid colors of the Ghanaian flag against his dark brown flesh.

"Why here?" she asked, not taking her eyes off the design she'd come up with herself. Even though it was in memory of his father, she was honored he'd tattooed something of hers on his skin.

"I got it over my heart, because that is where I will carry him always."

Her gaze met his. The impact of his choice hit her full force. "He would pretend to be so mad if he knew we got ink for him." She laughed.

"You don't think he would hate them?" Link asked, seemingly surprised.

She shook her head. "He'd secretly love it. He knows we only tattoo what matters most to us. As much as he hated the idea of us marking our skin, he always supported us. He'd always ask me about mine. Papa took an interest, even though he gave me a hard time about them. Was it the same for you?"

He sighed and rubbed a hand over his face. "He didn't really say much about mine. Just gave one of his snorts of disapproval. A few comments about running out of room."

She smiled, imagining her papa's mannerisms. "He probably thought your choices were explanatory enough. Pretty straightforward with all the car parts and gears. I'm sure he didn't need to guess. Whereas he had no clue what my flock of birds meant."

He nodded, but doubt clouded his vision. "Your turn. Where did you get it?" His eyes scanned her body.

She stood, deciding he needed to laugh. She unbuttoned her pants and shimmied out of them.

"You took your pants off for Roy?" His growl sent a delicious possessive thrill through her. He sat, hands fisting at his sides.

Emma bit her lip. "What if I did?"

He didn't answer her. Instead, his jaw flexed. His chest heaved in stuttered breaths as a war raged on his expression.

"Are you jealous?" she whispered, her smile faltering. If he was jealous, he wanted her for himself, didn't he? Her heart fluttered in her chest. The ember of hope inside her glowed red.

"I just don't like the idea of someone else's hands on you," he answered her through gritted teeth.

"Anywhere?" she asked.

His dark gaze met hers.

"What about here?" She pressed her hand to her breast.

A low growl was her only answer.

Sliding her hand lower, over her belly, and cupping her sex, she asked, "What about here?"

"Fuck no."

She smiled, joy glowing in her soul. *He wants me.* Did he love her after all?

Bending over, she untied her Converse and slipped her feet out before climbing onto the bed next to him. She slid off one sock and then the other, revealing the patch of black covering the new tattoo. "What about here?" She peeled the gauze back, uncovering her new ink. "So I can take him with me wherever I go."

He scoffed and pinned her to the bed, settling on top of her. "You did that on purpose."

She shrugged, a wily smile curving the edge of her lips. "I like to push your buttons, make you crazy, see how far you'll let me go."

"You should be punished."

"I was hoping you'd say that." She giggled.

His gaze raked over her face, only this time it was different. Sure, there was lust there, burning bright like the sun. But something else flickered in his eyes that hadn't been there before. Her heart thudded in her ears. Was it possible that this trip had left more than one thing tattooed on his heart?

28

LINK

Link stretched his legs out in the passenger seat, yawning. Glancing at the clock, he grabbed his water bottle and took a sip. He'd been out for two hours. His gaze flicked to the reason he'd needed said nap. Emma's small hands gripped the large steering wheel as she drove them along the highway in whatever part of Nebraska they were in now. A few stray blond, pink, and blue hairs blew against the side of her cheek. He couldn't resist tucking them behind her ear.

"Have a good nap?" She sent a warm smile his way, her eyes lighting up mischievously.

"Yeah. Maybe you can pull off at the next rest stop and I can drive?"

"No way. I finally got my chance behind the wheel of this Chevelle. You're gonna have to sit back and enjoy the ride." She shook her head.

"What if I have to pee?"

She motioned to his water bottle. "You got everything you need in here."

He chuckled. "What if I'm shy?"

She arched one of her eyebrows, shooting him a look that told him she wasn't falling for that. "Really? That's what you go with? You're gonna pretend your cock wasn't eight inches deep in my throat last night?" She lifted her hand to her jaw, rubbing it. "I'm kinda sore from just how not shy you were."

He stretched out his arm, laying his hand on the back of her neck and massaging while stroking behind her ear with his thumb.

"Mmmm."

"If I remember correctly, my mouth was pretty engaged too. You don't hear me complaining about a pulled tongue muscle," he joked.

She rolled her eyes. "How did this get turned on me? You were the one who said you were shy, and I was just pointing out it was bullshit."

Laughter erupted from his gut, spinning up in his chest and pouring from him until he couldn't breathe. Emma's light giggling followed his. When was the last time he'd laughed this hard?

After he'd caught his breath, he took another sip of his water before returning the bottle to the cup holder. Emma cleared her throat, a nervous tic. "What are your plans with the shop?"

He sighed, turning his focus to the sloping countryside whipping by. "Just keep doing what we're doing, I guess. Although, I might try to take on some more custom work and hire an actual secretary since Dad isn't here to do that part anymore."

A moment of silence passed between them before Emma spoke. "You know Geo is gone for a while. We could use a guitarist and singer."

A heavy anvil crashed onto his chest; his breathing stilled.

His shoulder muscles bunched and tensed, rising to his ears as he kept his gaze locked out the window. *What was she trying to ask him?* "What exactly happened with him? How did he end up in prison?" He changed the subject.

Emma sighed, turning the blinker on and switching lanes. "He got drunk, and there was one paparazzo in particular who liked to hound us, but especially Geo. Got in his face I guess—it was an accident. And now the pap is dead, and Geo is in prison."

"Jesus Christ," he cursed. "If you guys are having that kind of trouble, and after what happened with us at the karaoke bar, you should have bodyguards or security —something."

She scoffed. "I don't think we need to go to that extreme yet. We got out of there just fine. And the worst that would happen is I'd have to sign a bunch of autographs and snap selfies."

Was she really that naive? She could have been crushed. Or what if someone grabbed her and assaulted her? His hackles rose.

"Why didn't you ever pursue music?" she asked.

So, she wasn't going to drop it. "It was just fun. Kids messing around."

She shook her head, and he caught the tilt of it in his direction from the corner of his eye. "No, you're good, Link. Amazing. Your voice, and your ability on the guitar. Seriously, you could make it."

He clenched his jaw. Yeah, he'd wanted that at one time. But then he'd seen his father struggle, popping painkillers for his arthritis and wincing with every step. He'd come alive when he'd worked on this very SS Chevelle. Restoring classics was his true calling. "Dad needed the help at the shop. His arthritis was getting worse, and you were off doing tours."

Emma's sharp inhale made his stomach twist in anxiety. "I would have done anything for him. If he needed money, I would have sent it. If he told me he was having health issues, I-I would have—"

"It wasn't your job!" he snapped angrily. His father had been his responsibility. Emma didn't deserve to have anything or anyone tying her down. That was what his father and Link had both wanted for her.

"Why? Why do you think this was all on your shoulders?"

"Because he was *my* father." He closed his eyes, immediately regretting the words.

Nothing but the rumble of the engine and the whistle of wind through the cracked window made a sound. Emma's eyes shuttered, her gaze glued ahead.

"I didn't mean it like that." He tried to backtrack.

She didn't respond. Just clenched her jaw, the hollow of her throat bobbing delicately.

"Em, he never wanted you to stay in Shattered Cove. He always said you were destined for bigger things, better places." He reached out his hand to her thigh. The muscles tensed under his touch.

"So are you." Her voice was raw, as if all the emotion she wasn't showing was bleeding out from her throat, speaking as if she'd swallowed shards of glass.

His mind snagged on her words. *Are*, not were. "I'm just destined to take over the shop. Keep his legacy going."

She shook her head. "We could use another guitarist. You could—"

He pulled his hand back to his lap. "What? Join your band? Follow in your shadow? Leave everything Dad built behind?" His voice was growing more and more erratic as the pounding in his head increased. Panic rippled through his body at the thought of abandoning it all. The last piece of his father. The only home he'd ever known. The only life he'd lived. His lungs squeezed tight. The walls of the classic car closed in. He'd only drag her down.

"We could figure it out—"

"There is no *we*, Em. You have your life, and I have mine," he snapped. If they tried this out long term, not only would she get bad press and possibly have trouble with her label dropping her band, but in the end it would never work. He'd resent her for having to follow her around, not truly earning his spot, and having to give up his passion. Or she'd regret him and his need for small-town life.

"Right. How could I forget this was just fucking?" she mumbled, pain saturating every syllable.

Her words were like tiny spears puncturing his heart. He might have seemed stoic on the outside, but inside chaos was erupting. Pain and confusion. Fear and grief. Resentment and anger all roiled inside him like a whirlpool. They never should have started this. He never should have touched her.

He'd fucked up. And now, he needed to make it right.

29

EMMA

It had been two days on the road with mostly silence. They'd gone back to renting two separate rooms. Link had made that decision without talking to her—just handed her a key for her own room. She'd squeezed the cold plastic key card so hard in her hand it left an imprint long after.

The first thing she'd done was get rid of all the razors in her room—removing the temptation like her therapist had told her so long ago. And when the distraction had failed, she brought out her guitar, playing until her hands were numb and her voice was hoarse. All night long. It made the hours she was stuck in the car with him easier if she slept. She wouldn't think about the pain tearing through every cell. Not right now. She just had to survive this trip. And then . . . then she'd figure it out.

How could she have been so stupid to think this had turned into more than sex? Obviously, she'd been sorely mistaken. But what hurt more was the fact that Link had pointed out she wasn't Solomon's child. Had her papa felt that way too?

No. He loved me . . .

Did I let him down?

She swallowed the lump in her throat, biting on the side of her cheek, using one pain to distract from another. Nerves frayed, she stared out the window as the trees whipped by in the darkness. They were almost to the border of New Hampshire. They'd opted for a long, nine-hour drive rather than spending another night in a hotel.

"I'd like to get back to my own bed," Link had said. More like he wanted out of this Chevelle prison that kept him with her.

She'd given him everything—every part of her that was worth something. She'd been good enough to fuck, but not love.

The headlights from oncoming traffic blurred.

No. Not here. Not now. She wouldn't break down. She needed something. Just one moment of escape.

"Stop the car." Her voice came out as a whisper. "Stop the car," she repeated louder, her voice barely trembling.

Link glanced her way, his brows shooting up. "We just passed a gas station a couple miles ago. Should be another coming up soon, once we get to the border."

"No." She shook her head. "Pull onto the next road."

He clicked his blinker on and turned into a dark road. Cars from the main road they'd been on zoomed by as they drove on.

She pointed to a large warehouse building. "Behind there."

He followed her directions, pulling up under a lone flood light, illuminating the near-empty space. One large trash bin was situated against a chain-link fence on the other side. Bits of garbage were scattered across the asphalt.

"Can't you hold it until we get somewhere . . . safer?" Link asked, oblivious to her true intentions.

Her heart rate jumped. Her breath came out in pants as she climbed into the back seat.

His dark gaze met hers in the rearview mirror. Half his face was lit by the lights, the other hid in the darkness of the night.

"Come here."

"I don't think—"

"*Please*, Link? I need you to do this one thing for me."

He must have heard the desperation in her voice because he climbed into the back seat next to her a second later. His jaw was clenched, hands fisted at his sides. His head tipped down in shame. She didn't hesitate. Didn't give him time to think too hard and regret this. Emma wrapped her legs over his, straddling him.

His hands immediately found her waist, squeezing as his cock stirred under her. "Em—"

"Shhh. Just one more time. One more perfect moment where no one knows us. Where you chase away the darkness and keep me in the light."

He wouldn't understand what she meant, but hopefully he would hear her desperation. She held her breath, waiting for the oxygen only his consent could provide.

His cheek dimpled as if he had bit the inside. His eyes darted back and forth between hers as if waging a war before settling on her mouth. She leaned in, taking the choice from him. Emma melded her lips to his as she cupped his jaw. The scruff of his beard scratched against her palms, drawing her out of her head and into her body—away from her pain and into her pleasure. Link's mouth opened, his sweet tongue seeking entrance between her lips as his fingers dipped into the soft flesh of her waist. She reared back, panting, and ripped her shirt over her head before fumbling with her leggings.

"Pull your pants down." She tugged hers off.

The clink of his belt and the peel of his zipper only made her heart beat faster in anticipation. Her skin itched with the burning need to have this man to herself one more time. Because that was all this would be. This was goodbye.

His hard dick sprang free, standing to attention in all its thick, veined glory. She didn't waste another second. After climbing on, she straddled him. He flicked the head of his penis over her clit, teasing her. She lowered herself on him, holding on to his shoulders as he slid inside her. She fought the urge to close her eyes. No, she wanted to memorize every single second, every sensation of this. It would be all she had left of him.

He hissed as the tip of his cock knocked her cervix. She gasped. Using his shoulder as leverage, she rose on her knees before lowering back down, riding him slowly.

He reached around the back of her head and pulled her hair tie out so that her locks fell free. He dipped his head, lowering the cups of her bra before sucking one hard nipple into his mouth. The soft warmth of his lips sent a rush of emotions barreling through her. He'd taken her in every way imaginable, but never soft and slow. Never like this. He was gentle, spending time to lavish her breasts as if savoring this as much as she.

Pressure built, coiling in her womb, snaking out and tethering her to him with ropes of unrequited love. She wouldn't even try to deny it. She loved Lincoln Owusu. She'd give him the last piece of herself, knowing she'd never get it back, knowing they could never be. And then she'd walk away, so he could live his life and find happiness.

She kissed him, tipping her forehead to his. Hair fell like a curtain around them, blocking out the rest of the world, creating their own secret place hidden away from everyone else. Here, nothing existed except sighs of pleasure, locked eyes, synchronized breaths, and merging moans. He pulled her onto him harder, his cock reaching her soul. He groaned, his muscles bunching under her fingertips. They didn't exchange words. Emma let her body speak for her instead. Hers saying, *I love you*. His—she wouldn't know.

Despite his earlier comment, she knew this was more than sex to him. But the fear that permeated his every glance told her enough. This could never be. So, for one more perfect moment, she would be his and he hers.

She moved faster, taking him harder as a well of pleasure in her center sloshed, spilling out over the edges. Tingles raced down her limbs, curling her toes as she rocked her hips, merging their bodies in a symphony. Each bated breath was a low, electric chord, each thrust of her hips a crash of cymbals, their quickening hearts the drumbeat to her demise. They made love, colliding with eyes locked. His exhale, her inhale, until she wasn't sure where she ended and he began. Until nothing else existed but the flood of delirium-inducing plea-sure that rocketed through her body, burning her up like a flash of lightning.

His tongue stroked hers delicately, kissing her as she pulled away knowing that this time—this time she'd never find the pieces to be put back together again. He groaned out as his own orgasm chased hers, pulsing and throbbing inside her. She slumped on his shoulder, turning her face towards the fogged-up window, not ready to slide off him and end this experience just yet.

"Em . . ."

"I know." She slid off him, mourning the loss of him inside her as his cum dripped down her leg. She didn't want to hear his excuses. Her heart couldn't take it.

30

EMMA

Emma opened her eyes as Link shifted the car into neutral and pulled on the parking brake. It had been easier to pretend she was sleeping the last two hours of their journey than face the heavy silence of Link's guilt that permeated the inside of the car, tainting every breath she took.

The familiar weathered wooden sign for Shattered Cove Garage and Repair shop snagged her attention. She swallowed, her eyes drifting to the door leading to her father's apartment above the shop. Why were they here?

She sat, turning towards Link.

His eyes remained fixed ahead. "We have another meeting with the lawyer in a couple days. I figured we could start going through his stuff tomorrow if you're up for it?"

A twinge pulled at her chest as she swallowed the emotion that rose in her throat like bile. "Okay."

"I'll get your bag. I had Reese bring your bike here from Remy's." He pulled the handle of the door.

She was supposed to stay here? Alone? Her hand shot out

to stop him. "Can't I stay at your place for the next few days?" She couldn't sleep in their dad's apartment without Solomon. It didn't feel right.

Link's jaw clenched, his eyes darting to his lap. "I-I don't think that's a good idea."

Rejection plowed through her. She closed her eyes, inhaling through her nose to fight the sting in her eyes. Apparently, she had misread him the whole time. Emma exhaled and licked her lips. "I can't stay here without him." Her voice broke. She needed to get herself under control.

Shhh. Don't cry. Don't make a sound. We don't want to make him mad. Don't want to draw his attention to you. Her mother's words swirled from the dark recesses of her mind. She swallowed down everything as she'd always done, hiding herself behind a stoic mask. She still needed to know he'd be in her life. But if he knew how she really felt, Link would run for the hills. He'd made it clear this really was just a fuck. He'd used her and now he was done. *And I let myself be used, all for a scrap of temporary affection. God, I'm just like her.*

"Em." Link's hand reached out to hers, making it halfway before he faltered, slamming his clenched fist into the black leather seat.

"I'll get my bike."

He nodded.

"Drop my stuff off to Jaz's inn. I'll stay there." She pulled the handle and pushed open the door before walking towards one of the large bays. It was Sunday, so the garage was closed.

She punched in the number to the security pad and let herself in as the rumble from the engine revved and then faded as Link drove away, leaving her truly alone. She slammed her back to the door, shutting it with more effort than needed before crumpling to the ground. Heaviness threatened to suffocate her, descending on her chest. She sucked in a breath, again and again. Each inhale was tainted with motor oil and metallic notes that usually brought her comfort, reminding her of home.

She slapped her face hard, not once, but twice. The hot sting blossomed on her cheek, spreading down her neck.

Memories flooded over her, fighting for dominance in her mind. Her mother's boyfriends beating her. Finding her mother passed out with a needle in her arm. The shady men her mother had allowed in the house. The drug dealers. The pain. The screams. The bruises. The excuses. And then, like a blinding light, Solomon's face. He'd been so patient with her, drawing her out of her shell. Finally, she had been safe.

The last fight he'd had with her mom burst to the forefront of her mind.

"Marsha, where is the money?" Solomon asked.

"I spent it! Emma needed new shoes," her mother replied angrily.

Emma peeked out from her bedroom door, peering through the crack. She hadn't gotten new shoes, and from the disbelief in Solomon's eyes, he knew it too.

"Where were you yesterday and last night?" Solomon pressed.

Oh no. He was going to kick them out. Emma would have to leave again. Her stomach flipped and clenched, about to throw up.

Marsha stood straighter, a gleam in her eye. "You know what? I don't need to answer to you. We're not married. And as of now, we're done. I'm taking my daughter and leaving."

Solomon reached out, clasping her arm.

Emma gasped and closed the door, tears running down her face. No, Solomon wouldn't hurt her mom. He wasn't like the other men. Was he?

She listened, holding her breath as hot tears dripped down her cheeks, soaking the blanket she pulled up to her chin. After the initial raised voice, there was no yelling—only low, murmured tones. Minutes, or hours, for all she knew, later, there was a slamming door and then silence.

And when she'd woken the next morning, Solomon greeted her for breakfast with a sad smile.

"You're my daughter now. You'll stay here with me and my son as long as you want to."

She'd waited day after day for her mother to return. She never had. Marsha Sterling had abandoned her daughter.

Emma had come home from school one day and Solomon's drawn expression had morphed into sympathy at the small dining table. She'd known instantly something was wrong.

Her mother was dead. She'd overdosed and was found a week later in a drug den. The people she'd lived with hadn't even realized she was gone for a whole seven days. She'd left Emma for people like that. For the poison in her veins that had killed her. *Am I really that unlovable?*

Solomon was the only one who'd ever taken her in, loved her like his own. She'd never shown him every part of her though. She'd abided by her mother's words. Not wanting to risk being abandoned again, she'd hidden parts of herself. Link's words came back to haunt her. *And then I left Solomon when he needed me most.*

Emma shot to her feet, bending over the trash can before she vomited. Her limbs trembled as she wiped her mouth. She needed to get out of there. Away from the memories. Away from the pain.

She walked with leaden limbs over to hit the button opening the bay door. Approaching her motorcycle, she grabbed the helmet from the handlebar and strapped it to the back. Opting instead for a pair of sunglasses, she straddled the bike and twisted the key in the ignition. The engine rumbled to life. She hit the gas, shifting into gear and driving out of the garage before stopping to shut the bay. After returning to her bike, she revved the engine, skidding out of the driveway.

Wind whipped against her skin, blowing through her hair. She pressed harder on the gas, speeding faster and faster until everything blurred by.

What if I just steered into that tree? What if I just kept driving straight, even as the road bent ahead? She pictured the crash of the machine and the way her body would fly through the air, weightless and free for one stolen moment in time as a rush coursed through her veins. And then there would be pain for one split second before the darkness pulled her under for good.

31

LINK

Link coughed as a cloud of dust rose from the stack of boxes he'd moved from his father's bedroom closet.

Emma sneezed before opening the window. Warm spring air filtered into the stuffy room. Sunlight dappled the brightly patterned handmade comforter on his father's bed, still rumpled from the day he'd found his father clutching his chest on the floor.

"Wow. You were so little. And Dad looked so young here." Emma picked up a picture frame, turning it so he could see. The colorful background of the market in Ghana surrounded a younger Link and his father. The red clay ground contrasted with the bright patterns of the kente clothing they both wore.

"That was the last time we went together," Link commented as the memory flooded over him. "He was so excited to introduce me to our authentic foods. Fufu and palm nut soup. Banku and okro stew. Jollof rice."

"Oh, I miss his peanut soup and rice balls." Emma smiled wistfully, closing her eyes as the sun danced over her fair skin, making her seem to glow.

Driving away from her had been harder than he'd thought it would be. But this was for the best for both of them. There had been no missing the hurt in her eyes yesterday, but she seemed better today.

"Think he still has some Milo in the cupboard?" Link asked.

Where other kids had had hot chocolate, they'd had Milo —a chocolate malt drink that his father had called "tea." Whenever Link couldn't sleep, his father would make him a cup with milk and some bread to dip in it.

A twinge of pain crossed his chest. *That will never happen again.* How many small rituals were now only going to be a memory?

"Mmmm, maybe I'll make some for us after we get this room done," Emma said, bringing him back to the task at hand. He opened a box filled with files. His father never threw anything out.

One of the tabs was labelled *adoption papers*. He pulled it out and opened it curiously. He scanned the documents inside. "Em?"

She stepped closer, her strawberry scent wafting, reminding him of all the times he'd got up close and personal with that smell. He cleared his throat, cursing his body for the arousal speeding through his veins.

Emma plucked the file from his hand, her eyes tracing the page back and forth. "He was going to adopt me?"

"It's dated years ago. You had to be . . ."

"Seventeen . . . Why didn't he ever ask me? Why didn't he ever go through with it?" Doubt clouded her vision.

"I'm sure he had a reason. You know Dad; he probably set it in a pile, and it got lost in his never-ending to-do list."

She blinked, staring at the words. "Or . . . he didn't . . ." Her voice choked.

The broken expression on her face tore him to pieces. He couldn't hold back, pulling her into his arms. She relaxed instantly into his embrace, and fuck, it felt good to hold her like this again. To be the source of her comfort. "He wanted you."

She shook her head but clutched him closer. His chin rested on her crown as he closed his eyes. Every cell screamed at him to not let go, to pull her lips to his and kiss away all her doubts. *No.* He wouldn't do that. He couldn't.

Knock. Knock.

"Come in!" Link backed away from Emma so abruptly, she had to reach her hand out to a box to steady herself.

"Link?"

What was Rachel doing here? "Down the hall."

Emma's shoulders stiffened as a mask of indifference slid into place on her expression. The anguish he'd seen in her gaze only a moment ago was replaced by blue steel, giving nothing away. *How much more is she hiding in there?*

Rachel appeared in the doorway. Her lithe body was wrapped in a yellow sundress showing off her bronze, toned legs and arms. She'd been beautiful five years ago, but now she was absolutely stunning. She smiled, her eyes locking on to his with a shyness she'd always possessed. "I hope it's okay that I'm here?" She tucked a stray braid behind her ear.

"Yeah. Reese told me you were in town."

"Yes. I'm here for the month, maybe more. It just depends." She bit her bottom lip nervously before her gaze flicked over to Emma.

"Hi, Emma. You look great. I heard you're doing big things in the music world," Rachel complimented.

"Yeah. Thanks." Emma gave a forced smile.

Rachel's gaze focused on his as she wrung the side of her skirt in her hands. "I hoped we might . . . um . . . talk? I have an opportunity to come back to Shattered Cove. The Department of Marine Biology I work for in Texas wanted to open a chapter here in New Hampshire." Hope glittered in her eyes.

"I'm gonna go," Emma said, brushing past him, giving him another lungful of strawberries.

"Wait—" Link followed her, turning back to Rachel. "Give me a sec and we can talk, okay?"

"Sure." She nodded before he jogged after Emma, who was climbing onto her bike, sans helmet.

"Where are you going?" he asked.

She started the engine, not looking up. "I don't need anything from the house. Keep it or donate it."

Anger boiled in his gut. "Typical Emma."

"What the fuck is that supposed to mean?" Her eyes snapped to his.

"You're running away."

"You made it very clear, and from those papers we found, it seems you were right. You are his son, and I am just the charity case he took on." Her voice was steel.

"That's not true, and you know it. You're running scared—"

"You want to talk about running scared? You're a fucking hypocrite!" she screamed, her chest heaving as fury glowed in those blue spheres tearing him apart word by word.

"How so?"

"You have always been too scared to chase after what you want. You set music aside for Papa's shop. You let Rachel go to Texas and stayed here, knowing there was nowhere for you to grow. Knowing it was going to be predictable and safe." Her voice was laced with accusation.

He staggered back a step. Was that what she thought? That he'd settled? That he was going nowhere? "I stayed to take care of Dad. I told you he couldn't do this on his own. He was struggling with his arthritis—"

"Not when you were young. Do you know how many times he told me, 'That boy is going to do something great one day. Link's got heart and drive'?"

"He wanted me to take over the shop."

"He wanted you to chase your dreams. Why do you think he didn't give up control of anything at the garage? He wasn't a man of many words, but his actions said it all." Her voice broke.

Could it be true? How many times had he fought with his dad over giving him more responsibility and taking a step back from the business? Had his dad really not known that this work was his passion?

You've got too much to figure out in your own life, son. Leave the business to me.

The rev of Emma's engine blasted through his inner turmoil as she sped off, getting smaller and smaller down the road. The ground seemed to crumble at the revelation she'd just dropped at his feet like a bomb.

"Everything okay?" Rachel asked from behind him.

He turned around, rubbing a hand over the back of his neck. He'd wished this woman would come back to him for so long. Hoped she'd turned the job in Texas down and stayed here and started a family with Link. He'd expected a rush of emotions at seeing her again. Instead, he had only . . . apathy.

If Emma was right, that meant . . . that meant Solomon had thought Link was a coward.

32

EMMA

Emma followed Mr. Driscoll, the lawyer, inside his office. She hadn't wanted to endure a second with Link alone. Her eyes flicked over the hunched shoulders of her stepbrother. Was he weighed down with grief or regret? Probably both.

"Good afternoon, Lincoln. I'm glad you two could make it in. I have a few things to finish up with your father's estate," Mr. Driscoll said, taking a seat across from them.

Emma took the empty chair beside Link. His eyes burned into her, but she kept her gaze focused on the lawyer's desk.

The smell of old books melded with lemon cleaner filled Emma's nose as the lawyer talked about the breakdown of assets of Solomon Owusu's estate. She turned towards the warm ray of morning light glowing over her hand on the armrest of the wooden and velvet chair.

Mike Driscoll handed Link an envelope with his name on it in her papa's blocky handwriting.

Her eyes widened as she stared. *Is there one for me too?*

"Your father gave me this just a month before he passed," Mike explained.

"What is it?" Link asked, his voice wavering.

She hated that she still wanted to reach out a hand to comfort him. No. He didn't want her. They were finished.

"A letter, I believe, but I don't know the actual contents. You'll have to read that yourself," the lawyer said. "Is there anything else I can do for you? Any other questions you have?"

"Is there one for me?" Emma asked, heart racing.

The lawyer frowned as sympathy lit his eyes. "I'm sorry. There is just the one. But maybe its contents are for both of you?"

Her stomach sunk as another piece of her heart broke. *Or maybe I didn't matter as much to Papa as I thought.* It was like the whole foundation she'd built her life on was crumbling beneath her feet as she scrambled to find something real to hold on to.

"Anything else?" Mr. Driscoll repeated, this time looking to Link.

"No." Link shook his head and stood, reaching out to shake Mike's hand. He cast a glance her way. "Are you going to The Shipwreck to meet up with everybody?"

"Yeah. Just have to make a stop first. See ya later."

He hesitated a moment before turning his back and leaving. She waited for the door to snick closed and she met Mike's waiting and patient gaze. "I need you to help me with something."

* * *

Thirty minutes later, Emma walked out of the lawyer's door, heading down Main Street. Remy's café was across the road, but she was probably at The Shipwreck already. Her friends had decided to throw one last get-together before she left town to meet up with her band.

Thankfully, Remy, Jasmine, and the girls had taken her melancholy mood for the grief of losing her father. And it was partly that. But after discovering those adoption papers that he'd never filed, a new doubt had crept into her mind. *Maybe he didn't love me like that either.* Solomon had made it clear that even though at one point he'd thought of her as a daughter, something had happened to make him not go through with it. The year those papers were marked was the year she'd turned eighteen and worked on leaving this small town with her band. The year they'd started making a buzz. *Maybe he did feel abandoned by me.*

A creaking sign overhead drew Emma's attention upwards. *Shattered Cove Records.* Her gaze fell to the worn door where a *For Sale* sign hung. *I can't believe it.*

So much was changing in this small town. This place was where she and her band had recorded their first album. Old man James who owned it had given them a deal: if they'd repaint the front of the building, they could record for half off. The brick-red paint was now chipping off. She smiled at the memories of all the hours they'd poured into their music in this place, just trying to get it right. James had had them sign a group photo he'd taken. *For when you all get famous.* She shook her head. *I wonder if he still has the picture hanging in the lobby?*

Emma was so engrossed in her thoughts she didn't see the body in front of her in time. She collided with another person, sucking in a gasp as a dog barked.

"Oh my God! I'm so sorry," Emma apologized, reaching for the beautiful woman sprawled on the cement with several books scattered around her. The golden retriever sat next to its owner, sniffing her arm as if to check on her.

"It's okay," the woman said, gathering up the books.

Emma bent to help her, collecting a few in her arms before extending a hand. "I wasn't watching where I was going, and I was so stuck in my head. I feel awful. Are you really alright?"

She smiled brightly. "Accidents happen. I was rushing out of my shop anyways, so we were both preoccupied."

Emma turned her head to the side, noting *The Oyster Bookstore* sign. "Oh, you must be Pippa."

Pippa nodded with a smile.

"Charli, my friend, told me about the new owner. I'm Emma, by the way."

"Ah, yes. Well, I've been here a couple years now. But I know Charli. How's their little one?"

"Growing like a weed."

Pippa nodded. "Are you sure you're good?"

Emma blinked. "Of course. Why wouldn't I be? You're the one who got knocked on her ass." Emma forced a laugh.

Pippa just stared at her a little longer.

The words bubbled up. She wanted to tell this woman everything. Why would she trust a perfect stranger? She couldn't even tell her own friends what had really happened. But that was because they knew how she'd pined for Link her whole life. They'd pity her. Her friends had their own happy lives. She didn't want to ruin that—even for a second. She'd hide just a little longer. "I'm fine." The lie tasted bitter on her tongue.

"Well, if you ever need a listening ear, my door is always open." Pippa pet her dog's head and gave its ear a scratch.

Emma tucked her hair behind her ear. "Why would you offer that? You don't even know me." Or did she? Was she looking for a story?

Pippa shrugged. "We women have to stick together. God knows men won't be there for us." A long-buried hurt bled from her words.

Emma nodded. "Well, I, uh . . . appreciate it. I have somewhere to be, so . . . have a good day. And sorry again about running into you."

Pippa waved her off. "No problem."

Emma climbed on her bike and headed a couple streets over to the bar where all her friends were waiting. After parking, she slid her keys in her pocket and took a deep breath. Her mouth split into a big fake smile, and she locked her true feelings behind a wall of pretend. She could be happy for an hour. It would take everything in her, but she could do this one more time.

She pushed open the doors. A few heads turned her way.

"Hey, girl," Remy said, squeezing her in a hug. "We need to catch up. I feel like we haven't really talked in ages."

"You came to the inn yesterday morning for breakfast," Emma reminded her.

Remy waved her hand. "Yeah, but Atlas and the kids were there. You know, we need to have a girls' night soon. How about tonight?"

"Sure," she lied. But she didn't have the energy to explain that this was it. That she'd be leaving Shattered Cove right after this and not turning back. At least, not for a while.

"Hey, Rock Star!" Jasmine teased, coming over to their growing circle.

"Hey, Boss Bitch."

Jasmine rolled her eyes.

"I thought for sure when I got back from the trip Atlas would have put a ring on your finger," Emma said, steering the conversation away into safer waters.

Jasmine's affection-filled gaze flicked over to the man

who'd stolen her heart and become a father for her daughter. "I'm not in a rush. Besides . . . we have some news."

Remy's mouth dropped open as she squealed in surprise. "I knew it! I totally called it. I told Mikel you were glowing and being extra bitchy."

"Gee, thanks," Jasmine deadpanned.

Wait. Was Jasmine . . .

"I'm gonna be an auntie again!" Remy shouted loud enough for the whole room to hear. Mikel and Atlas walked over to their group. Remy patted Mikel's chest, beaming up at him. "I told you."

Mikel kissed her nose before clapping Atlas on the back. "Congrats, man."

Atlas's smile was so perfect, it was blinding. "Thanks."

Bently, sheriff of Shattered Cove and Jasmine's oldest brother, approached, his arm around his gorgeous wife, Belle. "You knocked my baby sister up?"

Atlas pulled Jasmine into his arms, her back to his front with his hand over her belly lovingly. "I did."

"I guess this calls for a round of shots!" Bently announced. "Charli, shots for everyone, except our expecting mama and Mikel. Give them the good sparkling cider." He winked.

Charli and Finn were behind the bar, setting up shot glasses on trays as Emma pushed farther into the room. Her friends' happiness was bittersweet. She'd watched them all fall in love. It hadn't been easy. And after seeing Remy and Mikel, she'd thought there might be hope for Link and her. But it wasn't to be. Her gaze pulled towards his muscular frame like a magnet at the other end of the bar. His back stiffened as if he could feel her gaze. His black orbs flicked to hers, locking her in a secret stare. Regret flashed before he blinked and turned towards Rachel again. If Link's smile directed at her was any sign, whatever Emma thought they'd shared was all in her head. Her imagination had gone wild. Their time truly had been a fantasy.

Remy's brother, Andre, leaned down to kiss his wife, Mia, on the lips. Rachel's eyes darted from them to Link, hopeful.

Emma's stomach clenched, spinning into knots. She needed to get out of here. She pushed her way to the tray of awaiting shots, grabbing the first one and downing it before grabbing another. Charli gave her a questioning look.

Emma climbed onto the barstool, holding her glass high. "To Jasmine and Atlas. May you enjoy every moment with your family. Your kids are lucky to have you as parents. And you all—Remy, Mia, Belle, Charli, and all the men who fell at your feet to worship the ground you walk on." Everyone laughed as emotion burned her chest.

"You guys fought the odds and created a relationship and a family that you should all be proud of. You are an inspiration. May the rest of us assholes be as lucky as you." She tipped the drink back, the alcohol burning its way down her throat as she climbed to the ground.

Everyone else grabbed their shots and downed them. Remy cast her a questioning glance, but Emma only smiled wider, hoping she didn't look as crazed as she felt. Her gaze traveled the room, memorizing the happy faces of her friends and some of Link's. Reese was here with his wife. Mason stood near the edge of the room, surveying the crowd like the ex-Navy SEAL he was, always the protector.

Rachel's hand rested over Link's chest. His hand wrapped around her hip. If she was the person who made him happy, Emma had to let go once and for all. Her eyes snagged on Link's. She was caught in the depths of his regret-filled black eyes like a mermaid in a net. Only she couldn't sing her way out of this. She'd tried. No, it was him who'd held the power. And it was time she took some of it back.

She turned around, weaving through the laughing couples busy stealing kisses and whispering secrets. Couples who'd seen the deepest, darkest depths of one another and stayed. They'd fought for this love. But you couldn't win when only one of you was willing to go to war.

Emma walked away and didn't turn back as she hopped on her motorcycle. She drove out of the gravel parking lot, skidding over bits of rock as she sped down the road, heading towards the highway.

She'd park her bike at the airport, and Callie could have it picked up for her and shipped to California. She wouldn't be coming back—not for a very long time. There was nothing here for her anymore.

She pressed harder on the gas, trying to outrun the pain tearing what was left of her heart to shreds. Shattered Cove whizzed by until it disappeared out her side mirror. It was really over. She couldn't return until she got over him. Until it stopped hurting to see him and know she could never kiss those lips again or feel his heart beating against hers with nothing between them.

This was truly the end.

33

LINK

Link broke away from his friends, searching the room as he walked over to the bar. Charli slid a cold beer over to him. He caught it, immediately reminded of how many times he'd sat in this very seat next to his father and enjoyed a drink and some laughs. All their conversations had been surface. Unless Link outright asked for advice, his father had always held his tongue, except for his passive-aggressive humor.

"You doing okay?" Charli asked.

He swiveled his head, glancing around the room once more. "Have you seen Em?"

He'd been a complete asshole to her. And after he'd had some time to think, he'd realized there was more truth to her words than naught. Link had been a fucking coward when it came to her. His father had given him one job, and that was to protect Emma. To look out for her. And he'd royally fucked that up after touching her.

"I think she left a while ago," Charli answered.

"Left?" Emma was gone? All their friends were still here,

albeit getting ready to head out before Finn and Charli had to open the bar for their actual customers.

"Mason said she took off like a bat out of hell. Did something happen on your trip?" Charli asked.

Link stared at the glass bottle in his hand. Condensation dripped, pooling between his skin and the glass. A heavy weight crashed over his shoulders. *Emma is gone.* That look in her eyes across the room, the resignation that had flashed in those soulful blues. It never bothered him in all the years she'd come and gone to Shattered Cove without even seeing him most of the time. *Because I avoided her.* Distanced himself from the illicit temptation. *I'm a selfish prick.* Guilt cinched around him with burning ropes of regret. *What have I done?*

"A lot happened," he finally answered Charli's question.

Her eyes filled with sympathy mixed with anger as she leaned in. "Tell me you didn't."

"Didn't what?" he asked defensively, suddenly aware of the few people in hearing distance. He didn't want anyone else knowing how badly he'd fucked up. Or the fact that he'd slept with the woman they all knew as his sister.

Charli's eyelashes fluttered as she looked away, opening her mouth as if to say something and then shutting it.

A soft, manicured hand ran up his arm, resting on his shoulder.

Charli shook her head and walked to the other end of the bar.

Link turned to face Rachel.

"You feel like getting out of here? Maybe we can go back to your place?" Rachel smiled suggestively, hope glowing in her brown gaze.

He should want this. He should take her hand and lead her out the door. For his own good, and even for Emma's. The farther away from her he was, the better off she'd be.

Link sighed, taking Rachel's hand in his. "I don't think that's a good idea."

Her smile fell.

"You're amazing. And what we had was special. But we aren't the same people we were five years ago. I hope you find what you're looking for, Rach, but it isn't going to be with me."

"Oh." She pulled her hand away from him, nodding. "I see."

"I really do wish you the best in life, and I hope you find your happiness," Link added.

She searched his eyes. "She's a lucky girl to have finally won your heart. I know from experience how guarded you can be."

He frowned. "Who?"

A small, sad smile turned up the corner of her mouth. "Emma. I saw the way she looked at you today, and you her."

He shook his head. "She's my sister. Of course she loves me, but not like that."

"You always were oblivious." She grabbed his beer and took a long gulp.

What? Emma loves me? "What do you mean—finally?"

Rachel set the drink back on the bar. "The whole time we were dating, it was obvious she viewed me as competition. But she never actually did anything about it. I asked her once. She told me she just wanted you to be happy, and if I was the one who gave that to you, then so be it."

The confession was a cannonball to his chest. Emma had loved him? For years? The image of the hope in her eyes being snuffed out the morning after their drunken hookup made more sense now. Why didn't she say anything?

Because I made it clear it was just sex.

He ran a hand over his locks. "Fuck."

And then she'd agreed to just sex, knowing it would mean more to her and tear her apart. His stomach churned. The intensity of just how badly he'd screwed up surged over him like a rogue wave.

"Go after her," Rachel urged.

He shook his head. No, he'd hurt her in the worst ways. *Do I love her?* Christ, yes. And he hated how they'd ended things. These last few days had been miserable, and that was with her just down the road, not gone. His heart ached, his head spinning and pounding at the revelation. The things he felt for Emma were nothing like what he'd felt for Rachel once upon a time. Emma invoked so much passion and lust, it scared him. At the thought of anyone trying to hurt her, a fierce protectiveness roared like a hungry lion inside his chest. *But I caused her more pain than almost anyone.*

And what would his dad think? He'd asked him to protect her. How devastated would his father be that Link had touched his daughter? That he had fallen in love with her? They'd be the laughingstock of most the world and would ruin her chances as a rising star and the legacy his father had built from nothing.

But regarding his father's wishes meant hurting Emma. *Fuck!* He stood, heading straight for the door. He needed some air. Needed advice. Needed his father.

How could I fall in love with the one woman I can't have?

34

EMMA

Emma gripped the blade as the red droplets fell against the white porcelain sink. Eyes burning, back aching, she hunched over in the tiny bathroom, swaying as the bus continued the drive towards their next destination. Another stage, another show of pretending she had it all and she was happy. Driving her farther from Shattered Cove and the man she was cursed to love unrequitedly. Away from the only home she'd ever known. Farther from the friends who had become sisters to her wrapped up in their own hard-earned happy-ever-afters.

She was drifting in a cloud of grey that grew darker and darker, like the sun was setting on her world. The alcohol barely worked to numb the pain. In the two weeks since she'd left, she'd pulled the blade out more than once. This was the quickest relief. The only way she could take control of the emotional riot raging in her soul before she broke down. She couldn't afford for the dam to break—surely it would drown her. She'd stuffed so much down for so long. That inky blackness would suffocate her in its oily darkness.

Emma tossed the razor in the trash bin and rinsed her arm. She'd needed to go deeper this time and make an extra cut for the same relief. Pressing the paper towel onto the wound to stop the bleeding, she closed her eyes and sat on the closed toilet.

The latch clicked open. Asher's dark eyes fixed in horror on her arm. "What the fuck happened?" he boomed.

Emma blanched. "N-nothing. I just, uh, cut it on the, uh . . . thingy when I reached under the sink for more toilet paper. The bus swayed, and I lost my balance."

Asher eyed the half-full roll of toilet paper, clearly catching her in a lie. His brows drew together as he shut the door behind him, locking them in together. "I thought you stopped this?" He reached under the sink and pulled out a first aid kit before holding his palm open for her hand.

She sighed. Asher had seen the marks in high school. He was the one who'd suggested the bracelet. He'd always been good at hiding secrets.

"I did."

"You gonna let some asshole who didn't see what he had in front of him this whole time drive you back into carving yourself up like this?" he asked, grabbing a tube from the kit and rubbing some antibacterial ointment onto the cuts.

The pain morphed into a dull burn of shame. She hissed and blinked away tears. "I just needed to take the edge off."

"Then fuck him out of your system or have a drink and write a song about him. Don't hurt yourself." Asher pressed a gauze onto the cuts and taped it to her arm.

"And become a sex addict like you?" she teased, hoping to lighten the mood.

"I hardly think I qualify as an addict. I'm just a young man sowing my wild oats, living the dream of being a rock star." He winked.

Asher clipped her leather cuff back on, where it hid the white gauze perfectly. He lifted Emma's hand until she was standing, squished against him in the tiny room. His arms wrapped around her, holding her tight.

"That motherfucker might not know what he had, but we do. We got your back, Em. Someday you're gonna find a man or woman who will worship the ground you walk on and never let you go. Hell, you already have us five." Asher spoke softly in her ear.

Maybe he was right. Or maybe it was time she stopped chasing a happily ever after. She would live for the moment. Fuck everything else. "You're right. Fuck him."

"That's my girl."

Knock. Knock.

"What the hell is taking you so long? I gotta piss," Ravi called through the door.

"Eating pussy! Come back later," Asher shouted to Ravi before turning back to Emma and whispering, "Promise me you'll come to me instead of doing this next time."

Emma nodded, not able to speak the lie.

"You're gay." Ravi deadpanned through the door.

"And I'm pretty sure the alphabet mafia would take my rainbow card if they knew I liked doing it. So keep it down." Asher sniggered.

Emma couldn't stop her giggles as he put the first aid kit back under the sink.

"Come on. Play along," he whispered.

"Ohhhhh," she moaned between fits of laughter.

"Yeah, baby, you taste so good!" Asher yelled.

"Asher! Yes, right there, right . . . YES!" Emma shouted an orgasm so fake it was porn-worthy.

Asher opened the door and wiped his face with the back of his hand. Ravi leaned against the other side of the hall, his arms crossed and an amused smile playing on his lips. "Nice try. Now move before I piss all over you."

"Now, that would be kinky. Maybe we should do like the papers say and have an orgy," Asher joked.

Emma smacked his chest and headed towards her bed in the back of the bus.

Asher followed, scooping her into his arms and laying her beside him. "After that fake orgasm, I think I at least deserve some postcoital snuggles. You know, gotta release that oxytocin." Asher tucked her back to his front.

She lay on his arm and closed her eyes, content. Emma inhaled, relaxing into his warmth. Asher would make the perfect partner to some man someday. "Why couldn't it have been you?" she whispered.

"Because you don't have the right equipment."

She chuckled. "So it's my fault?"

He ran a hand over her head, smoothing the hair out of her face. "Love you, Em. Always."

"I love you too, Asher."

He was one of her best friends. He'd seen her through some of the hardest days and lowest points, and she'd been there for his.

She closed her eyes, grateful for his arms and longing for another's. Her smile faded as reality came crashing down. Numbness settled into her bones once again, stealing any joy she'd captured in the last few minutes.

Emma was alone. Even here in her best friend's arms, in the tour bus with the men who'd become her brothers, she was separate. Icy fingers of loneliness spread out and sunk into her marrow. Her arm stung and burned under the leather, reminding her just how broken she was. All was lost, but she'd survive this because . . . because why? What was her reason for doing any of this anymore? Why fight when giving in was so much easier? Why breathe when holding her breath brought less pain? Why wake when sleep was within reach, offering her a reprieve, swallowing her into the darkness?

35

LINK

1 MONTH LATER

Link was back at The Shipwreck, peeling the label from Sand Dune's summer IPA. He pulled out his phone and tapped Emma's name on his contacts. His call was sent straight to voicemail for the millionth time. He grumbled, setting his phone facedown on the table before scraping a hand through his overgrown beard. It needed a trim, but he barely had the energy to drag his ass down to work or the bar. Reese and Mason's eyes bored into him from across the table.

"What?" Link snapped, taking a long gulp from his drink. It was a good night to get drunk and forget. He could live with the fact that his life sucked. But he couldn't stand the idea that Emma was out there hurting because of him.

"What's up with you lately?" Mason asked.

"I got papers from the lawyer last week. Emma signed over her portion of our dad's will to me. The shop's all mine." And it had cemented the shame over his choices. Did she do it because of what he said? Did she think she was any less Solomon's child? A pang tightened in his chest.

Reese and Mason exchanged glances.

"You must be really happy. You've wanted the garage for a while now." Reese scratched his chin.

Link finally had what he thought he wanted, and it left him somehow even more empty inside. What was wrong with him?

"You talk to her yet?" Reese asked.

"She won't answer or call me back." He'd told the guys he and Emma had had a falling out, but not the details.

Mason sighed and shook his head, his eyes snagging on a woman at the bar with neon-colored braids and a golden retriever by her side as she handed a pile of books over to Charli.

Since when did they let dogs in here? And when did any woman turn Mason's head? In the years Link had known the man, he'd never seen him date or look twice at a woman. Link had teased him about it, and Mason had always said he didn't have time for distractions raising his daughter by himself. Aspen always came first. Was he still grieving his wife after all these years? Would Link ever get over Emma?

"You really fucked up." Reese's laugh grated on his nerves.

"Thanks for pointing out the obvious."

"If you really loved Emma, you'd man up and go after her and grovel until she hears you out." Reese took a sip of his scotch.

Link's eyes widened, glancing around to see who was close enough to overhear their conversation. Thankfully, the alternative music drowned out most of the voices. He leaned in. "What the fuck are you talking about?"

"Oh, for fuck's sake, are you that stupid?" Mason grit out. A man of little words and even less patience.

Did everyone know about his feelings for her? Link grit his teeth, leaning forward. "I can't. What would my father say?"

"Not to be harsh, but does it matter?" Reese asked.

Link swallowed, emotion rising in his chest. Hope and grief. Longing and anger.

"It's not like you're blood-related. If you love her and she loves you, what's stopping you?" Reese asked.

"Look, man, I recognize the guilt that's eating you alive. You have the opportunity to fix this. You can make this right. Don't waste your chance like I did," Mason said, his eyes growing dark.

The man's wife and their tragic story was a wake-up call. Life was short. We never knew when our last day would be. His father's death should have taught him that.

His body trembled at the thought of leaving to go after her. How would it work? She was on the road seven months out of the year and recording for most of the others. There was no way he could run the garage and be with her too. "I can't leave everything I've spent my life working for and what my father built." Defeat bled from his tone.

"No one is saying you have to. You just need someone reliable and equally committed to the future of the company to oversee things while you're not there." Reese shrugged. "I wonder where we could find someone like that."

"You'd do that? Take on that responsibility?"

Reese nodded. "Of course. That place is home for me almost as much as it is for you. I grew up in that shop. Besides, I just want to see you happy, bro."

"I've been meaning to ask you anyways . . . You think you'd want to become partners? Maybe we could work out a buy-in?" Link asked.

Reese's eyes widened. "Seriously?"

"Absolutely."

Reese stuck out his hand to shake Link's. "Done."

He returned the gesture, sealing the deal.

"You gonna go get your girl?" Mason asked, finally pulling his eyes from the woman at the bar.

Link sighed. Fear twisted his gut, his lungs squeezing tight at the thought of leaving everything he'd known. But the idea of not making things right with Emma, of never telling her how much she truly meant to him, was worse. She deserved to know just how lovable every inch of her was inside and out. She deserved someone to take care of her, protect her, and cherish her. He could only hope it wasn't too late for him to apply for the position.

* * *

Link rushed through the door to his apartment and packed a bag while trying to get through to Emma once again. No answer. He skimmed down his list of contacts and typed out a quick message to a friend who'd be able to get him in touch with one of her bandmates. He needed to know where she was, so he could make this right.

Link opened his dresser drawer, his eye catching on the lone envelope sitting on his desk. His father's letter.

He picked it up, broke the seal and pulled out the paper. Two letters were inside. One had his name and the other had Emma's. *He left Emma a letter after all.* Shit. Link's cowardice had caused Emma even more pain. It was time he stopped being afraid.

Son,

If you're reading this, I've passed on. I know you're probably feeling pretty lost right now, and that's okay. But you're not alone. You still have Emma and the good people of Shattered Cove.

I wasn't raised to talk a lot about feelings or get involved with anyone else's business. In that, I think I failed you. I tried to lead by example, but I am human.

I came to realize something this year—something I want to talk to you about, but I'm waiting until the time is right. Till Emma comes home next time. It's thanks to Emma, actually. She pointed out how much you loved the garage. And I . . . I realized she was right. All your life, I thought I'd held you back somehow. You are my only son. The last piece left of your mother that I had. I think I didn't push you because I was selfish, wanting to keep you around.

But I've seen how much you love this old place, how it has become a part of you. I only ever meant it to be a stepping-stone, a way to support the two of you. That's why I kept control of the business so much and turned down your ideas for expansion and custom work. I didn't want anything holding you back for the moment you pulled your head out of your ass and saw what has been staring you in the face the whole time.

That girl won't wait around forever. I did my part not legally adopting her so that you could be with her when you realized Emma's been in love with you since you brought home that damn guitar. In our Asante tribe, adopted or related-by-marriage siblings cannot ever be together. You would be disgraced and possibly cut off from our family in Ghana.

I hope you never read this letter and I get the chance to talk to you about all this in person. But just in case, here it is.

I am so proud of the man you are today. You are the most precious thing on this earth to me besides my daughter. I've always been harder on you because I knew you needed the push to do things. Sometimes, you have to get out of your own way.

I love you, son, and I'll always be with you.

Take care of our girl,

Papa

.   .   .

He knew? Link collapsed onto the floor. His father knew—everyone knew. *Maybe I did too, but I was too afraid to face it.*

That was why his papa didn't adopt Emma? *Oh God. She thinks he didn't want her.* She needed to know. He had to get to her. He choked back sobs, wiping a few stray tears that got away. His father not only approved of his relationship with Emma, but he was proud of Link. God, how long had he waited to hear those words?

Link stood on shaky legs, urgency moving his limbs as he grabbed his bag and Emma's letter before heading out to the car he'd built from the ground up with his dad. The future of Shattered Cove Garage—rebuilt classics and custom work. The same vehicle he'd taken on the trip that changed his life with Emma. *I need to get to her.*

His phone pinged with a text message from his friend.

Looked like he was going back to where it started: Las Vegas. Only this time, what they had wouldn't stay there.

36

EMMA

Emma wiped the bead of sweat from her head as she entered the penthouse suite. Loud, hypnotic music thrummed through the room as she walked along the hallway, her stomach twisting at the memories of the last time she had been in this very suite here in Las Vegas. Her body was still amped up from the show they'd just played, her heart thudding. She went straight for the bar set up in the corner, pushing past some scantily clad groupies surrounding her bandmates and a few guys.

"You made it!" Callie yelled louder than necessary. She rubbed some of the white powder from her nose and reached for the bottle of vodka from Emma's hand. "Allow me." She poured an inch into the glass.

Emma picked it up and downed it in one gulp, relishing the burn. She'd become accustomed to it this month. She grabbed the vodka back from Callie, opting to drink straight from the container this time.

"Yes, girl! That's what I'm talking about. Let's celebrate! You guys totally rocked that show."

Emma squinted as she lowered the bottle to take a breath. They'd done well for being down one man.

Geo wouldn't talk to her. The prison had turned her away because she wasn't on his visitors list. Promising backstage passes to the guard had gotten a message through to Geo, but he'd still refused to see her.

Emma closed her eyes at the rising pain. She'd come straight from the prison to the show. Emma wanted to be alone, but the penthouse was filled with people. Emma surveyed the room. Asher's head tipped back on the couch, his mouth slack as another guy's head bobbed up and down between his thighs.

Ravi snorted one of the lines of cocaine spread out over the glass table Link had fucked her on.

The pungent smell of weed enveloped her as a man she didn't know approached her with a wolfish grin. He was attractive—dark hair, green eyes. *Not Link.*

He offered her a joint. "Hey, beautiful."

She opened her mouth to reply, but Nicky beat her to it. "Get out of here with that, man. Emma doesn't do that shit."

Green eyes winked at her, and he strolled away like he didn't have a care in the world. Her eyes darted to the drugs on the table. She'd never let something strip her control like that.

"You okay, babe?" Nicky asked.

She nodded, forcing a smile. "Yeah. Of course." She just needed to capture some of that control for herself. Needed to erase the memories from this room. But it was like finally sleeping with Link had embedded him in every cell of hers. She couldn't be rid of him no matter how hard she tried. And without him, the grief from her father was suffocating. She was a shell of who she'd been before. Her restraint waned and shattered. The healing cuts on her wrist under the leather bracelet were evidence of that—along with the ones on her thighs from when those hadn't been enough. Asher never thought to look there.

She walked around in a heavy cloud. The hazy grey was getting dimmer. Cold tendrils of darkness cinched around her ankles, tugging her down. She needed to breathe. To escape. To get ahead of the pain bubbling up, leaking through the cracks like thick oil.

Leo disappeared into one of the rooms with two women. Maybe he had the right idea. Maybe she needed to fuck Link out of her system. It obviously had worked for Link. She turned to Callie, who was chatting with another blonde, running her finger over her arm suggestively.

The phone in her back pocket vibrated. She pulled it out. *Link.* Again. The pain she kept buried inched towards the surface, making the room spin. Tears burned her eyes. Emotion clawed its way up the back of her throat. Her hand trembled as she squeezed it. She shut the phone off and tucked it into the back of her pants once more.

The music switched to "Dear Agony" by Breaking Benjamin. The heavy drums and guitar made her gasp in a breath. Her hand reached out to Callie's. Both women turned to look at her.

Emma nodded towards the bedrooms, grasping for escape. There were a million reasons she shouldn't be doing this, but she pushed them away with a vengeance. She didn't want to think because thinking led to remembering and remembering led to pain.

Callie's mouth turned into an all-out grin as she bent and whispered something into the blonde's ear. Blondie nodded and licked her lips, her eyes raking over Emma. She linked her arm into Emma's, leading her and the other woman to a vacant bedroom. Emma shut the door. Callie's mouth peppered kisses up her neck, to her jaw, inching closer to Emma's lips. She wasted no time tugging off Emma's black T-shirt. Emma lifted the material from her body, still holding the bottle of vodka. Emma's stomach pitched. This felt wrong.

She turned her head before Callie's lips could mold to hers. Emma pushed Callie's shoulder back and nodded to the other woman in the room. Blondie came forward, pulling Callie into a kiss as they stripped each other's clothes off, piece by piece. Callie kept turning to check on Emma, as if to make sure she had her attention.

Emma's stomach twisted as she downed more vodka, until she had no choice but to take a breath. This was going to be a mistake. But she didn't care. If it saved her from one more moment of this agony, she'd pay the price.

Callie unhooked her bra, running her fingers over her hard, pink nipples. She was beautiful, available, and more importantly, wanted Emma. Too bad Emma only fell for people who couldn't love her back. What did that say about her?

She took another gulp of the half-empty bottle of vodka, pushing away the question. The room spun as she swayed forward. Blondie and Callie had moved to the bed, pleasuring each other. Callie crooked her finger to Emma.

Stumbling forward, Emma placed one leaden foot in front of the other. Everything inside her screamed for her not to do it. The music blared from the built-in speakers in the penthouse. The two women stared at her, no doubt waiting to bring her multiple orgasms. She'd just played their best show ever. And she felt . . . nothing. Nothing but pain. Nothing but a squeezing pressure on her body, slowly suffocating her. Her grey existence had turned into black despair. Darkness crawled beneath her skin, spreading out in inky despair, leaching the life from her, clawing her wide open and exposing the oily black sludge she'd buried deep within.

No. She shook her head, running into the bathroom and stumbling into the sink. The vodka bottle crashed onto the marble floor. She closed the door, locking it before she slid to the ground. Crimson droplets of blood ran down her arm. But she couldn't feel it. Emma tore off her leather cuff and picked up a shard of glass as she gulped in a breath. She couldn't *feel* anything anymore but the sinking sense of being pulled under.

Placing the broken bottle against her arm, she didn't hesitate. She sliced into her flesh. *Nothing.* Again, but this time deeper. Just a hint of a burn reached her senses but no rush.

She screamed, her tears bursting through the dam. All the years of pain and hurt, every emotion she'd stuffed down exploded to the surface like a volcano erupting and sending searing hot agony bursting from her.

Her mother walking away, leaving her.

Her father abandoning her before she was even born.

Solomon, the man who she'd thought had loved her like a daughter, storing those adoption papers for her to find someday.

Maybe it was better he hadn't left a note for her. What if he confirmed she'd disappointed him? Hot tears poured down her cheeks like an ocean of regret. Link's face flashed in her mind. The anger, the disgust at what they'd done. Why was she so unlovable? *I hate me too.*

It was too much. She needed to get control of the pain. Her arm rose and fell. She slashed it before switching to the other arm. Digging for the relief buried deep within her wrists. But the euphoric feeling didn't come. Her arms throbbed—pain without the relief. She looked down and gasped. They were both sticky with warm, red blood dripping, a stark contrast to the white marble. Her head pounded, growing fuzzy. The room spun. She was so tired—exhausted from years of pretending she was okay.

She lay down. The cold floor sunk into her skin. A chill settled deep into her bones.

The man over the speakers was begging agony to let him go as he suffered ever so slowly. It was like he knew this feeling—this utter exhaustion from just simply having to breathe. She needed one moment where she was free. Like how Link had made her feel the last time they were here.

Emma sobbed harder. Saltwater melded with blood. There was so much of it. She should care. She should do something. Go get help. But why? What was the point when she'd have to feel all this hurt again? Everyone was better off without her.

She'd cut to feel, to grasp a thread of control over the emotional pain, trading it for physical. Instead, she was left numb and cold. Darkness clouded her vision. Nausea rolled in her stomach. Panic jolted through her. She didn't want to die alone. Didn't want this to be the end. But she was so tired. The door was so far away. She'd exchanged her grey existence for the darkness after all—those black tentacles dragging her below the surface. She'd lost the fight within.

"I'm sorry," she whispered. Sorry for not being enough. Sorry for being born.

She closed her eyes, taking one last ragged breath before surrendering to the darkness as it overpowered her, burying her in frigid, lonely hopelessness.

37

LINK

Link had to call Nicky's direct line and wait to get approval to be escorted to the penthouse suite. Music throbbed through the elevator before the doors even opened. He gave a nod to the bellhop and walked through the hallway to the room he and Emma had shared all those weeks ago. The room smelled like sex and pot. Barely clothed women danced on furniture. One couple was having sex on one of the couches, while others hunched over the glass table he'd taken Emma on, snorting thin white lines.

Jesus Christ. Where is Emma? His gaze snagged on Nicky's. He was smoking a blunt while a woman was giving him a lap dance.

"Where is she?" Link shouted over the music.

Nicky's bloodshot eyes met his, hazy and unfocused. Nicky patted the woman's hip, urging her to move off him before he stood, setting his oversized joint in a vase turned ashtray. "Look, she's had a rough day, and I don't want to add to that. The only reason I'm letting you in here is because you said you were gonna make things right with our princess."

Link couldn't help the jealousy that boiled in his gut, curling up his limbs. His chest puffed out. "Where is she?" he repeated.

Nicky's eyes scanned the room. "I saw her walk off with Callie. Maybe you'd better wait here." He headed towards one of the bedroom doors.

"No fucking way," Link growled, keeping to his side. Was she with someone else already?

"I mean it, man. Maybe you'd better stay here." Nicky lifted his hand.

"Just open the fucking door!" Link shouted.

Nicky twisted the knob, and Link's breath clogged in his throat. A dark-haired naked woman lay over another, kissing her. Link's body locked up, pain and regret knocking a hole in his chest.

"Where's Emma?" Nicky asked.

Was he so high he was blind?

The dark-haired woman sat, eyes widening before she drew a blanket over her exposed body. The blonde turned, mouth agape and eyes wide.

Not Emma.

The relief that skated through his body was like ice water on a hot day.

"She went to the bathroom a while ago," Callie answered, running her hands through her hair.

Link's attention darted to the closed door to his left. He tried the handle, but it was locked. "Emma?"

No answer.

"Emma, open the door." He jiggled the handle.

She wasn't answering, at least not loud enough that he could hear over the music. Worry cinched his gut. Had she done some of the drugs? Was she in danger?

"If you don't open this door, I'm gonna break it down!" Link shouted.

Nicky's hand landed on his shoulder. "Dude, calm down. I guess she doesn't want to talk to you."

Link roared, backing up to ram the door, ignoring Nicky. Something was wrong. He ran, jamming his shoulder against the door, once, twice. Wood splintered on the marble floor as pain radiated through his arm. But the sight that met his eyes stole his breath, making his heart stutter. His ears rang as fear like he'd never known crashed over him, pulling him under.

"Oh, fuck!" Nicky shouted, wrenching him out of his shock.

Link didn't think. He moved. There was so much blood and broken glass. Crimson stained her arms, stomach, and lap, pooling under her limp form curled on the cold ground.

He lifted her into his arms, seeking out the source of her injuries. Red slashes in all directions crisscrossed her wrists and up her forearms. He laid her back down gently to pull off his T-shirt before ripping it. "Call an ambulance!"

"On the way," Nicky said, dropping next to him.

The music cut off as the rest of Emma's bandmates crowded in the small room. Someone gasped.

"Is she breathing?" Nicky asked, checking her pulse for himself. His worried gaze met Link's, his mouth forming a grim line. "It's there, but it's faint."

"Put pressure on the wounds," Link directed, tearing strips from his shirt.

"Oh my God!" Callie screamed.

"Get these people out of here!" Asher yelled at her.

Link held the strip to one of her arms. Nicky moved, so he could tie it on tightly. They did the same with her other arm.

Link picked her up, his heart racing, adrenaline coursing

through his body. "Hold on, little bird. Just fucking hold on." He kissed her cheek, cool to the touch. Her pale skin was now grey and sickly.

How could he not see she was hurting so much? Was this because of him? He never got to tell her how much he loved her. Regrets and fear twisted and tumbled inside with a hurricane of emotions as he carried the woman he loved towards the elevator, past a few lagging partygoers.

It opened, and four paramedics climbed out with a gurney.

"What happened?" one of them asked.

He laid her down, not wanting to let her go. What if this was the last time he got to hold her? "Her wrists are cut." The words choked out of him. *Emma tried to kill herself.* He backed away, knowing he had to move if he wanted her to have a fighting chance.

"Has she taken any drugs or medications?" The paramedic looked up at him as two others attended to Emma's seemingly lifeless body.

"I don't know." He turned to Nicky.

"She doesn't do drugs. She had a lot of vodka though."

Questions drowned into background noise as one of the machines started to beep.

"She's going into cardiac arrest."

They pushed the gurney onto the elevator, tapping the buttons. Link moved to get on as one of them opened a bag and took out paddles.

"Clear!"

Emma's body jolted on the gurney as a paramedic pushed his chest. "Sir, you can't come with us."

"She's my life."

"We have to go if you want her to live."

He staggered back. The doors closed as Emma's body jolted for a second time. *No. No, no, no, no, no.* Not her. He couldn't survive without her. He hadn't even told her he loved her yet.

After a few moments, Nicky tapped the button, calling the elevator back. He handed Link a shirt. Link took it numbly before pulling it over his head. He stared at his hands, covered in Emma's blood. *Why didn't I see she needed help?*

Flashes of their conversations assaulted him. Moments when Emma had mentioned this life wasn't all it was cracked up to be. Asking him to come with her. Hinting at something and then pulling back. He should have pushed. He should have gone with her. He should have . . . it didn't matter. It was too late.

A hard slap met his back, returning him to the present.

"Let's go," Nicky said, heading onto the waiting elevator. Had Emma died in here?

The rest of the bandmates climbed on. Callie was the last one, hugging her arms into herself.

"You stay here," Asher snapped.

Her tear-filled eyes widened. "What? Why? As the manager, I need to be there. It's my job to make sure you guys are taken care of."

What?

"And you failed!" Asher screamed.

Nicky put a hand on his chest as if holding him back. "Calm down."

"You didn't know either! It's not my fault!" Her shrill voice grated on his ears. The woman he loved's life hung in the balance, and these idiots were still fighting. "Get the fuck in here and let's go!" he boomed.

Callie darted inside as Leo hit the button for the doors to close.

They rode down in silence except for Callie's sniffling.

His hands fisted at his side, his skin tight from the dried blood. Their last conversation played on repeat in his head. A sinking feeling told him it was already too late.

I've lost her.

38

EMMA

Cold, sterile air burned Emma's nose as she blinked her eyes open. A white ceiling. Lights and machines hung above her. Hospital. *Why am I in a hospital?* She tried to sit, immediately regretting the action. *Why does my chest feel like I was crushed by a water buffalo?* She lifted her throbbing arms, covered in gauze. Memories flooded over her. The broken bottle. The blood. Link's voice. She closed her eyes as tears welled up and poured out of her. She didn't even try to hide them this time. She looked around the empty room, finding a call button for the nurse.

A few moments later, a young RN walked in with a careful smile and kind eyes. "How are you feeling, Miss Sterling?" She grabbed a cup with a straw before bringing it to Emma's lips.

Emma sipped the cool water, blinking through tears. "I'm sorry."

The nurse's eyebrows drew together as she nodded. "I'm your nurse, Melanie. I'm just going to take your vitals, and then I'll go get the doctor. Okay?"

Emma nodded.

Melanie pulled open a laptop and recorded whatever she needed to as Emma allowed herself to be prodded.

"How long have I been here?" Emma asked, her voice hoarse.

The nurse checked her watch. "Since about midnight last night, so coming up on fifteen hours." *The guys must be so worried. Did they call Link?* Panic gripped her already aching chest. Nausea rolled in her belly.

When the nurse was done, a grey-haired doctor walked in, knocking on the open door. Melanie gave him a full-on smile as she positioned the hospital bed up.

"How's our patient?" the doctor asked.

"She just woke a few minutes ago. Vitals are good," Melanie answered.

He turned his attention to Emma, his blue eyes assessing her. "Hello, Emma. I'm Doctor O'Malley."

"Hi," Emma answered feebly.

"You gave us quite the scare, you know?" He took a seat on the round stool as he crossed his arms at the side of her bed.

"Sorry."

"Your heart stopped twice on the way to the hospital," he said without emotion.

She gasped. She'd died?

"Was it everything you'd hoped it would be?" he asked.

She whipped her head to look at him, stunned by his question. "I-I wasn't—that's not . . . I didn't want to kill myself."

He kept his gaze on hers and remained silent.

"I just wanted the pain to stop. Sometimes I cut to help relieve it. I guess I took it too far this time," Emma admitted, looking down, ashamed.

"I did see the healed wounds from before. You'll be lucky to not have nerve damage this time." He motioned to her bandaged arms.

I just wanted the pain to stop. Just needed to fight off the darkness a little longer.

"I believe you—that you didn't intend to end your life. But what you did could have killed you if your boyfriend hadn't gotten to you when he did."

Boyfriend? He must mean one of the band. Oh God! Who had to find me like that? How could I have done that to them?

"Since you're over eighteen, I cannot hold you against your will if it wasn't intentional. But I have to do an assessment to make sure you don't still pose a risk to yourself. Okay?" the doctor asked.

Emma nodded.

He asked her a list of questions, and she answered truthfully. A heavy weight was bearing down on her; she was still lost in a cloud of grey, still numb inside.

"I'd like you to remain here for observation for the day at least. You lost a lot of blood, and that took a toll on your heart," O'Malley said.

Emma nodded. *God, how selfish could I be? What would Link think? We just lost Dad, and now this. I've been so selfish.*

"You know, it is extremely valid for you to want the pain to end."

Emma looked up at the doctor.

"I don't know your story, but I don't blame you for wanting to end your pain," the doctor continued.

"You don't?" she asked, astonished.

He shook his head. "I find it extremely human of you."

She sighed, some of the weight on her shoulders lifting.

"But if we lost you, we'd lose everything you were going to accomplish. And every life that was supposed to be touched by you wouldn't be. You are important. So are all the things you will create and the lives you will change."

Tears streamed down her cheeks once again. Why was she crying over everything all of a sudden? It was like a dam had burst forth, and she couldn't get it closed again.

"But none of that will happen if your life ends," he finished.

Emma licked her lips, tasting her salty tears. "Thank you."

The doctor nodded and then motioned to the nurse still standing on the other side of the room.

Melanie handed Emma a few pamphlets.

"These are a few of the best rehabilitation centers in the country for people who self-harm. My professional advice is to go and get help," Dr. O'Malley said, rising from the chair.

Realization hit. She'd sworn not to become addicted to something that could control her life. Sworn she would be the one to hold the power. She'd wielded a razor blade, mutilating her own skin in an attempt to grasp just a piece of that illusive control. But it had all been a lie. It was all an illusion of red.

"I'll think about it," she promised.

"Your boyfriend is outside. Should we send him in?"

Emma nodded, preparing herself to face one of her angry bandmates.

"You've got a whole group of people here for you who've been hounding the nurses for updates. You've got a lot to live for," he said before he left.

Melanie followed him out.

Emma closed her eyes, trying to take a deep breath, but her chest ached as it stretched from her attempt. She winced.

"Emma?"

Her eyes shot open. Link walked in, eyes bloodshot and blurry with tears. *What is he doing here?*

He took the seat next to her, leaning in. "Why? Why didn't you tell me?"

A sob burst from her. Pain radiated in her chest. "It was an accident. I didn't mean for it to go that far."

He placed a hand over her cheek, using his thumb to wipe the tears away. "What were you trying to do?"

She couldn't bear to see the disappointment in his eyes. Instead, she stared at his wrist. There was no hiding this from him anymore. He was here for Christ's sake. But keeping the truth buried inside for so long made it hard to find the words. How many times had she swallowed the confession down?

His thumb rubbed soft circles on her collarbone as he waited patiently.

She owed him this much. "Sometimes, I cut myself because it makes me feel more in control of the emotional pain. And it helps me feel something besides numb."

He didn't say anything, so she glanced at him.

One tear had fallen over each side of his face, leaving a wet trail down his brown cheeks before disappearing into his beard. "How long?"

She swallowed. "Since I was a teenager."

"How could I not see how much you were hurting?" His voice was raw.

"Because I didn't want you to. I'm really good at pretending."

"Why would you hide that from me?" He trembled.

"I hide it from everyone. Well . . . I mean, Dad knew. I think he saw the marks one time."

His hands dropped to hers. "Dad knew?"

"He never really said anything directly, but he took me to counseling for more than a year."

His brows drew together. "I remember that. I thought it was because of your mom."

She shook her head.

"The bracelet. That's why you're always wearing it," he said, his eyes lighting with realization.

"I had gone five years without relapsing before Dad . . . well . . . and then lately it's been . . . hard," she admitted. After the hell she'd put him through, he deserved answers.

"This is my fault."

"No!" Her stern voice even caused her surprise. She lifted her arm to his cheek this time, locking eyes with Link. "This was in no way your fault. I made these decisions. I wasn't trying to . . . end my life . . . just the pain."

He tipped his forehead to meet hers. His sweet breath was tinged with hints of coffee.

"When I . . . when I cut myself, it didn't hurt inside as much."

"Em—" He choked. "When I found you, I thought—I thought I was too late."

She pulled back. "*You* found me?"

He nodded grimly. "I came to tell you I was so wrong. That I love you. And I want you in my life. I'll give up the shop. We can go on the road together. I'll be there for you. Take care of you."

Her heart thundered in her chest. Was Link saying what she thought he was saying? "You love me?"

"Yes."

"Like love me, love me? Or . . .?"

He kissed her forehead. "I loved you like a sister." His lips melded over her mouth, his kiss resuscitating her body, as if breathing life and color back into her world. "And now I love you with every fiber in my body. You're part of me. What I feel for you, I've never felt for another person."

She sucked in a sharp breath, her mind spinning with the revelation. She'd hoped for so long, and now he was giving her the words she needed to hear. "You came here to tell me you loved me and were coming on the road with me?" she clarified, still not able to believe it.

Hesitation flashed in his eyes.

"What?"

"I came here to tell you I loved you. But now I see how much you need me."

Oh. He's giving up the garage to take care of me? "That garage is your passion. It's a part of you. I didn't see it before, but you can't abandon your dreams for me. It's Dad's legacy."

"You're more important," he said.

She took a deep breath, eyes dropping to the bed before she scooted over to one side, flinching through the pain.

"You okay? Do you need me to get the nurse?" he asked, concern marring his features.

"I need you to lie with me."

"Won't I hurt you?"

She shook her head. "Just don't touch my arms."

He slid onto the bed, scooting his arm under her neck and situating himself on the tiny mattress, so as not to squish her. She lay against him, inhaling his scent as comfort wafted over her. Her eyelids grew heavy as she snuggled into his chest, listening to his heartbeat.

"We'll get through this together," he promised, his voice rumbling.

She closed her eyes, savoring this moment. But guilt tainted her happiness at having Link here with her.

He pulled out his phone. "Gotta text Nicky and let the guys know how you're doing. They've been here all night with me. Callie too."

Emma didn't respond, exhaustion pulling her under into a deep sleep.

. . .

Wind whipped across Emma's face, growing stronger. Cold water lapped at her feet as she stood in the shallow waters of the grey ocean. Her papa stood across from her on the shore. Next to him were her mother and Link.

She'd been here before.

"Papa? Mom?" She glanced between her mother and Solomon.

Her mother shook her head. "I'm so sorry, Emma." She turned around and walked away.

A piece of Emma could understand the pain in her mother's eyes and the choices she'd made. She wasn't ready to forgive her yet, but now she could empathize with the struggle for control over an addiction.

Emma took a step forward, but the water was deeper somehow, coming up to her waist.

Emma turned her attention onto her papa. "I love you, Papa. Thank you for everything you've done for me. I'll always keep you in my heart. I'm sorry if I ever disappointed you."

Her father gave her a sad smile. "Read the letter."

"What letter?" She stepped forward only to be sucked under the water. She kicked and struggled to the surface, sucking in a gasp of air.

Her father was gone, leaving only Link at the shore. Her arms throbbed, blood pouring from them, coloring the water red as they grew tired. No matter how hard she fought, the shore got farther and farther away. She screamed for Link.

Only this time, he ran towards her. His hand reached out for her.

"Link!"

"I've got you. I'm coming with you," he said as a big wave crashed over them, sucking them under. Emma broke the surface, her arms and legs on fire. Link was nowhere to be found.

"Link!" She searched the dark water below, diving deeper. He was gone, sucked under, and it was all her fault.

. . .

Her arms became lead weights, sinking her lower. She screamed for him, but no sound came out.

He'd come to save her, and instead, she'd ended up dragging him down too.

39

EMMA

Emma's eyes opened as she sucked in a breath of air untainted by saltwater. Link stirred beside her. He was here, safe by her side. It was only a dream. Or was it a warning? He was willing to give up the thing most precious to be there for her. But at what cost? That wasn't an equal relationship. She didn't want him to have to take care of her or worry that he would break her. He'd resent her for that codependency eventually. Witnessing Remy's and Jasmine's and even Charli's relationships, she'd learned that what makes a relationship really work was that give-and-take. The partnership of equals. It wasn't his job to take on the responsibility of her mental health. That would be unfair—and unhealthy. And as much as they both wished, it wasn't him who could fix her. Her emotional wounds were deep. Here in his arms, she was safe and belonged. But she still carried an emptiness. A crack with a hole she'd tried to fill with pain, and sex, and music. Was this the same hole her mother had tried to fix with drugs? Why didn't she ever get help? *Why haven't I?*

The doctor's words ran through her mind. Her pain was

valid. And she needed help Link couldn't give. *I have to love myself before I can love him the way he deserves to be loved and allow him to love me back.*

Emma's eyes darted to the plastic bag on the small table by her bed. The black skinny jeans she'd been wearing and the white bra, covered in blood, lay inside, along with her phone. She opened it, searching for her cell. Instead, her fingers caught on a folded paper. Pulling out the letter with her father's handwriting, she looked over at Link's sleeping form. *How is this possible? Did Link bring it? Where did it come from?*

Emma unfolded it carefully. Her heart stuttered at the familiar scrawl.

My sweet Emma,

My daughter, I'm guessing it's been a while since my passing that you're reading this. You always did things in your own time, dancing through life to your own beat. You have this beautiful, magnetic energy that attracts everyone around you.

You've always felt so deeply. So, I know you've probably taken my passing hard. I wish I could be there to see the moment when you and Link finally give in to the sparks between you—the day you walk down the aisle and promise your lives to each other. Know that I'll always be watching. And I'll be cheering for you. I'm so proud of you. You brought so much joy to my life. I can never thank you enough.

You never asked, and I never wanted to disturb the growth you'd made, so I kept this to myself. But I feel this is my last chance to tell you what happened the day your mother left. After she said she was leaving and taking you with her, I knew I could never let that happen. She was in no shape to take care of herself, let alone a child. So, I told her if she really wanted what was best for you, she would walk out that door alone. And I would take care of you until she got help and could be the mother you needed. She had tears in her eyes as she agreed. She left you with me so you could have the best chance at life. She knew she would only take you down with her. The reason she didn't come to say goodbye is so she wouldn't change her mind. I offered to help her into a rehab, but she said she wasn't ready.

Sometimes staying is the worst thing a parent can do for a child. And sometimes leaving is the best act of love someone can give you.

You are the most exceptional woman I know. You have so much strength and creativity. I saw your shine long before you became a star to the world. You never stop chasing your dreams and what you want in this life. Keep fighting, baby girl.

And take care of our boy. Sometimes he needs protecting too.

Love, your papa

Droplets fell onto the page. Tears streamed down her face as she tried to memorize each word he'd crafted for her, as she digested all he'd written. Her mother had abandoned her, but had it been the right thing to do? *Yes.* She sucked in a ragged breath. A hurricane of emotions pelted her from the inside out.

"The letter was inside the envelope the lawyer gave me. There was one for me and you inside. I'm sorry I didn't open it right away." Link's voice made her turn to look at him.

"He really did think of me as his daughter?"

"He didn't adopt you because he knew I loved you."

Her brows drew together in confusion. "You mean he knew *I* loved *you*."

Link shook his head. "That's why I distanced myself from you. Knew I'd just hold you back from your dreams. And I figured he'd be so angry that I had feelings for you."

"We've wasted so much time assuming." She shook her head.

"From here on out, we talk, okay? You tell me what you're feeling and what you need. And I'll be right here for you."

God, why did he have to be so perfect?

Take care of our boy. Sometimes he needs protecting too.

"You know, for so long I thought that the piece of me that was missing was you." She stared into his eyes, willing him to understand. "It turns out you were just a temporary fix."

Sometimes leaving is the best act of love.

"What are you saying?" He swiped the hair that fell into her face, tucking it behind her ear.

"I need to go away for a bit. I need to get help."

His eyes narrowed, but he nodded. "Anything you need. Do you want me to take you somewhere?"

She shook her head. "You can't give up the shop for me."

"But—"

"I'm going away—alone. I don't know how long I'll be gone . . . I mean, I don't expect you to wait for me." Her gaze darted to the side of the room. Of course, when they finally got together, her problems would ruin it.

His finger tipped her chin to force her to look at him once again. "I'll wait forever for you. Whatever you need. I mean it. You get the help you need."

She swallowed, leaning in before taking one long, deep kiss. He was so gentle with her, cupping the sides of her face, stroking her cheek with his thumb like he was trying to memorize every sensation of her as well.

He was everything. But sometimes, even that wasn't enough. The realization that she could have all the purest love in the world but still be damaged was scary. Would she always be this way—broken? Her physical injuries would heal in time, but would her heart? What about the festering wound from her mother's abandonment? Would she ever be whole?

Link's tongue slid into her mouth, the sensation stirring up want and desire, but above all, a love like she'd never known, finally given the permission to be freed. She whimpered, pressing her body closer to his despite the bite of pain. He pulled back, leaving her breathless and wanting.

"You'll fly free one day soon, little bird," Link said, still cupping her face in his big, calloused hands. His black eyes focused on hers, love shining brightly from their depths as if the man had swallowed the sun.

What have I done to deserve the love of this man?

"How do you know?" she asked, her voice breaking.

Link's thumbs rubbed over her cheekbones, his intense focus swallowing her up. "That's why I call you little bird; because you were meant to fly. And I'll be here ready to cheer you on every step of the way and to give you a soft place to land when you need to rest."

40

EMMA

1 MONTH LATER

Emma relaxed into the couch in her therapist, Dr. Ruby's office. The woman sat across from her in a pink pencil skirt and white blouse with gold bracelets dangling from her wrists. Her amber eyes locked on Emma's in rapt attention. Dr. Ruby tucked a dark strand of hair behind her ear, her pink nail polish contrasting her warm ochre skin.

She'd gotten access to her phone for an hour that morning and had taken a first glimpse at the media storm raging with different assumptions as to why she'd been admitted to the hospital. Callie was no longer working with them. The label had deemed her a liability after the truth of what happened that night and the fact that she had been the one to arrange suppliers for most of the drugs had come to light. Her new manager and the label's PR company were taking care of that mess and were not too happy with having to delay yet another round of concerts. Her career was hanging on by a thread. But instead, she'd focused on the texts waiting in her inbox from Link.

Link: *Miss you, beautiful. Spend my days thinking about you and hoping you're doing better. I love you, little bird. Can't wait to have you in my arms again.*

She smiled. She wanted that, but only if it was truly the best thing for him too. As long as she didn't bring him down.

"Why don't we talk about your father's letter today?" Dr. Ruby suggested.

Emma picked up the yellow pillow with red tassels by her side, running the threads through her fingers as she agreed. "What do you want to know?"

"I've read it, like you requested." She handed it back to Emma.

Emma folded it neatly and slipped it into the pocket of her hoodie.

"I'd like to know what you thought of what he said about your mother."

Emma took a deep breath as rejection and old emotions rose to the surface, tinted in anger. "I feel confused. Angry. Rejected. But more so like I don't know how to feel anymore."

"If your mother had taken you with her, what do you think your life would have been like?" Dr. Ruby asked.

Broken memories of drug dens and a dirty apartment without power or clean water flashed through her mind. "I wouldn't have been safe or cared for most likely."

"Having an adult point of view to look at a situation can help in many cases, but it doesn't negate the emotions and the hurt caused by those actions when you were a child. Tell me about the but."

"The what?"

"When you tell yourself you'd be unsafe if your mother had taken you with her—so you were better off with her leaving—what is the 'but if only' that pops into your head? What is the internal argument that comes to your mind?"

Emma took a sip of water from the bottle before setting it back on the coffee table between them. "But if she had taken me, maybe I could have saved her. Given her a reason to get clean if she saw how much I was hurting from her decisions."

Dr. Ruby was silent for a moment as if letting Emma's confession ruminate. "That is a lot of responsibility to put on yourself as a child."

Emma nodded.

"You told me you have nieces and nephews. Do you believe it is their responsibility to save their parents?"

"No." Emma shook her head at the absurd statement. The therapist remained quiet.

"I understand it isn't logical. I just thought that maybe if I'd been good enough, I could have helped her."

"It is *never* the child's responsibility to take care of their parent or caregiver. You evolved into that role as a way of survival, your basic evolutionary instincts in order to make the best out of an exceptionally difficult situation." Her doctor leaned back in the yellow chair. "I want you to close your eyes."

Emma did as she instructed.

"Take a deep breath and imagine you as a child when you felt most scared and vulnerable," Dr. Ruby guided.

Emma fought the surge of emotion that rose in her chest, clogging her throat.

"Don't hold back. Just take time in this safe space to feel what you couldn't back then."

Tears escaped Emma's closed lids at the image her mind painted of her so lonely and scared, worrying about how many days her mother would be gone this time and when she was going to have food.

"Now, I want you to imagine you are there as you are now

with your inner child. Give her a hug and tell her all the things you needed to be told back then. Comfort her."

Emma imagined stepping in front of a large mirror. Instead of her reflection, it was her as a child. Dirty smudges stained her pale skin. Dark bruises marked her sunken eyes, rounded with fear as she hugged her bony arms to her too-skinny body. Emma kneeled, getting on her level. She reached through the glass, wrapping the child in a tight hug. *It's going to be okay. Soon you will be taken in by the best man in the world and his son. They will love you and protect you, and you will never go hungry again. You will be loved.* The child relaxed into her, letting out sobs.

Emma opened her eyes and gasped.

Her therapist handed her a box of tissues. "How do you feel now?"

"Emotional. Sad. But also relieved."

"Whenever you hear that inner voice trying to cast blame on you for your mother's choices, I want you to do the same exercise. Remind yourself of how vulnerable you were as a child in that difficult situation."

"Okay."

"How have the urges to self-harm been?" Dr. Ruby was always straightforward but kind in her approach.

"It's . . . less. The medication I've been taking is helping me have more good days than bad."

She nodded and scribbled something on a pad of paper in front of her. "How are you sleeping?"

"Better."

"Do you feel rested when you wake up?" Dr. Ruby's attention focused back on Emma.

"Yes . . . but how long will this take? To feel whole?" Emma asked.

Her mental health was the priority, but her band couldn't

wait too long before they'd have to make some decisions. The label company wouldn't hold off forever. The new manager had negotiated an extra thirty days off for Emma's rehab. But she wasn't feeling halfway there yet.

Dr. Ruby set her paper and pen on the coffee table between them and leaned forward. "Healing is not linear. You can have everything going right in your life, be surrounded by people who love and care about you, and yet still have the urge to harm yourself."

Emma's stomach sank. "Don't I just need to learn to love myself? Isn't that the key?"

Her therapist offered her a sympathetic smile. "Loving yourself is vital to your healing and to living a happy and enriched life, but unfortunately it isn't a cure-all. Love doesn't heal all wounds completely. You will always have scars from your childhood trauma. You may feel broken at times. But there is beauty that comes from pain. Your scars tell a story. And you have an audience."

"Will it always hurt this bad?" Emma asked.

"No. And yes. You may go years with everything being better. You may even come to a point where you feel almost completely healed. But some event in your life may trigger things for you, or your depression may spike, and you'll go through a difficult period. You will have to learn how to live with and manage your depression. You will have to use the outlets we discussed when the urge to cut happens: distracting yourself, using other sensations, talking to your accountability partner or a therapist." Dr. Ruby sat back to take a sip of water before she continued. "You have to grieve your losses. The loss of your childhood. Your mother. Your biological father. And the man you view as your father . . . this will take conscious effort from you. A choice you make every day to not stuff down feelings that are uncomfortable for you. That will drastically reduce your urge to harm yourself."

Emma took a deep breath, crossing her arms in front of her as she digested this. She was disappointed that she would never be "normal" and intimidated by the work ahead of her. But Dr. Ruby was right; if she committed to this healing, she had a whole audience of young men and women who could hear her story. What if she could save just one person from ending up devastated on the bathroom floor, bleeding to death all alone?

No matter what it took or how long, she'd get through this. She had to because she had people counting on her.

The image of her inner child flashed to the forefront of her mind. *I'm doing this for me. I may not have had the power to save my mother, but I can save myself.*

41

LINK

ANOTHER MONTH LATER.

Link wiped the sweat from his brow as he closed the hood of the Chevelle. It had needed a tune-up, and his hands had itched for something to keep them busy. He'd already been to the gym and had dinner. But sitting alone in his house watching mindless television wasn't enough to keep his mind from worrying over Emma.

He'd had no contact with her since she'd left the hospital and he and her bandmates had driven her to the airport. She was somewhere in California at a rehab center that looked more like a spa from the pamphlet he'd glanced at and then the website he'd scoured for hours.

Would she come back after all this was done? Even if she did, how would they work things out? She was going to be on tour for seven months out of the year, and she'd told him she wouldn't let him give up the shop.

The rumble of a motorcycle got closer. His stomach flipped. Every single time he heard that sound he got his hopes up that it was Emma, but it never was.

He wiped his hands on one of the rags as he leaned

against the steel table in his garage. Sure enough, the motorcycle passed by. He couldn't even bother to look. He picked up the bottle of beer, gulped it down and wiped his mouth before washing the rest of the oil from his hands in the sink. He crossed his arms over his chest, staring at the front bumper of the Chevelle. Memories of working on this very car after it had been towed into his father's garage, half-rusted and in need of a total restoration, blinked through his mind like an old television reel. He'd learned so much from the vehicle. And it held so many precious memories in it.

"Thinking hard over there."

Link's gaze whipped up. Mason walked into the garage.

"Want a beer?" Link offered.

"Nah, gotta get to the bar for my shift tonight. Wanted to check in on you."

Link opened his arms. "As you can see, it's another exciting night for me. Too wild for a man like yourself." Link inhaled long and deep before letting it out. *Maybe I should get out of here.*

Mason snickered. "Well, I happen to know it's about to get a lot more exciting."

"Oh?" He straightened and headed for the driver's side door.

"I figured you'd know what to do with this one." Mason winked.

A flash of blond drew his attention to the entrance of the garage.

Emma.

She took a few steps forward, walking around the front of the vehicle. Link met her halfway, until they stood at the hood of the classic car. His eyes raked over her, drinking her in like water in the desert. From her pink Converse to her black, ripped skinny jeans, and the faded, long-sleeved band shirt to her soft, exposed neck and delicious lips he ached to kiss. Those blue eyes, unsure and watery, were no longer bruised and sunken.

"You're here," he said.

"And that's my cue to leave." Mason gave a mock salute out of the corner of Link's vision. He couldn't tear his eyes off Emma, afraid she was only a mirage.

He reached out his hand, needing to touch her. His palm coasted across her cheek to her neck, grabbing hold as he wrapped his other arm around her waist. Tingles raced up his arms, winding through him, setting his body ablaze. "I fucking missed you so much."

She blinked, tears rolling down her pink cheeks. "I missed you too."

He kissed her forehead, tucking her into his chest. Her arms hugged him tightly.

"I love you. So much," he confessed.

"Me too."

He pulled Emma back far enough to search her face. She wiped the tears away. The spark in her eyes was brighter than it had been the last time he'd seen her. He had so many questions, but he just wanted to savor every second she was in his presence. He'd wasted enough time when it came to Emma.

He wasn't sure how, but they would work this out. The alternative was life without Emma, and that was no life at all.

"Link?" She said it like a plea.

"What do you need, sweetheart?" His body thrummed, every nerve ending alive and ready to do her bidding. Lust coursed through his veins, his senses heightened and aware.

She lifted her hand to the back of his neck, dragging his face to hers. "I need *you*."

"You sure?"

"More sure than I have been of anything else in my life," she promised.

His mouth crashed to hers, months of concern and missing her snapping what was left of his control. Link pressed his tongue to the seam of her lips. He groaned as her sweet taste filled his mouth. *She's really here.* He gripped the back of her head, pulling her closer like he'd wanted to do every day since she'd been gone. He wasn't letting her go this time.

His fingers clasped the hem of her shirt, tugging it up a few inches before he stopped. *Gentle. Slow.* "Is this okay?"

She kissed him again. "Yes."

Slowly, he lifted the garment over her body, exposing a black lace bra, her hard, pink nipples poking through it.

She reached for the hem of his shirt. He helped her, pulling it over his head and letting it drop into the growing pile of clothing on the floor.

"Link?"

"What?" He panted, trying to not give in to the urge to rip the rest of her clothing off and fuck her into oblivion.

"Look at me." She pressed her hand to his jaw.

His eyes locked on to hers.

"I won't break. Please don't treat me differently. I want *you.*"

He swallowed. "You sure?"

"Fuck me."

Emma's pants were down to her knees in a heartbeat. He picked her up and set her on the hood of the Chevelle. She gasped with surprise, her eyes widening. Her pupils so big and dark, they were now only rimmed in cerulean. He stripped her pants the rest of the way off, along with her panties. Backing up, he hit the button to close the garage bay door.

"Don't want the neighbors to see?" she teased.

He stalked forward, spreading her legs wide before he

stepped between them. He ran his knuckle down her cheek, leaving a black streak from the oil that he'd missed staining the back of his hand. "I don't share what's mine. And if I haven't been clear enough, that means you. You're all mine, little bird."

She gave him a saucy, defiant look. "Oh, really?"

Link unbuckled his belt and pulled out his steel cock.

Her eyes zeroed in on his erection as she licked her lips.

"Say it." He slid his fingers through her already slick pink folds.

"I want your cock," she moaned, head tipping back.

He grabbed her hips, pulling her to the edge of the bumper. Her nails dug into his shoulders with her need.

"Admit that you're mine," he growled, fisting his cock, tracing the tip over her clit.

Her eyes met his, hazy with want and shining with love. "I'm yours. Only you." She screamed out as he thrust inside her. He grabbed the back of her neck, keeping her gaze on him.

"That's it, baby. Look at me. I want you to see who's making love to you."

"Move."

He slowly rocked his hips, her body bouncing. The car suspension creaked under her as he fucked her slow and deep.

"Please, Link. I need more," she begged, her voice breathless and wanton. Her body was pink and flushed. He used one hand to pinch her nipple through the lace while the other surrounded the thick flesh of her ass and thigh, pulling her against him with every thrust.

She moaned, unintelligible curses leaving her mouth. "I'm so close. *Please*, Link. Give me everything."

He dropped his other hand to her hip, thrusting inside her hard and fast. She held on to his shoulders, clinging to him as he drove her higher and higher until she broke apart, sending his own orgasm tearing through him. Her name on his tongue was a roar. His every muscle tensed. He squeezed her so close he wasn't sure where he ended and she began. They were one soul, comprised of nothing but particles of ecstasy floating somewhere above the universe.

She shuddered with aftershocks, their bodies slick with sweat. He pulled out of her. After picking her up into his arms, he carried her into the house through the side door, naked except for her bra. He laid her on his bed, her eyes half-closed, body limp. Link curled next to her, pulling her back to his front as he worked to catch his breath.

After a few moments of silence, he leaned and kissed her shoulder, tasting the salt of her sweat.

"You waited," she said.

"Did you think I wouldn't?"

"No. I just—I guess I don't know how to start this conversation," she admitted.

He nuzzled her neck. "Just tell me. I'll listen."

"I . . . I learned a lot while I was gone."

"Mm-hmm." He traced his thumb over her belly.

"I started some medication after I was diagnosed with persistent depressive disorder bordering clinical depression." The words tumbled out of her, and then her belly stopped moving as if she was holding her breath.

"Is it helping?" he asked.

She exhaled. "It's not perfect, and I'm still trying out which one is for me, but I have more good days than bad."

"What can I do?" He was so helpless in this situation. He needed something to do—anything.

"You know a lot of people talk about the light at the end of the tunnel and the darkness sucking them down? But not a lot of people talk about the grey in between. It's like a fog that makes it hard to see the light. You know it's there, tempting and teasing you with its subtle warmth shining on those around you, but you can't even feel it unless you find a way to climb out of the mist.

She took a breath as he tried to envision her metaphor.

"My life has been a series of monochromatic grey. It's like I'm somewhere in the middle of light and dark. I know the sun is there, but I can't feel it. And on my bad days, the cold blackness of my depression tugs my ankle, trying to pull me down. When I cut, I get these glimpses of warm sunshine." She took another deep breath, preparing herself for the admissions pouring from her heart. "When I was with you, it was like seeing color for the first time."

Link's chest squeezed, and his eyes stung. His heart broke that she felt so lost. His arms tightened around her.

"In the grey, you feel numb. An outsider to an alien world. It's like living in the shadows—the in-between. Purgatory. Why bother getting out of bed? The thought crosses your mind as you desire to isolate yourself despite feeling lonely. And that's the tricky part. One wrong step and you can fall into the thick blackness. Monsters live there. Sometimes their cold tentacles reach up from the inky pool, wrapping around your ankles, trying to pull you under."

She continued, hot tears dripping onto his arm. "That's when you should scream for help, because by the time those currents of hopelessness pull you under, it's next to impossible to cry out because you're drowning. You can't get out of bed. You can't sleep, or you sleep too much. You just want to escape, willing to trade anything for one minute's relief." She trembled. "But that's when the darkness does something even more sinister. It plays with your mind, until you're convinced it's better down there, so much that you crave even more. More darkness. More silence. It tricks you into thinking everyone in the light will be better off without you. And then you stop fighting, ending it all to stay in the quiet depths."

He cleared his throat, raw with heartache. "Is that how you felt?"

She nodded. "That bathroom floor was rock bottom for me. And I don't ever want to be there again. I'm learning to find my way out."

"I'm so proud of you."

Her breath stuttered. "I'm learning to love and forgive myself. To ask for help. It's hard to show my needs to others. It's hard not to hold things in. I used to think it meant I was strong, not showing my emotions. But I see now how that only hurt me. True strength comes from within, from loving myself enough to feel those emotions and then deal with them. To express myself in healthy ways. True strength means loving myself enough to ask for help."

"You are so strong. So brave," he encouraged.

"I don't feel it."

"Strength isn't about swallowing down emotions but being strong enough to face that feeling and show you're human."

She laughed. "You sound like Doctor Ruby."

He smiled against her shoulder.

"The urge is still there. But each time I refuse, it gets quieter," she confessed in a whisper.

He ran his hand over the raised, newer thick scars, the stark reminder of her darkness that night.

"I'm so sorry," she sobbed.

He turned her around so he could face her, cradling her face in his hands gently. "Shhhh. Hey. Sweetheart, you were hurting, and I'm the one who's sorry I couldn't see it."

Her eyes blinked open, vulnerability glowing in her gaze. Droplets of tears stuck to her blond lashes. "That isn't your fault, Link. Don't take the burden of my choices on your shoulders."

"I won't if you won't blame yourself for your mom leaving."

Her gaze wavered. "I'm working on that."

He kissed her. "That's all I can ask."

After another moment of silence, she asked, "What are we going to do about us?"

"I told you I'm ready to pack up and follow you to the ends of the earth."

She sniffled. "But I want what is best for you. You shouldn't have to give up your dream for me."

He tucked a piece of her blond hair behind her ear, tracing the edge of her jaw with his knuckle. She shivered.

"What if what's best for me is you? What if I told you, you were my dream, my future?"

Her eyes widened a fraction. "You want me . . . after everything? With all my problems? I'd only drag you down."

He shook his head, his voice steady and firm. "I want every piece of you, scars and all." After pulling her healing wrists to his mouth, he took his time to kiss each jagged scar.

Tears poured from her eyes, and she sniffled every now and then.

When he finished, his mouth hovered over hers. "When you feel the urge to hurt yourself, let me be there for you. You're gonna have bad days and good days, and I'm gonna be there for all of them." He kissed her gently. "I'll dance with you in the light, carry you in the darkness, and love you in the grey."

42

EMMA

A week later, Emma handed Link the handle to her suitcase. He loaded it into the car as she turned around to give Remy and Jasmine a hug goodbye. Mikel and Atlas spoke to Link, along with Mason and Reese.

Little Phoenix, Remy's son, clung to her leg. She smiled and reached out to grab him, tucking him into her arms. "I'm gonna miss this cute little face." She kissed his chubby tan cheek as he giggled.

"What about me, Auntie Emma?" Zoey and Lyra asked in unison.

She handed her nephew over to his mama and opened her arms wide for the two little girls. "You know I will. Should I bring you back some presents from my tour?"

"Yes!" Lyra clapped her hands excitedly.

"Peas!" Zoey added jumping up and down.

Emma stood. "I think I can manage that."

Reese clapped Link's back before loudly laughing, drawing her attention to the man she loved with all her heart.

"I'm so happy for you," Jasmine said, tears gathering in her eyes. She waved her hand. "Sorry. It's these pregnancy hormones."

"Me too."

News would come out soon about her and Link's relationship. Her new manager thought it would be better to get ahead of the story before it could become a scandal. She and Link had already done an interview with someone from the media. The story would be breaking later today, making it clear that there was no relation between the two of them and nothing nefarious had occurred. Of course, the world loved drama and she would face some heat, but she wouldn't be alone. Her boyfriend had her back, and so did her band.

"I've got everything covered for the next two weeks. Enjoy your vacation," Reese said to Link.

Link's eyes met hers, and a giant grin split his face. "I will."

He'd join her on the road for a couple of weeks, and she'd fly to him when she had more than a day off. They'd make this work long distance for the tour. And then the band had agreed to buy Shattered Cove Records. They'd stay here to record their next album and make this their studio. A part of her felt guilty asking them to relocate back to Shattered Cove for a portion of the year. Had they just agreed because they thought she was so fragile after what happened? She had a long way to go to make up for how much her choices had affected them too.

Her phone rang in her pocket. She pulled it out. Auntie Yaa's name flashed before she answered. "Hello, Auntie."

"*E te sen?*" she asked in Twi. *How are you?*

"*E ye,*" she answered. *I'm good.* "How are you?"

"I am very well." Her Ghanaian accent reminded her so

much of Solomon. A twinge of longing and sadness crept over Emma.

"Are you on the road yet?" Yaa asked.

"Almost. Just saying goodbye to our friends."

"Okay, I won't keep you. Just wanted to wish you safe travels. You and Link have to come here for a visit when things slow down. I'll show you where my brother and I grew up. You can meet some of our other family," her aunt offered.

"That would be amazing, Auntie." Emma smiled. She'd love nothing more.

"You should have the wedding here too."

Emma coughed, her eyes widening. "What are you talking about?"

Her aunt laughed. "You and my nephew. Don't you think you two have wasted enough time dancing around one another? Time to make it official."

Emma blushed. Did she want to marry Link? Absolutely. But was she ready? No. They needed time. "I'll have to wait for the question to be asked." She bought herself some time.

"Okay, dear. Safe travels and let me know if you guys need anything."

"Goodbye, Auntie."

The call ended. Link walked over to her with a questioning look.

"Auntie Yaa wanted to wish us safe travels."

He scratched the back of his neck, an amused look on his expression. "Yeah, she called me earlier."

Did she ask him to propose too?

Emma shook her head. Before she could even think about marriage, she needed to work on herself, her relationship with the band, and the complications of a partially long-distance relationship with Link. Marriage was far down the line.

"Dad, can we go to Pippa's now?" Aspen, Mason's daughter, asked him.

A panicked look crossed the usually stoic man's expression before it was gone. "You were just there."

"That was last week," she whined. "I need more books. You can drop me off and go get coffee or whatever at the café."

He let out a deep, frustrated sigh. "Fine."

Emma turned to Link. "What was that about?"

He shrugged. "I don't know. Who's Pippa?"

"She owns The Oyster Bookstore on Main Street," Emma supplied.

One eyebrow drew down and Link's forehead wrinkled in concentration. "I don't think I've met her yet."

"She's got colorful braids, she's gorgeous, and has the cutest dog."

Recognition sparked in his gaze. "A golden retriever?"

She nodded.

"I think I saw her at the bar one night when I was there with Mason and Reese. Mase couldn't keep his eyes off her."

"And another one bites the dust," she joked.

"Huh?" He looked at her, seemingly utterly clueless.

She patted his chest. "Never mind. Ready to go? We'd better get on the road if we're gonna make our flight."

He leaned and kissed her until their friends reminded them there were children present. She pulled away, breathless and so full of joy she thought for sure her skin was glowing.

His dark eyes stared through her, down to her soul. He smirked, like he was happy with what he saw. "I can't wait to find all the fun new places we can sneak off to. There's probably a lot of dark corners in a concert stadium behind the scenes." He winked.

"I can't wait that long. First class has a bigger bathroom on the airplane," she whispered so only he could hear.

His hands tightened around her waist. "You're a bad girl." His voice was rough in her ear, sending shivers over her skin, leaving gooseflesh in its wake.

"Just for you." She gave him a chaste kiss. "Only ever for you."

EPILOGUE - LINK
1 YEAR LATER

ink stood in the back corner of the stage, his eyes trained on Emma as she stepped up to the mic in front of a roaring crowd. The diamond ring was burning a hole in his pocket. He was going to wait until they got back to the hotel room. Their private suite was being set up with candles and flower petals at that very moment.

"Thank you so much for the warm welcome, Los Angeles," Emma said. The cheers rose again to an ear-splitting level.

Emma turned to look at him, a smile on her face, her blue eyes surrounded by dark kohl, glowing with life. She'd come so far in this past year. Long distance wasn't easy, but he made a point to spend at least a week with her every month.

Emma spun back to the microphone. "This next song is straight off our new album and poured from my heart." She waited a beat as the crowd clapped and whistled. "You see, sometimes I struggle with depression." Her breath against the mic echoed in the stadium as the audience grew silent. "I'm sure some of you remember the story in the news about me being in the hospital just over a year ago. There were a lot of assumptions made, and I'm finally ready to share my story."

She wrapped her fingers around the mic, her dark nail polish matching the all-black ensemble she wore: tight jeans and a lace corset top with long sleeves. It was khol and red, feminine and edgy, reminding him of that racy outfit she'd worn in the hotel when they'd gone on the trip of his lifetime. Her golden hair now had strips of red through it.

After pulling up her sleeves, Emma raised her arms as a shocked gasp reverberated through the room. His body tensed, his gut cinching tight. Link's attention remained glued to her, watching for any sign she needed him.

"Sometimes the pain of life gets to be too much. The scars we carry inside become too difficult for us to handle. Sometimes we just want it to end. Sometimes what doesn't kill us makes us wish we weren't alive." Her head turned as she surveyed the room, most of which was hidden thanks to the overhead spotlights shining on her. "But I'm here to tell you that life is worth the fight. And this song is for all of you out there who live in the grey, in the shadows, putting on a mask for everyone around you so they think you're okay."

Phone lights blinked on all through the stadium as the first chords of Emma's new song began to play.

"This struggle seems all too familiar.
   This path overworn.
   These lungs gasping for air.
   This heart shattered yet again.
   To love is not to breathe.
   To give in is to die in darkness.
   To quench this thirst is to starve my soul.

.   .   .

They tell me breathe. Just breathe.
When the flood comes and darkness reigns,
Hold on just a little longer.
Go on a little farther.
Fight. Fight for the light.

Escape cuts just a little deeper until the ecstasy flows over,
Drowning me with endorphins coated in red.
Sick of all these disguises.
Time to get off my stage.
Got to channel this rage.

They tell me breathe. Just breathe.
When the flood comes and darkness reigns.
Hold on just a little longer.
Go on a little farther.
Fight. Fight for the light.

Who am I really?
A shell, numb and hollow.
Darkness pulling me under.
Suffocating in the open.
Alone in a crowd.
Silent screams swallowed by a fake smile.

They tell me breathe. Just breathe.
When the flood comes and darkness reigns,
Hold on just a little longer.
Just a little farther.

Fight. Fight for the light.
Fight for you.
Fight for me.
Fight for your life."

The crowd roared, phone lights waving. Asher, Leo, Nicky, and Ravi all stepped away from their instruments and surrounded her in a group hug. Link wanted to be out there. Instead, he cheered her on from the sidelines. He stuck his fingers into his mouth and gave a loud whistle. "That's my girl!"

Her bandmates backed away before taking up their instruments once again. Emma's cheeks were flushed and wet as tears of joy glittered under the lights. She gave him a wink before grasping the mic once again. "I'd love to thank the one person who's been with me through it all. He's followed through on his promises to hold me through my dark days and celebrate the good ones. I wouldn't be where I am today without this man. Can you give my boyfriend, Link, a warm welcome?"

What? No. Link held up his hands and shook his head as she motioned for him to join her across the stage in front of tens of thousands of people.

"Come on. Don't be shy," she teased.

He sighed in resignation and stalked across the stage, pulled her into his arms, and gave her a kiss that made the flush on her cheeks deepen. If she wanted to put him on the spot, he'd give it right back to her.

Several catcalls and oohs and ahs came from the audience.

Emma's eyes sparkled with mischief and adoration. "Link, I love you more than life itself."

"I love you too, sweetheart. You could wait until after the show to tell me that though." He chuckled.

She shook her head, tucking her hair behind her ear nervously. "I wanted an audience for when I told you that I wanted to spend the rest of my life with you. I wanted them to know just how much of an amazing man you truly are—willing to give up everything so that I could fly. Lincoln Owusu, will you marry me?" She kneeled, holding his hands in hers as his heart raced in his chest.

What? She's proposing?

"Say yes!"

"I'll marry you!" someone from the crowd called.

He shook his head, and fear flashed in her eyes.

Link pulled her to standing. "Of course you would make the first move. I had this all planned out." He pulled the ring from his pocket. It glittered in the spotlight as the crowd gasped for a second time. "Yes, I'll marry you, little bird."

The biggest smile he'd ever seen split her face as she jumped into his arms, her arms snaking around his neck. He caught her with one hand, wrapping her legs around him. The audience went wild.

Emma pulled back enough to kiss him, long and hard.

God, he wouldn't ever get enough of her.

She broke the kiss and held out her hand expectantly. "I didn't know you were going to ask me too."

He slid the ring on. "You always knew what you wanted before I got the nerve to act on it. Fearless as ever."

"It's beautiful." She lifted the grey teardrop-shaped diamond closer, blinking away fresh tears.

"A grey stone, to remind you every time you look at it that I will always be here to love you in the grey."

. . .

Thank you! We hope you enjoyed reading *In The Grey*.

Now, turn the page for a sneak peek of Chapter One in the next book, ***Brave Love***, (Book 7, featuring Mason and Pippa's story).

Or visit the website below to order Book 7 in the Shattered Cove series right now.

WWW.AMKUSI.COM/BRAVELOVE

Also, don't forget to read Ash's note to you. It's right after the sneak peek.

SNEAK PEEK OF BRAVE LOVE: CHAPTER 1

Pippa

Pippa pushed one of her cotton candy-colored braids out of her face as she focused on the computer screen in front of her. After moving her mouse, she clicked the order button. She probably didn't *really* need more books, but it couldn't hurt to have a few extra copies. They seemed to be flying off the shelves of her store these days. Enough so that she could finally hire some more help.

A snort came from her side where Lady, her golden retriever and service dog, looked up at her with her brown puppy eyes.

"Oh, don't look at me like that. More books mean more treats."

Lady's ears perked up with the word.

Pippa chuckled and got to her feet before grabbing some books that needed to be re-shelved. "Come on. I'll get you one from the office."

She locked the door and walked through the shop,

checking to make sure everyone was gone before she closed down for the day. Her stomach grumbled. *When was the last time I ate?* Oh, right, the protein bar for lunch. The clicks of Lady's paws padded behind her. *I'll have to take her to get them trimmed soon.*

She passed the large sculpture she'd made herself of a woman reading a novel, her expression one of fascination and pure joy as her hand reached out as if to turn the page. The entire sculpture was made from pages of books that she'd gotten from Goodwill. Recycling stories that gave so many joy and an escape into something beautiful was a hobby of hers. Several of her smaller sculptures were scattered around the store. Some were more realistic, like the beehives on the counter, while others were more fantastical like the mermaid perched in the folds of an open book with one page textured to look like waves.

Pippa's wide hips knocked the shelf to her right, causing a book to fall sideways. She straightened it and made her way to the aisle with a white sign with black letters in a quote by Lloyd Alexander. *Fantasy is hardly an escape from reality. It's a way of understanding it.*

She smiled to herself. Inside the doors of The Oyster Bookstore was her own oasis. Here, her imagination could run wild. She'd created the very place she'd dreamed of as a little girl, stuck in hospital rooms day after day. There was greenery in every corner, plants that kept the air clean and the colors vibrant. Each row had a separate quote. Instead of boring "Self Help" signs, hers said, *In life, nobody will help you until you're willing to help yourself.* Instead of "Parenting" she had, *Children learn more from what you are than what you teach. - W.E.B. Dubois.*

Pippa placed the two books on the shelf and inhaled. The smell of books never got old. If someone could bottle it up in a candle, they'd make a fortune off just her.

She walked into the bathroom. "Anyone in here?"

"Me," came a small voice and then a sniffle from the last stall. *Was it the little girl I saw earlier?*

"I was just closing up. Do you need anything?" Pippa asked.

More sniffles came from behind the wooden door.

"Are you okay?" Pippa asked, concern growing in the pit of her stomach.

"I . . . I um . . . I'm bleeding."

Pippa's eyes widened. "Do you need a doctor? Can I come in and help?"

The latch unlocked a moment later, and a young girl with strawberry-blond hair stared up at her, her arms crossed as if she were hugging herself. Tears stained her freckled face.

Pippa reached out, checking her over for signs of injury. "Where are you hurt?"

She shook her head. "I'm not. It's . . . I think I got my . . . you know?"

Realization flooded Pippa, and her shoulders relaxed. "You mean you got your period?"

The girl nodded. Her eyes slid to the floor, suddenly taking interest in the scuff marks.

"Is this your first one?"

Another nod.

Something clicked into place for Pippa. She might not be able to do a lot of things, and she'd been through a lot of shit in her life. But this right here was her moment. Pippa knew exactly what this young girl was going through. So, she'd do what she wished someone had done for her way back when. "This is something to celebrate!"

The girl flinched and looked up at her with an incredulous expression.

Maybe I'm coming on a little too strong. "You've become a

woman today. That is something so sacred and special, and I am honored it happened in my bookstore."

"I bled on my pants," she said shyly.

"It happens to all of us." Pippa waved her hand in front of her face. "Nothing to be embarrassed about."

"I don't . . . I don't know what to do," the girl admitted.

"Well, it's a good thing I have a lot of experience in this department." Pippa walked out and opened the cupboard by the sink before pulling out the box of pads and tampons she kept under there just in case someone needed one. *Empty.*

"Crap. Well, I don't have any in my house either because I use a cup."

"A cup?" The girl's eyebrows rose in question.

"A menstrual cup. It's a reusable silicone cup that you . . ." Pippa trailed off as the young woman's panicked eyes frantically moved around the room.

"Hey. It's okay. This happens to everyone with a uterus at some point. I'm gonna help you out, so you can feel prepared. I'm Pippa, by the way. What's your name?"

"Aspen." She sniffled and then her cheeks bloomed red. "I don't want to tell my dad. This is the most embarrassing day of my life." Her tears started again.

Pippa pulled her into a hug, holding her while she cried. "The first time I got my period, I was in class and everyone laughed at the huge blood stain on my pants. No one told me. Not one person stopped to let me know. I went to three classes before a teacher noticed and told me to go to the nurse's office."

Aspen pulled away. "Oh my God."

Pippa nodded. "Then I had to call my dad and tell him why I needed him to come get me at school, and then he had no idea what I needed and came home with these giant pads. I was mortified."

"Where was your mom?" Aspen asked.

Pippa took a deep breath. The pain of losing her mother had faded with time, but it was still there, a hollow ache inside. "My mom died when I was a kid."

"Mine died when I was a toddler. I don't even remember her," Aspen admitted.

"That sucks."

"Especially right now." Aspen's voice was a whisper.

"I'm gonna help you, so you don't have to go through all the embarrassment I did. But there is no shame in having your period. This is something that is normal and natural, and it happens to more than half the earth's population." Pippa smiled, hoping to help alleviate some of Aspen's concern.

"Will you tell my dad?" The young girl tucked a piece of her reddish-blond hair behind her ear, her blue eyes pleading.

"Where is he?"

"At the Stardust Café across the street."

Pippa smiled. "I'll do better than that. You go sit at the front desk and use the sweater I have draped against the seat to wrap around your waist. I'll go get him. What's his name?"

"Mason Wright."

"Okay. I'll be right back."

Pippa led Aspen to the front desk. She took a quick turn around the store, checking that no one else was inside before she left. She made sure to lock the door behind her, and she crossed the street, holding on to Lady's leash.

Opening the door to the bakery, she had one thing on her mind, and that was helping a young girl out and saving her some of the pain and embarrassment she'd endured growing up without a mother to navigate some of the more sensitive matters in a girl's life. Pippa was so distracted, she didn't see the mountain of the man in front of her. She slammed into something hard and warm as hot liquid burst from a cup, pouring all over the hulking man in front of her. Lady barked once.

"Fuck!" he yelled. His deep voice sent a shiver through her.

Pippa looked into the deepest sapphire blue eyes she'd ever seen. His full lips turned down on only half of his face. The other side of his face twisted, his flesh marred with thick pink swirling scars. Her head tipped upwards—this man towered over her five-foot-one frame. He must have been more than six feet. The scars continued down his thick neck, disappearing under his plaid shirt. Her gaze wandered over his bulky chest to the massive arms with defined lines of muscle. She swallowed, her lady parts waking up, alert and hungry. Her eyes flicked back to his.

Anger radiated from him. "Take a picture. It will last longer." He turned to the counter, his voice softening just a bit. "Remy, I need a mop."

Remy, the woman Pippa had come to know from her frequent stops into the specialty gluten-free bakery and café, appeared behind the counter. "Sure thing."

"I'm sorry. I wasn't looking where I was going. Can I buy you a replacement?" Pippa asked.

The man kept his back turned to her. "No."

She should have slowed down, but still, he didn't need to be an asshole about it. Pippa sighed and led Lady to the front counter as Remy walked out with the mop.

The man reached and took it from her. "I've got it."

"Thanks." Remy's eyes flashed to hers as the grumpy asshole started cleaning up the mess. "Hey, Pippa, what can I get you?"

"Uh, well, actually. I wondered if you could tell me which one of your patrons is Mason Wright?"

Remy smiled, her eyes focusing over Pippa's shoulder. "He's the one you just ran into."

Pippa's gut knotted as she closed her eyes. "Oh, fuck."

To continue reading Mason and Pippa's story, visit the website below to get your copy of *Brave Love* today.

WWW.AMKUSI.COM/BRAVELOVE

Now, turn the page to read Ash's note to you.

DEAR READER, A NOTE FROM ASH

"There is a story within you waiting to be told." - Unknown

Every time we sit down to write a character, we always infuse a little of ourselves into them. They come to us, and sometimes we're not always sure what story they are trying to tell until we're three-quarters of the way through the manuscript. Emma's story and her struggles have more than just a little bit of me (Ash) and my experience in it.

I feel we always write what we know best. That's why this series has been so close to our hearts. Living a life with trauma leaves lasting scars. I've been on a journey of finding self-acceptance, forgiveness, and love. And I thought that was the key to healing completely.

Oh, how I was wrong. I sat at my desk, writing out my feelings in the middle of the night because I couldn't sleep—yet again. My two children were dreaming peacefully in the other room, like my husband, and the urge to hurt myself arose. The dark grey had seeped into my bones after eight years without relapse. I was stunned. I was full of so much pain, and I didn't know why, all of a sudden, it crashed over me like a tsunami.

I have a husband who loves me more than life itself. He's been my rock and always believed in me, always accepted me as I am. I have two wonderful daughters so full of life, living in a family without trauma—much different than the one I grew up with. I'd been working on radically accepting myself and making myself happy, loving myself. What was missing? What was wrong with me? Why did I still want to mutilate myself?

I started therapy soon after that and got on some medication for my depression. My therapist told me, "Healing isn't linear." And that just took a huge weight off my chest.

Loving yourself, grieving your losses (stolen childhood, people abandoning you, relationships lost, and stolen innocence), and accepting yourself will go a LONG way in your healing and growth. It is what will save you when that darkness becomes too much.

Throughout the years since that moment, I've learned that there will always be pieces of me that will remain damaged. Scars that won't completely heal. I will always be just a little bit broken. I can choose to wallow in that and take it as defeat, or I can tell my story and ask for help when I feel those grey and dark feelings coming along. I can fight.

I can forgive myself. I can accept my faults. I can love myself through the grey. And so can you.

I'm choosing to fight for me, for my family, and for everyone who's reading this, so you can know there is hope. We may not be perfect, and we may relapse, but we can always move towards the light. We may always be just a little bit broken, but we can turn it into beauty.

I beg you, if you ever experience suicidal thoughts, or

thoughts about hurting yourself, that you seek help. Keep fighting. The world needs you. *I* need you.

National Suicide Prevention Lifeline: 1-800-273-8255

JOIN OUR NEWSLETTER

The best way to get updates about new releases, sneak peeks, pre-orders, giveaways, and more is by joining our newsletter.

You'll also receive a FREE short novel that's not available on any retailer to read.

Visit the website below to join now.

WWW.AMKUSI.COM/NEWSLETTER

THANK YOU

Thank you for reading *In The Grey*. We hope you are emotionally satisfied with Emma and Link's love story. If you enjoyed this novel, please consider leaving a review on your favorite retailer and sharing it with your friends and family.

Also, you can start reading the other books in The Shattered Cove Series right now!

Remy and Mikel in **A Fallen Star (Book 1).** The eBook version is FREE on all retailers.

Andre and Mia in **Glass Secrets (Book 2).**

Belle and Bently in **Defying Gravity (Book 3).**

Jasmine and Atlas in **The Lighthouse Inn (Book 4).**

Charli and Finn in **His True North (Book 5).**

Mason and Pippa in **Brave Love (Book 7).**

Lastly, if you haven't read our first complete series, **The Orchard Inn Romance Series**, make sure you get your copy so you don't miss out on three wonderful love stories.

Thank you again for reading *In The Grey!*

Cheers,

Ash & Marcus.

ABOUT A. M. KUSI

A. M. Kusi is the pen name of a wife-and-husband author team, Ash and Marcus Kusi. We enjoy writing romance novels that are inspired by our experiences as an interracial/multicultural couple.

Our novels are about strong women and the sexy heroes they fall in love with, are emotionally satisfying, and always have a happy ending.

Discover more about us at:

WWW.AMKUSI.COM

To receive updates about new releases, giveaways, sneak peeks, pre-orders, and more, visit the website below to join our newsletter today:

WWW.AMKUSI.COM/NEWSLETTER

After you join the newsletter, we will send you a FREE novella to read.

To contact us, use this email address amkusinovels@gmail.com.

Happy reading!

facebook.com/amkusi

instagram.com/amkusinovels

pinterest.com/amkusinovels

ALSO BY A. M. KUSI

A Fallen Star (eBook FREE on all retailers)

(Book 1 in The Shattered Cove Series)

Glass Secrets

(Book 2 in The Shattered Cove Series)

Defying Gravity

(Book 3 in The Shattered Cove Series)

The Lighthouse Inn

(Book 4 in The Shattered Cove series)

His True North

(Book 5 in The Shattered Cove series)

Brave Love

(Book 7 in The Shattered Cove series)

The Orchard Inn (eBook FREE on all retailers)

(Book 1 in The Orchard Inn Romance Series)

Conflict of Interest

(Book 2 in The Orchard Inn Romance Series)

Her Perfect Storm

(Book 3 in The Orchard Inn Romance Series)

www.ingramcontent.com/pod-product-compliance
Lightning Source LLC
Chambersburg PA
CBHW061316190726
48288CB00002B/523